CHRISTA

Christa

DEBBIE O'BRIEN

Christa
ISBN: 9780645325058

www.facebook.com/debbieobrienaustralia
www.instagram.com/debbie_obrien_author
Also by Debbie O'Brien
A Million Stars
ISBN: 9781649996442
BonBon Street
ISBN: 9780645325003
Pen Pals
ISBN: 9780645325003
www.debbieobrienaustralia.com

'The night's too quiet, stretched out alone
I need the whip of thunder
And the wind's dark moan.
I'm not Able, I'm just Cain
Open up the heavens,
And make it rain.'

Tom Waits

Prologue

Exhaustion leaned her against the verandah post, palms flat, one hand across the other to act like a cushion for her behind, head tilted back so it too, touched the post. The position felt comfortable, her neck, elongated, welcomed the final warmth as the sun drew its fingers back across the earth. The earlier burning rays softening in the farewell felt like an apology for the damage they had punished them with for so long, they had stopped counting the days. Closed eyes hid for a moment the endless damage the sun had caused, waking them each day to taunt them, sucking the life from every living organism before departing, as she did now with a grace that made you long for her return.

Part of her ached for long shadows, the kind made by towering pines or spreading oaks instead of the mottled pattern cast by the spiny tea tree onto the powdery dust. It was almost a wistful look that crossed her face as she tried to let only gentle thoughts settle inside her head. She could hear the children laughing as they played, the tiny bit of water in the bath was enough to amuse them, yet not enough to wash them entirely clean. They were safe, the oldest one would call if they weren't. In the distance the sun reached out to grasp the ridge as if trying to save itself from slipping over the other side, stretching a giant hand along, each finger of beam reaching out before being defeated by the pull from the world beyond. The final red line slid away, throwing pretty colours high in a last wave of goodbye leaving only a reflection on the evening star.

Sunset was her moment of the day to steal for herself, and one she savoured. Dinner was prepared, the children not yet hungry enough to argue into the witching hour, and her man still yet to come in from the paddocks. Sometimes it was just a few minutes, others, in summer when time had no meaning and the sun stayed high in the sky for longer, she could sit with a mug of tea, to watch the entire performance as the children played, and it was too hot to send them to bed. He came now, the slamming of the truck door crackling the air, the noise rippling across the stillness as she straightened to greet him. This too was a moment she savoured, the sight of him completed her world each time. He ambled more than walked, the slowness to his purposeful stride a conflict in itself. The violet-blue of the twilight mixed with the puffs of inevitable dust behind him looked almost solid, something she wished she could capture in a jar to delight in its colours on another day. Removing his hat, he banged it on his leg as he approached sending more dust particles into the air to swirl and settle into the cracks which now laced the paddocks beyond. His slow smile was something she looked for to judge his day before he reached her. The routine of stomping his feet and shaking his body, to rid himself of the dust, so as not to add another layer to the house when he stepped inside, often gave him time to hide the worst from his face in a bid to lessen her concerns. He leaned in to brush her lips with his, his eyes running down her body in a way that made her feel like a girl again.

'Do you never tire of it?' His eyes as blue as a summer sky held a hint of amusement. He knew her so well. Every movement and thought, when she was near, seemed to absorb into his body. He never judged, held her up on days when she was down, and rejoiced with her on the others, his quiet way wrapped around her and part of her wished today, this day, had stayed a bit longer.

'Never' she replied, 'it is hope, hope tomorrow might be better or hope it won't be worse than today. No matter what the outcome it is never goodbye, only farewell until the morning comes again.' He smiled and the skin crinkled around his eyes.

'You make no sense my sweet, but I hope tomorrow is better than today, and I hope tomorrow you cannot see your sunset for the storm clouds I need to fill the skies.'

Reaching out she squeezed his hand.

'It will come, my love, eventually it will come.'

The children heard his voice and called for him to watch them play. He hung his hat on the peg and slid the boots from his feet. She leaned back again and watched the muscles as they played down his arms, he turned to grin at her and the warmth of him filled her even though they were apart. The screen door banged twice behind him, and she sighed as the dust fell and scattered across the boards before glancing up one last time to make a wish for rain on the evening star. It shone brightly now as the sky darkened behind it to a rich navy blue, and she turned away before the other stars came out to twinkle in their bid to outshine.

He was leaning on the door jamb, laughter filled the room, and she ducked under his arm to help them out.

'Leave them a bit more, they are having fun. Empty it and run them some more, they look like three little pigs in mud not three who would come out clean.'

She looked at him.

'We may regret it tomorrow, we have so little water left, we should save it.'

He looked sad.

'Give them a memory of joy, we will run out of water anyway, give them one joy.'

As she lifted each of them out they wriggled, trying to cover their bodies with their hands, suddenly embarrassed by their nakedness now they were standing. Pulling the plug the thick sludge of muddy water slid slowly away, she pushed the last down with her hand, replacing the plug and filling the bath so it would now nearly reach their waists as they sat. He had moved away, and she heard him return pushing her gently out of the way to hold one hand up to the children, who were now anxious to re-enter their water playground. From behind his back, he produced the washing liquid and squirted generous amounts into the water before swishing his hand wildly to make the bubbles form and rise. The children squealed in delight and stomped their feet in excitement as they waited to be lifted back in, each wanting to be the first.

'But Daddy, we are not dishes.' The oldest wriggled her toes as the bubbles covered her feet on her descent. 'They're cold' she giggled, and her eyes were wide with the sensation of them on her skin. The twins pushed each other to be next and he lifted one for her so they could go in at the same time. She had thought they would splash and had stepped away to avoid it, yet they sat stunned, unwilling to move and spoil the cloud around them.

'I'm so sorry,' he said. 'I thought you were some dirty pots and pans when I saw you, I thought Mummy had gone completely mad and had forgotten where the kitchen was.' They giggled at the crazy face he made. 'Let me look, ahh yes, these are children under here. Look Mummy we have found them.' He winked at the children. 'I thought she might have put you in the cupboard with a lid on your heads and would pull you out to cook supper.'

The children's smiles were wide, and he took handfuls of bubbles and placed them on their heads, he showed them how to make a beard and they marvelled at their appearance when she held up a small mirror. Their bright eyes matched his and she hoped the boys would grow to be men as good as their father. She didn't wish for better, she could not imagine a man better than him. She reached in a hand and felt the water cooling. She showed them how the soap made the bubbles disappear when it submerged in the water, and they were happy to watch them fade away. They were tiring, getting cold, and he helped as they rubbed them dry with worn towels and dressed them in singlets and flannelette pyjamas. She combed their hair flat against their heads and it did her heart good to see them clean for once. As she ushered them out, he helped her gather the towels and told them to choose a story for him to read while she cooked their meal. A smile played across her lips as he removed his shirt and pants to quickly wash in the soapy remains. If only it could wash away the heartbreak as easily as he removed the outward toils of the day she thought. As the potatoes boiled and steam filled the kitchen, she glanced in to see them all laying back against his fresh shirt as he read aloud the books they had chosen. He glanced up and winked, his mouth still moving, they owned so few books the stories were embedded in their minds, and they no longer had to read the words. The little one's eyes battled to stay open, and he tickled them to keep them awake.

After they had eaten and the children were tucked away in bed, they sat together, her head on his shoulder as he spoke quietly of the stock he had found. Another ten laid out by the dam, their bodies worn out from scratching on the cracked earth searching for a drop of water or a blade of grass. He had shot them where they lay, a miserable but necessary job to end their suffering. His voice was empty as he spoke, and she knew how bereft he was at their loss. These cattle were not just income, these cows he had raised, chosen their fathers and sold their young, he had brought some of them into the world, helping their mothers in their labour, reaching in to straighten their legs in the birth canal so they could slide from her body. They were a part of him, and their suffering was almost more than he could bear.

She closed her eyes and thought about the journey, the journey which had brought her here. The journey she had thought was hard until she found him. The journey which could have led her to so many places, and yet it had led her here, to him, and the three little souls who filled their world. As poor as they were she felt rich, this life, his dreams, were more than she could

have ever wished for. This man had given it to her, and she could
never repay him.

Chapter 1

Christa

Christa always felt she was halfway to somewhere. Never quite in a group, never quite out, even when she was small, she was just there, hedging around the edge to add a number to make up a team, never really noticed by anyone. Sometimes she felt like a ghost, drifting and swaying, listening but never speaking, gliding along on a light breeze that pushed her through life, gentle but with enough force so she never resisted. To resist took effort and would make her seen, seen by those from whom she hid. Noise created anger and change, and change was not always good. For Christa, the path of least resistance lessened other burdens she seemed destined to bear. Maybe this was the problem, so used to being told what was good for her, she believed they knew best, and of course they did, after all, they were the grownups.

Her mother had been the first, eventually dumping her with her aunt when she was five.

'Only got halfway through the pregnancy when you popped out, lucky to be here you are, double trouble then, double trouble now,' her mother would say.

She couldn't remember a lot about her mother now. Memories had faded but she remembered the sentence, said often so she would feel grateful for all her mother had done for her. Getting clothes from the donation bin under the cover of darkness, along with a broken toy or a torn book, and feeding her cereal for every meal, was something she was expected to be thankful for, and she was. On a cold night, a worn rug was better than no rug at all, a toy to play with, broken or not, or a book to feel and study the pictures, dreaming of other places while she waited for her mother to come to after the syringe fell from her arm. Yes, she had felt grateful, just as she was sure every other child felt thankful for their comforts.

One other thing she remembered very clearly was the smell, the smell of beer and cigarettes and cheap perfume. It wasn't until she started school did she realise, not everyone smelt like it. When the pretty mothers dressed for tennis came into the classroom, the sweet smell of them lingered in the room and she would hold her nose up and close her eyes hoping it would not fade away. It was the little things that lifted her throughout her days.

Halfway to the age of ten, her mother took a turn in the road and never reached back to take her daughter with her. Her aunt, though kind, was young and had no room in her life for a five-year-old. Although some days they ate proper meals with vegetables and her clothes were now new, purchased from the local variety store, her aunt did not bat an eyelid if she wanted to go out and party with her friends. Often Christa was left on her own, the one-bedroom flat not the ideal place for a child either, stuffed with old furniture which had been begged or borrowed as well as piles of magazines full of the latest fashion trends, their glossy covers, to Christa, all looking the same. Sometimes her aunt stayed out all weekend, often not returning until after lunch on a Sunday smelling like her mother had, and with dark smeared makeup under her eyes.

How are you going lovely, she would call out when she got home, although Christa would already know she was there. Sitting at the window watching out to see if her aunt was returning alone or, if not, if she would have to grab some snacks and retreat into the hall cupboard out of sight until her aunt's friend left. Sundays were fairly safe she was usually alone, it was the other days you could never be certain.

Christa's little nest below her aunt's coats consisted of a piece of foam, a crocheted rug her aunt had picked up at a fete, and a pillow so thin it was just a barrier to keep her face off the foam, with no support in it left for her head to nestle. Still, it was the best bed she had ever known, and she could close the door which made her feel safe and gave her a private little space of her very own.

Her aunt had put one of those stick-on lights on the wall and all she had to do was wave her hand and it turned on. Often, in later years when she was reading, she would wave her hand around, an unconscious habit formed from her time in her cupboard as the light went out every three minutes, and a quick hand wave allowed her to not lose her place. Halfway down the stairs one day, on her way to school, a neighbour asked a few questions of her and a few days later some people came to school and took her to a new place. They already had her clothes and an old teddy she had grown attached to.

Christa learned early to retreat within herself, each foster home bringing its challenges. She did meet others along the way, ones whose parents and families had decided they could live a better life without them. Some were argumentative and aggressive, while others, like herself, were content to get through each day without conflict. The older she got, the more she hid behind the veil of shyness. From temporary accommodation to semi-permanent care and back again, each time it seemed, being introduced to a new caseworker who, looked tired and asked questions, but never gave any real answers. Christa was often moved on because she did not talk. To her, if she didn't give anything out, they couldn't give anything back or take the tiny piece of her she knew to be true, but to some foster parents her silence irritated and they spent hours trying to get her to *come out of herself* to no avail, so they moved her on, hoping she would find someone who could.

In some foster homes where there were two or three of them, she witnessed how others reacted, some loud and defiant, every action wanting and demanding the attention they so craved. She met others who had struck a chord with the carer and found a true home but even here they were very protective of what they had and did not like another coming in, scared and jealous of any kindness she may receive in case theirs would be taken away. Each time it seemed she slipped through the cracks as the institutionalism of the agency laid its blanket of cover and she did nothing to ruffle it.

Christa liked school, her silence meant she went unnoticed most of the time, and usually by the time she was, for a good mark or a clever assignment, she had been moved on to a new school, a new place, and a new situation. All the schools gave her regularity, routine, and a strange sense of belonging, of being like everyone else. No matter who they were, rich or poor, they all had to go to school, and the uniform set them all on the same level, although hers were always second-hand. It didn't bother her to always be the new girl, there was usually someone willing to make a new friend, someone ostracised from the group and who had been roped in to show her around. They were always ready to fill her in on the hierarchy of the place. Christa would then be pulled onto the sidelines as they were accepted back into the group, and she tagged or was dragged along as well.

Halfway through her teens, Christa had a stroke of luck, a group home was found and along with five others, she moved into a recently renovated home with around-the-clock carers who came and went on different shifts. All were enthusiastic.

The children looked forward to a relaxation of rules, being in charge of their own lives to a degree and a place they could at last call home. The counsellors were young and keen to set programs in place for improving self-esteem, teaching new skills, and showing them they were now accountable for their actions. These few were determined to make a change.

Christa had to share a room. Emily had breezed in, a face full of smiles and a laugh you could hear as she turned the corner of the street. Emily had plans and as soon as she could leave the system, or they would let her go, she would be gone, off to travel and explore, live on the edge yet smart enough not to tumble over it. Christa wished she too had a plan.

Emily said her mother had died when she was fifteen, so the system had not yet taken a hold on her, nor worn her down and she had just been glad to have somewhere to go while she struggled with her grief. Emily's mother instilled the benefit of education and filled Emily's head with dreams and tools for her survival. As the cancer ate her body, she had at least left a legacy of love and respect for herself and others. Christa struggled to understand how this, now silent support, lifted Emily higher. Emily's optimism frightened her, Christa knew the moment you put faith in something or someone, they would let you down, almost every day of her life had proven to her this very fact.

Christa didn't know how to dream, nor thought, if you did, they could come true, they certainly never had for her in the past. Day after day Emily wore her down, loudly at times, pushing her to get up, study hard, dress up, and laugh out loud, Christa had only done it once and the feeling in her body as if she was losing control had been terrifying. The giggle rising in her throat, the gushes of air behind it as she had watched Emily dance crazily around the room, hairbrush in hand, and totally out of tune singing the popular song of the day. The laugh had surprised her and even Emily had frozen as the sound bound out across the room, alien and unexpected. Emily had grabbed her then, delighted, and Christa had felt a crack in her armour as the tiny piece tore away and for a moment her mind scrambled to catch it, stick it back on, but as Emily twisted and twirled, their hands held tight, Christa had let it go, praying as she did this lovable magical girl would be someone she could learn to trust.

Emily coming into her life, and the work of the counsellors, awakened in her a tiny light, a low beam to the future. Maybe there was more? Was it time she started to think ahead to when no one else would make decisions for her? It hurt her head sometimes and scared her. What would she do without the routine of school? What did people do? How did they make those decisions? How could she not be like her mother?

Emily accepted Christa's quietness, and let her own chatter fill any void.

'Can't wait to get going, we'll need to save harder though, I've got a bit from my Mum, but it won't last long.'

Christa's head shot up.

'We?' Her insides felt suddenly warm and calm. It felt like a fog spreading inside her, seeping and searching, finding crevices she did not know existed, it was like a smile too, widening to the brink of laughter yet not willing to release the glow that had built up to let the world know how she felt. Christa wanted to hang on to it, wrap it in a bow, and never let it go. Somebody wanted her and wanted to be with her.

Emily continued, unaware of the impact one little word had made on her friend. She presumed Christa would agree. The difference between them, one who had known a mother's love and one who had never felt it, seemed to hang in the room then curl itself up and hide away as the glow hit Christa's face and Emily, in Christa's mind, became someone she could maybe rely on. For Emily, the moment drifted unnoticed as she tried to summon other plans and ideas, but this was the only plan she could think of, and she was determined to see it through. As was her way, Emily voiced all her thoughts and emotions openly, laying everything on the table for others to add to, or take away from. She was not bossy, more 'encouraging people to think like me', was how she liked to put it.

'Thought we could catch the train to Brisbane, cheaper than the bus and we can still work on our student ID for travel which should be valid until the end of the year at least. From there we can work our way across and up to Isa, you know, Mount Isa, should be able to pick up some work there. We are not particularly good at anything, but we can learn. See how it pans out. Hey Christa, what do you think? Wouldn't mind going out to a station, I could be a jillaroo, what do you think? Can you ride a horse? I can, haven't done it for a while, and I suppose it will be a bit different than the ponies I've been on, but, how hard could it be? Maybe they just ride motorbikes, have you been on a bike? Or, Chris, Christa! Are you listening?'

Christa was, yet never felt the need to answer, as Emily would only pause long enough for a breath and launch straight into the answer she wanted to hear anyway, long before Christa could open her mouth. Christa smiled at her friend and nodded so Emily would continue.

'Maybe they'll do helicopter mustering, wow wouldn't it be cool, ever been in one of them?'

Christa did look up this time as silence descended the room and she looked at her friend. Emily was gazing at the ceiling as she let ideas run around her head and paused to daydream each one.

'I'll beg Mr Jahid to give us more shifts at the store, I'm sure he will have some and if it's a late one we will have time to study while we are at work, kill two birds with one stone as they say, a double bonus, what do you think?'

The counsellors had encouraged them all to get part-time jobs, and they had said, apart from giving them spending money and responsibility, it would give them something to put on their resumés. Christa noticed the other boys in the house with new headphones and the latest electronic devices, but Emily had helped her open a bank account and assured her she would be grateful in the end to not waste her money on things she could live without. Mr. Jahid also encouraged the girls to dream big and varied their jobs from tidying up to being allowed to use the register and greet customers. As his trust in them grew, he allowed them to occasionally be responsible for closing the shop and giving him an early night for a change. He enjoyed their chatter and felt a fatherly responsibility towards them, he would miss them, but also knew from experience, the opportunities this great country could offer them. Christa could see the many pieces were coming together to push her in a certain direction, it did scare her but with Emily to push her along she hoped it was karma finally coming her way in, fingers crossed, the very best way.

Emily tugged at her oversized jumper, moving it so it bunched up at the front, she shuffled her bum off her foot which was curled up under her on the bed, and grimaced. Christa could see her coming back to earth and braced herself for the next onslaught.

'Ow, Ow,' Emily jumped up hopping around the room, her foot giving way as she tried to wake it up and the pins and needles tickled then stung as the nerves again received their flow of blood. 'I'll go ask Drew, he's coming too, be good to be three, a bit safer, what do you reckon?'

In seconds she was gone, hobbling and still talking to whoever was in earshot or to no one at all, Christa never knew. Christa shook her head and realised her mouth had dropped open as her mind caught up with the conversation. Drew! What?

Emily had certainly kept this a secret, she blushed deeply. Drew, he was her daydream.

Drew heard Emily coming. He knew she would have some fresh idea to tell him and some sort of plan she had made. He didn't mind, she had given him a push and he liked her chatter, it filled the empty void of silence that usually surrounded him. Unlike the two girls, Drew had left his home willingly. His family seemed normal on the outside but somehow, he never seemed to fit in and really could not work out why. His twin sister Sarah had left not long after, each of them happy to take their chances away from an over-strict mother and a father who complained about them all day.

Bloody kids look at the mess, no better than dogs, he would yell, then want to spend time with them to make up for it but only on his terms. Keeping up appearances to be the good father for their neighbours and friends to see, it was as if he was saying *look at what I do for them and how they repay me.* People would nod and smile, yes, they could see, his children showed no respect. As his ego was boosted higher by their approval, his opinion of his children was lowered. Drew's sister had escaped to a boyfriend and was happy enough on the surfing circuit with him, living a life free from rules and regulations, a hippy-like lifestyle with no thoughts for the future. Drew knew whatever happened, she was better off living in the back of a kombi van than being poisoned by their mother's evil heart and their father's angry stares.

Where Sarah had flown under the radar, for Drew it had been harder. No friend's parents had been willing to take in a teenage boy, usually the one they had was trouble enough, let alone what they ate. Two growing boys could eat anyone out of house and home. A school counsellor had known someone on this trial experiment and Drew knew he had been in the right place at the right time to get a position. Leaving had never been hard and his parents had never bothered to seek him out since. There were two other boys here as well, Kent was sixteen, a long timer in foster care after being taken from his drug addict parents, and Jake who never spoke but followed Kent around like he was a god and Jake was his bodyguard. Drew had nothing in common with either of them.

It had been Emily and her bright optimism that had caught his attention. The live-in carers encouraged them to feel like a family, so hopefully when the day came, they would all at least have each other. Everyone knew the resources were not available to them once the magic age of eighteen was reached and the current caregivers were pulled in other directions no matter their attachment to each of them.

Christa was a mystery to him. She was quiet yet when she looked at him with those big eyes, he felt a tug inside and somehow wanted to protect her.

'Drew. I think we should all ask for more shifts at the shop, I'm sure he'll agree and ...' Emily paused as a thought caught her. 'It will give them a break as they know we are all heading off soon so it would make sense for them to have a relax now, don't you think?' Drew smiled, Emily was hardly in the door and was already finished with her question, he also knew she would broach the Jahid's with exactly the thought, placing it in their heads as if it was their idea for a break and Emily was only the vessel to voice it. He had to give it to her, she had a knack for manipulating people and her smile wiped away any creeping doubt in their minds. Deep down he knew Emily was kind, though Drew did think her enthusiasm covered a lot of fears which sometimes led her in the wrong direction, and covered inner scars she would never admit.

'Have you got your licence, maybe we can buy a car, no, a bus will be cheaper for a while on the student card. Maybe once we are on the road, after all, they sell cars everywhere don't they?'

Drew had not answered her once, he just let her work it out on her own, truth be known he was also never quite sure if they were questions or just statements. One thing he did know, if her plan was ridiculous, he would interject with his own opinion. Drew did have his licence it was one thing his father had allowed him to do, though he hadn't had anything to practise on since. Drew wasn't shy, just quiet, he liked his own company and did not suffer fools lightly. He had agreed to Emily's crazy ideas as he had no other plans, and he thought the girls would need his protection. Somewhere in this great brown land, he would find his niche, what he wanted to do with his life, he was sure, somewhere, it was waiting for him. Travelling with Emily and Christa would be fun, it would bring him out of himself and give them all the confidence to move forward with their lives. He didn't care if he never saw his parents again, but he missed his sister, his twin, and now, the only family he had.

Emily wandered around his room running her hands over things as she pondered and talked and laughed to herself. She felt like his sister, someone he had known his whole life even though in the scheme of things they had only just met. Emily was almost infectious, though the other boys steered clear of her. Drew wasn't aware anything had happened, but they seemed almost scared of her and moved out of her way in the hall or ushered her in ahead of them to the bathroom. Drew knew it would come out eventually if he was supposed to know, yet for him it was not something to make his business and it amused him to see the power she could display without being any different in her attitude. One thing for sure, with Emily, you knew where you stood, she had a way of looking at you if something displeased her. In the olden days, Drew could imagine her as a queen running an empire, her subjects bowing before her as they glanced up to see the mood of the day, yet none would be able to pinpoint when she had ever been in a bad mood, but they would all know they had to obey.

The closing of the year seemed to rush towards them. Drew would be out almost as soon as school was over, his eighteenth birthday already seemed a long time ago and it was only his schooling that had kept his place here. Emily was next in the last week of November and Christa, in early December. The counsellors had argued a case for them, but this was a halfway house, not a permanent home and the program had a closing date. The powers that be had a long waiting list of neglected children to cross off their list and present to the public as a trophy for what the government had achieved. It gave them a cloak to draw around all those who were left to wallow in a mostly inefficient system full of ladder climbers with no care, and dedicated believers who banged their heads against the wall trying to fight the system.

Emily kept them both enthused and amused. They all avoided the end-of-year formal, money was the reason they stated, but their hidden emotions also played a part. For Emily the gushy girls with their plans for gap years financed by parents were a bit too much to take, her mother's death still too raw she claimed, to be surrounded by the selfish and ungrateful. For Christa and Drew, the lack of family to encourage them to make it a special occasion or congratulate them for their achievements was a chasm they couldn't fill, and it saddened them to watch others whose lives overflowed with love and support. To make up for it, Mr Jahid was sad to see them go, and his quiet shy wife pressed a coin into each of their hands as she half curtseyed in front of them.

'For luck,' she said and withdrew to stand with her husband as both their eyes filled with tears. Christa realised they genuinely understood their struggles, as they too faced prejudices every day no matter how hard they tried, and she for one, would never forget their kindness. Tiny little pieces of each of them would now be with her, and Christa wondered how her final mosaic would turn out. Did the shiny bright pieces ever outweigh the larger ones? Did bigger chunks of time make things more important, or could these tiny moments change her life? How long it would take her to find out was unknown and she didn't know if they could ever erase the darker moments of her past.

As they left the shop Christa glanced at Drew and Emily. Drew's eyes also gleamed brighter than usual, and Christa saw him gulp as if trying to control the emotions inside. To have someone care was hard to take and difficult to control, the contrast between what they had never known and these feelings from almost strangers created a struggle inside. Others saw this as normal and they did not even notice the depth of the love being shared, yet to Drew and Christa, it was a welcome drop of kindness into their deep and empty wells.

Emily was striding ahead, almost unmoved by the emotions being held in check around her. She had been loved, and shown love, up until recently, whereas Christa and Drew soaked up any skerrick of it cast their way. Neglect always left its mark.

'Hey Em, wait up.' Drew saw her pause, but she only turned slightly as if urging them to catch up. 'They are such good people, so nice and they are sad to see us go, I hope the new kids work out for them.'

'They'll be fine, I'm sure we are not the first people they've employed, now if we pick up our bus tickets and get some money out of the atm, we'll be set, all ready to go.'

Drew was a bit shocked and looked at her quizzically, it was like a wall had suddenly gone up and Emily had closed off one section of her life. Drew began to see there was more to her than the bright smile she displayed to everyone. I wonder if this was the side of her the other boys encountered first. As his mind puzzled she then stopped and gave him a smile that would bring any man down. Drew suddenly felt weak and almost useless as he tried to fix in his head a way to fight against it. He did not feel about her in that way, but suddenly his whole body was betraying him, and he felt the warmth creeping up his neck as his mouth tried to find words yet failed. Phew! He would have to be careful or this whole travelling thing could fall apart quickly. Drew shook his head and glanced at Christa. She too had stopped and the shadow which ran across her face for just a second told him she had seen it all and he was suddenly ashamed as if he had betrayed her and this little family they were becoming. As quickly as it came it was gone as she hung her head and started to saunter away.

'Come on you two, let's get this done, I still have to clean my room and pack.'

Drew watched as Christa's shoulders seemed to weigh down her body and again felt weak as Emily playfully clutched his hand and made him run with her to catch up. As they reached her, Emily grabbed Christa's as well and let out a squeal of joy.

'Yeah! Let our gap year begin. It's going to be so much fun. I just know it.'

'Not a gap year Em, more like the rest of our lives really, it's not likely we'll be back for university or anything.'

'Oh, don't be a sour-sop Christa, we are going to have such a good time our whole life will be like a gap year. Just wait and see. In thirty years, when we are all sitting on a porch with the grandbabies on our knees, you will look back and say Em, you were right, we've had the best life ever.'

Christa had to laugh, Emily would not be as easy to live with as they all thought but at least she would brighten every day. Christa also knew she would do whatever she could, to help Emily reach her dreams.

'Well Em, if we are going to be nursing grand babies in only thirty years we better get going or we won't have time for everything else on your list.' Drew gave Christa a wink as he said it and her shy smile made them think all was good between them again.

Emily raised both their arms up high and cried *let's go* as she swung them down again. The energy seemed to shoot between them like lightning and they laughed loudly and surged forward towards their future. With Emily pushing them on, how could they fail?

Chapter 2

Emily's enthusiasm never waned. As time after time they were knocked back for their lack of skill in well-paid jobs, she remained upbeat and was always the centre of attention. As they moved from one fruit picking to another, zigzagging from apples near Stanthorpe in the south of Queensland to strawberries at Eumundi, and blueberries in Bundaberg as they moved north. The last few months had been exhausting, exhilarating, and just plain fun if Christa was truthful. She had come out of herself a bit and following Emily's wise guidance, had put her modest savings in the bank and they worked for their daily expenses. They were lucky at some places, getting room and board and although the pay was never great, it was enough, and they all felt grown up and were proud of their self-reliance. Christa was glad they had Drew, he seemed to have grown five inches since they left the home, but his body was still catching up. To describe him as lean was an understatement, lanky more like, but his presence had deterred a few unwanted advances, and Christa's heart still fluttered when she saw him.

Christa and Drew had grown close, they all had. Emily liked to tease her, but Christa knew she was happy for her if Drew was what she wanted. They shared the occasional drunken kiss and felt awkward about it the next day, but their lifestyle and different accommodations had not taken them any further. With both of them from broken homes their caution was a safeguard to ensure they had not learned or inherited, the recklessness of their parents. Emily's constant chatter and encouragement about working towards the future had sunk in and although they worked hard, and played hard at times, they wanted to be the ones to break the cycle and make something of themselves, so no one could ever come in and tell them it was time to move on, or where to live or to have to scrape for a meal. Christa knew Drew was her one but did not want to shatter what they all shared at this moment, a romance in the mix could change everything. If it was meant to be, they would know when the time was right, although Christa had to admit it sometimes took a lot of self-control when he sat watching her after a late night or a big day of work. The look held a dreaminess that would cross his face as if he was taking her with him and she hoped he was seeing the same future she was.

They were still scraping by on their student travel passes but also knew the time was coming when they would have to pay more or invest in some wheels of their own. They were gobsmacked by the changing landscape as they moved away from the coast and started to see the open plains. The sky looked so big it seemed to go on forever with only wispy clouds to fracture its path to the horizon. The sun sucked every particle of moisture from the earth, just as any breeze stirred up the dust, twisting and turning it to resemble a tiny tornado before pushing it across the paddocks only to disappear leaving the scattered remains of what it had found.

They marvelled at the people who scratched out their living in tiny towns, some with no more than a pub or a general store and wondered what was at the end of the roads which turned off to far-flung stations and the isolated families who lived there. Red kangaroos stood in the shade of solitary scrubby trees and emus ran along fence lines as they passed, the males shooing and scolding their chicks as the hen, larger than her mate was always alone, her job done and her only interest to look after herself until her next mate was found and the process repeated itself. Christa thought they were probably like many of the mothers she had heard about from other foster kids, selfish and moving on from mate to mate to fill their desires and needs, the difference being, at least the emu left their offspring with someone who cared.

The day they got to Mount Isa was like a celebration. It was the furthest they had ever travelled and to all of them, it was the gateway to the outback, the road beyond disappearing in the distance towards the Northern Territory and the vast emptiness which is Australia's heart.

Emily had reached her dream, beyond here more dreams were to be made but for now she had fulfilled the promise to her friends she would lead them to the outback. They had survived so far and now the real adventures were about to begin. The excitement of realising this dream bubbled up inside, they all felt it and for Christa, it visualised in her head as bubbles forming and bursting making her tingle all over. Ahead was the outback, not scary, more wondrous, full of legends and new beginnings. There was more though, they had become a family, each looking out for the other, pooling resources at times, and supporting each other in every way. Christa knew, with her friends' support, that her confidence had grown, and could see now how love made you feel safe. Often in her life, she had not known where she would sleep next, if she would get a meal or if it would be another night she would have to flee, now it never seemed to matter, with Emily and Drew by her side it seemed to always work out, and on their terms as well. Christa could feel the lump of anxiety that had always lived in her chest thawing as happiness rubbed against it and ground it away.

The huge chimney stack in the copper mine rose high towards the sky, reminding them all where the lifeblood of this town lay. The hum from the mine rumbled constantly, a backdrop they would become so used to, they would soon not hear it anymore. They pulled their backpacks from the undercarriage of the bus, shaking off the dust they were coming to accept would be a constant part of their lives out here. The driver smiled and raising his hand in farewell checked his mirrors and pulled away from the curb. Christa had to laugh, the smile on Emily's face said it all, and her friend even looked speechless, but just for a moment.

'Look at us, we made it. Wow, can you feel it, the dust, the flies...I'm sure there will be flies! It's bigger than I thought, look at the stack, it's as famous as the town you know, the Isa stack maybe we should take a photo.'

Drew reined her in.

'Maybe we should find our accommodation first Em, plenty of time for sightseeing later. I don't know about you but I'm hungry and sitting for hours on the bus made me tired from doing nothing.'

'Come on, get your stuff, we can grab a bite as we go, it will be cooler inside this mall than out here as well.'

Christa swung her bag on her back and headed inside the shopping centre. It contained one major chain store, a supermarket, and a few specialty shops, not much, but all they would need. The donut place had a few empty chairs, and they overindulged on hotdogs with masses of mustard and sauce followed by extra-large iced donuts and a coffee each.

'Gosh, so good.' Drew pushed his chair back, rubbing his belly with satisfaction as he spread his long legs out wide. Dusty boots and socks held down by some leather sock guards which Christa knew, made him feel attached to the land. Drew looked at home and was satisfied in a way she had not noticed before, yet had seen grow as their journey progressed. Even after a long day, Drew had spent time yarning, as he liked to say with each property owner they had met. She had often seen them crouching, running soil between their fingers before looking out across whichever crop they were discussing or running their hands over an animal's rump discussing its formation and breeding. Drew seemed to absorb it all and Christa knew he was storing it all away, learning as much as he could whenever the opportunity arrived, she did not think he had found his true role yet, but each step gave him knowledge for the future.

'So, where's the backpacker's hostel, who's got the address?' Drew was always anxious to know they were settled for somewhere to sleep; the one time they had slept in a bus shelter he had been beside himself pacing most of the night to make sure they were safe.

'It's alright Dad,' Emily teased. 'I've got it here and I googled the directions, five minutes' walk tops. It's all organised they know we're coming. Seriously you are such a grandpa sometimes. Pity it's the weekend or we could have stopped in to see what jobs are about.'

'There she goes' he whispered to Christa, 'not even waiting to draw a breath. I bet you we'll be there before one of us can answer her.'

Christa had to smile, and they slapped hands sealing the unspoken bet, though Christa knew he would win. They glanced at each other to confirm their conspiracy then both blushed and turned away. Without them noticing Emily had halted and caught them in the act.

'So, what is it now, another silly bet to see how long I talk for?' They both looked guilty, and she gave them a disapproving look. Christa chanced a glance and then dissolved in laughter as she saw Drew too, was trying hard to look serious. The minute their eyes met he could hold it no more and as Emily stalked off in disgust, they both exploded with laughter and then ran after her pleading for her to forgive them.

'You two,' she said crossly. 'Why don't you two just get on with it, all this lovey-dovey eye shit, just do it and get it over with.'

They both stopped stunned and embarrassed by her words, neither knowing what to do nor how to fill the soundless void between them. Emily turned again this time with her hands firmly on her hips and her shoulders slumped forward.

'What, do you think no one notices?' Standing, legs apart, her backpack nearly as big as herself, and with an angry look like a snappy terrier on her face, broke the ice and they both swept in to hug her.

'We were only playing Em,' said Christa.

'Yeah, don't get mad Em, you'll spoil my reputation. If I date Christa my cool, handsome guy image of travelling with two girls will be ruined.'

They all laughed as he fake-combed his hair and puffed out his chest, yet a part of Christa hoped it wasn't true, and he was only saying it to cover his true feelings and make Emily smile again.

As if a magic wand had touched her, Emily was back, full of smiles and the chatter started again.

'Well, just so you know, it doesn't bother me. We would have been there by now if the both of you would pick up the pace. It'll be dinner by the time you two old ladies get a move on. Geez, the things I have to put up with. Now Drew, do you think we have enough cash to buy a car? Might be handy, especially once we leave here, and we could buy a tent too, I was thinking if we camp out, we can save more and buy something a bit better. Might look into it tomorrow. Wonder if there are many staying here, well I suppose we would have known by now if you two girls hadn't been taking dolly steps to get here.' With her biggest smile, Emily turned in the door of the hostel ready to charm whoever was at the desk off their feet. They had no idea what was about to hit them Christa thought.

charm whoever was at the desk off their feet. They had no idea what was about to hit them Christa thought.

Chapter 3

The station track was full of bulldust holes and Christa tried to steer the ute around them. The pump had been damaged, and they needed the parts out at the bore site pronto. As the kitchen hand, she had been the only one available at camp to take them.

Christa had learned a lot since they had arrived and preferred the unskilled jobs around the homestead, to work out in the yards. Muster had started and the cattle were being rounded up and walked in from the far-flung corners of the station. Emily had been snapped up to go as she had riding experience and had been excited to meet the stock horse she had been assigned for the season. As she had babbled on telling Christa the background of the Australian stock horse and how it was bred from thoroughbreds and Arabians and something about Spain and Welsh ponies thrown in, Christa had glazed over and wondered what other snippets of knowledge Emily had hidden away in there. Drew had gone out to, he would ride if needed but mostly would be with the support vehicles helping to set up camps and temporary yards if needed. They were all swagging it, and Emily was talking now swags might be the way for them to go once they left the station. It was clear to all Emily was embracing the whole experience in more ways than one.

They had been at the pub for a meal the first night they arrived in Isa, and the barman had pointed them in the direction of a group of stockmen who were in town for the night. Luck would have it they could use a hand and the next day they were bouncing their way along one of the very same tracks Christa had wondered about on their way here. Emily and Drew had been full of excitement, and it only grew when they learned they would be getting the full jackaroo/jillaroo experience. Christa had been more reserved and worried they might thrust her on a horse and send her out into the wilderness, she had only ever seen a horse once in real life and the very thought of it made her tremble inside. Christa wasn't sure what she expected, American movies full of fancy ranches and cowboys in spurs were her vision.

The homestead was modest but at least had a few trees and a rough fence around it to protect the feeble attempt of a garden. The dust seemed to swirl at any movement, and they had been told the muster was early as the dry had gone on too long and any money they could make now was more than a carcass would be worth in the paddock if this drought continued. Everyone was nice and the station cook required a hand, which Christa was only too happy to put hers up for if it would keep her off a horse's back. What she hadn't known was how long her days were about to be. They were the first ones up and last to bed after the clearing and cleaning were done. It was fun though, Christa could see how hard they all worked and the planning that was going into the highlight of the year. After muster, there would be some time to relax. The cattle would be drafted, branded, ear tagged and vaccinated. The young males would be marked, the females preg-tested, and the bulls would be reselected. Christa didn't think she would ever understand some of the conversations. As the days went on they laughed with her as they told her the meanings of all the words, retelling her horror when she found out what marking was, but not once was anything said in a way to make her feel stupid. There were others like them, who had travelled here for the experience, fell in love with the job, and the land, and stayed. Most of them knew what it was like to be the new hand and were happy to see the newbies trying so hard. From then on Christa no longer looked at the washing up as a chore when the thought of cutting out the young bulls' manhood at marking time, could have been her alternative.

The outer bores had been turned off to make the cattle start to make their way in towards the yards. As they sought out the next bore, it in turn would be turned off and the ever-growing herds would soon merge as they walked, in what seemed to Christa, an ever-lessening circle toward their fate. Supplies had to be packed for each camp along with supplying the three meals a day plus smoko or morning tea as she knew it. Watching tiredly those first few days as Emily flirted her way around the camp, Christa wondered if she had made the right decision in taking this role. Cookie followed her gaze and smiled at her.

'Don't worry love, a few days and we can have a rest and your young friend there, well, she might not be enjoying herself so much after twelve hours in the saddle every day. You'll be right, it gets easier.'

Christa gave him a weak smile.

'Thanks, Cookie, I'm enjoying it, really I am.'

Drew hung close when he could, drawing her out to mix with the group after her chores were done. Christa noted the sideways glances they were given and with the men outnumbering the women, Drew was staking his claim. Christa felt a warm glow whenever he looked at her and knew it was only a matter of time before they cemented their relationship. Out here in this harsh land amongst the heat, the flies and the isolation, you made your mark, became stronger inside, and took opportunities before the wind gathered them up like dust and blew them away.

The last day dawned, and it seemed everyone was in camp for the night. Christa wondered how so much food could be consumed in one sitting all the time whilst preparing the next.

Dusty boots seemed to tramp in and out of the dining area all day and the flies seemed to have multiplied tenfold overnight. Christa tied her hair high on her head hoping a cool breeze would find its way in to soothe her. She felt jumpy and on edge. Drew and Emily would be going at first light tomorrow and it would be the first time Christa would be without them. She felt almost sick about it and was surprised at how deeply she was already missing Drew, although he hadn't even left yet.

Dinner was noisy and there were lots of jokes followed by laughter filling the air. As the sun said her final goodbyes, Cookie nudged her and said he would finish up so she could join in the fun. Christa slid into the seat next to Drew and he took her hand and guided it into his lap. Emily was the centre of attention and had earned the respect of everyone with her attitude and willingness to learn the work. They also watched while she flirted with each of them, waiting keenly to see where her irresistible smile would fall. Out here Christa had never felt so safe in all her life. As the night cooled around them and the flies dropped away from the screens to wherever flies go at night, Christa's heart was pumping to a beat she was sure every-one could hear as Drew increased the pressure on her hand. She knew it would be tonight before he left, he wanted to go, but he didn't want to leave her, and he wanted her to know just how much he cared. It was like they were having a conversa-tion through their fingertips, no words were exchanged but as his calloused hand rubbed hers, Christa was sure she could hear his unsaid request. Could she feel it too? Would it be ok? His hesitations, ... if you only want to be friends... and the pres-sure from her as she squeezed her reply.. yes, yes, I want it too. Drew glanced at her as more laughter ran around the room, his shy smile just for her and awkwardness too, as they played this out in their quiet way in front of everyone. The head stock-man pushed back his chair and signalled it was time to wind it up and get some rest. Drew never let go of her hand and head bowed, had nodded goodnight, and led her out the door. The room which moments ago, had been so noisy was now deathly quiet, and the door banged twice behind them as they stepped out into the night. Christa felt the warm blush move up her face and was glad of the darkness enveloping her. A few chuckles were heard and then Emily's voice.

'Thank God, finally! I thought I'd have to tie them together if they didn't do it soon.' There was a roar of laughter and Christa stopped, smiling but embarrassed too, as to how she would face them in the morning. Drew was grinning ear to ear and whispered.

'Come on, they mean well, don't worry.'

They heard the screen door again and scurried around the corner towards Christa's room. Drew pinned her against the door kissing her with a passion she didn't know he had. As he turned the handle they swung with the door into the room. Kicking it closed Drew's mouth never left hers as they scrambled, buttons flying, boots kicked from their feet in a frenzy. It was fast, passionate and everything they had felt in the past few months poured out. From the shy glances to the stolen kisses, it all combined to bring them both to a place they had never been before. Panting and smiling, Christa could not believe the feelings inside, it was like he was part of her, and she never wanted him to leave, her heart was singing a tune she had never heard before, and she wanted to laugh and cry all at the same time.

Christa looked up at his face, the moon's soft glow through the window highlighting his features. He was filling out she realised, not with weight but with maturity, his eyes were closed, and a single tear glistened on the edge of his lashes, he felt it too, she could see it and he was scared to open his eyes in case she didn't feel it as well. She ran her fingers up his chest and as he braved a look hi tear fell and splashed onto her face.

'I can't believe you,' he said and gulped. 'I can't believe us!' His smile said it all as he rolled onto the bed beside her. Their hands kept moving, exploring, caressing. Christa snuggled closer knowing already how empty she would feel when they moved apart and not wanting it to happen, ever. For the first time in her life, everything was perfect, her past blurred away and the future looked full of so many opportunities. Drew held her close, murmuring sweet words in her ear, telling her secrets she knew were only for her to know. As his voice drifted away, Christa's mind seemed full yet light, like a cloud, soft and gentle floating on a summer breeze. Sleep eased its way in and as she drifted off to slumberland Christa was already dreaming of the man who lay beside her.

Chapter 4

The morning had flown in a whirlwind of last-minute packing and breakfasts being almost inhaled as no one wanted to be the one who held them up. The dust seemed to fill the air and hang like a curtain behind them as they disappeared in front of it. Drew had popped his head in last minute, but they had already said their private goodbyes in her room and Christa knew how excited he was to be having this adventure. Cookie had given her a wink and a, how was your night comment before they were heads down, bums up until the dust settled and Christa realised how quiet it was with everyone gone. Cookie made some tea and produced a slab of cake he hadn't been able to fit in the last container. Christa sank onto the kitchen stool and looked at him.

'It's like a whole day rolled into a morning isn't it?' he said wearily.

Christa laughed.

'I suppose this is how every mother feels in the morning when she finally gets the kids off to school. Now I know what organised chaos is, some of them are hopeless aren't they?'

'Well, we can take it easy for the rest of the day, do a bit of a stocktake and a cleanout while we can, because once the choppers arrive it won't take them long. They'll walk the cattle about fourteen kilometres a day along the fences and the bush pilots will push the wild ones in so they can join the herd, it will be just as busy here the closer they get, and we'll have the extra teams attached to the helicopters. Those guys are crazy, but I tell you, not as crazy as the bullcatchers if they have to bring them in. Let's get to it and hopefully we can have an early night for a change.'

Christa and Cookie worked solidly for most of the day, he enticed conversations out of her she never thought she would have. He was a kind man, and he loved his job. He took three weeks off each year to visit his elderly parents, he told her, but otherwise, this was his life, and he loved it. He loved the banter and challenges of being an outback cook and always tried to be a mate and a confidante for everyone on the station.

'It's my job to be happy,' he told her. 'To fill their bellies and be the smiling face they see every day. They all know they can drop in for a cuppa and a chat, the new ones feel like they have a friend, and the long timers a family. They are my family too, every one of them, some stay and some move on, some hide from life here and some get the confidence to take it on head-first. I've seen all types but if you watch them, each one of them stops for a moment during the day. You look over and they are just standing, or leaning on a rail taking it in. There is something about being out here, looking out at the nothingness and feel-ing a connection with the land no matter where you go from, it never leaves you, and you never forget the lessons she teaches, this is God's country, Christa. Listen to her and you'll always be ok.'

Christa didn't follow but somehow understood. The look as he spoke softened his face and she could see it was his heart talking. The stockmen also talked about the connection with the land and whether they were from a traditional background or from across the sea they spoke about the land in rever-ent tones. The land was their mother, their worst enemy, their protector, and their spirit. She wound her way around them throwing the worst of times at them and then drawing them in, bringing them together and celebrating with them. If they could survive everything she threw at them, they could survive anything, yet still, they bowed down to her and she made them humble, kind, and grateful for whatever she sent their way. Christa felt moved by everything he said, she had never felt like she belonged anywhere and as she walked to her room she stopped and looked out past the yards to the emptiness beyond. Soon it would be full of dust and noise as the men and horses guided the cattle in and they were separated into new mobs. It was exciting and Christa was looking forward to seeing the whole process and getting caught up in the atmosphere of the muster, even if was right at the end. She couldn't wait to see Drew again and knew Emily would want to know all the details, they hadn't had a chance to chat in the turmoil of the morning, but Christa could already hear her friend's voice prodding and poking her, even from here. As she stood, Christa felt the peace settle over her, she understood it now, here she did not feel alone, no matter the distance to the nearest neighbour, let alone town or city.

Sydney seemed so far away, almost a dream, and it was as if the land was easing her past and healing her spirit as well. Christa was so grateful she had met both Emily and Drew, without them she could not even imagine where she would be. She smiled, she certainly never imagined she would be here. Somehow Christa knew she would never go back, to live in a city now would suffocate her, she didn't think this was her place, but she was getting closer and dreamed one day she would find it, a special place where everything fell into place, right down to the last puzzle piece. She could see it in her mind as if it was a premonition, the last piece as it clicked into place. The outlook blurred but now she knew she would feel it, she would just know, know when it was right.

In her room, Christa kicked off her boots and gathered her toiletries and towel. There would be no competition for the showers tonight and she intended to take advantage of their absence and have an extended one to give her hair a good wash without someone banging on the door. Sliding into her thongs almost felt like a holiday as the soft rubber, so light on her feet, allowed her toes to spread and the air to circulate her feet. Christa stepped out the door and quickly closed it behind her as she saw the swirl of dust headed her way from behind the station ute which then pulled up in front of her. Christa held her breath, and as the dust began to settle the window slid down and she bent her knees so she could see who it was.

'You can drive can't you Christa?' The boss looked at her as if no wasn't the answer.

'Um yes, yes I can, I'm only on my P-plates though.'

'Those things don't matter out here Luv, our son drives and he's only ten. Look, I need you to take some parts and tools out to Jimmy's Bore, the cattle broke into the turkey's nest and did some damage, and I've got no one else I can spare. You'll be right, Cookie will give you the directions, and Johnno, the bore runner, he's out there, he had to use the same part over at Matilda so makes more sense for me to send it out than him to waste a day driving in and another back. Needs to be done before the rest of the cattle get there.' Christa knew she must have looked a bit concerned as his face softened and he reassured her.

'You'll be right. I'll put everything in the back here and a swag in case you want to stay the night before driving back. Johnno will look after you, no worries. Tell him if he needs a hand I can send young Drew over from the mob as well, I just need it done. Cookie will pack you some food and I'd leave early before it gets too hot.' Nodding his head, he went to pull away then stopped.

'You know if anything happens, to just stay with the vehicle, there is plenty of water in here and the worst thing you can do is walk away. Easier to find a ute than to find you wandering around out there. Keep to the track and you'll be fine.' This time he did go, slower now so the dust barely lifted off the ground.

Christa felt a ball of anxiety mixed with excitement roll up inside of her. She was always the one who held back, a bit reluctant to try new things, it's where Emily had been such a bonus, she just barrelled straight in. You can do this she said to herself, it will be an adventure. As much as she consoled herself, on the inside her nerves still jumped around as she finally headed to the showers.

Chapter 5

Cookie had reassured her she would be fine and even stood outside to wave her off until she could no longer see him as the dust rose behind her. He had given her a continuous stream of advice and reassurance, always coming back to the first rule of the outback, never leave the vehicle. Too many lives were lost because they had wandered away from the one thing which would protect them from the elements, and which could be spotted far more easily from the air and the ground. Christa had tossed and turned all night, mainly worried by the physical act of driving. Yes, she had a legal piece of paper which said she could drive but apart from the leadup to obtaining her licence she had never driven a car on her own. The counsellors had taught them at first, and then received funding so they each had professional lessons as well. Again, it had been Emily who had insisted she complete the hours and go for the test.

'Don't think I'm going to let you sit back like Lady Muck while I drive you around everywhere.' Emily had said. Oh well, Christa thought, at least there is not much out here I can run into.

The track seemed to twist and turn, and Christa wondered why when the land didn't seem to require it to, except through a few dry creek beds. Why didn't they just drive in a straight line? At times she could see as far as her eyes could see as if there was nothing between her and the far horizon, not a bush or a tree or an animal, and then the track would seem to sink and all she could see were the sides of it and she wondered how many vehicles it had taken to wear away this section of the track. She had stopped once so far and laughed at herself as she had checked behind her before opening the door as if another car would suddenly appear out of nowhere at the exact moment to overtake her. Sitting on the bonnet munching one of the sandwiches Cookie had packed while looking out toward her destination her anxiety dropped away. She had made it this far and not damaged the car and apart from the few kangaroo hops as she left, Christa thought she had done quite well. It was more than peaceful, and Christa again recalled her conversation with Cookie and how he described this place. It was a warmth. Not like a blush, they rolled up your neck onto your face, but a warmth all over which fitted exactly inside her body, and once it was there it would never leave. It was part of her now and the more she lowered the walls she had built up as a child, the more Mother Nature captivated her and opened her mind to listen to the land, her surroundings, and her inner self. Christa was learning a different kind of survival to the skills she had been forced to learn as a child, the outback for all its harshness, was teaching her in gentle ways.

The sun was certainly starting to bite, and Christa slid off the bonnet stepping toward the door. Suddenly she froze. Lying neatly under the door was the biggest snake she had ever seen. Christa's eyes were wide and her mouth wider. It was moving its head, raising it as if it was trying to find a way inside. The second rule of the bush, or was it the third? Her mind was frozen and trying to work out things she did not want to know right at this minute!

1) Always have water. 2) Never leave the vehicle. 3) Oh god what was three?

Have food? No, have shelter ... no, I have the truck. If you see a snake stand still! Yes, three was the snake. Without thinking she was already doing the right thing. Her mind tried to work out what kind it was, they had a chart up in the dining room, but she had never really stopped to look properly and they all, to her, looked the same. Eastern brown, western brown, tiger? Whatever it was it would be deadly, and she wanted to get as far away from it as possible.

The snake turned and seemed to look straight at her, and Christa almost reeled back in horror. Stay calm, keep still, her head screamed at her as the snake lowered its head to the ground. The snake turned as if to leave and the way its body rippled underneath as it moved made her skin crawl as if she could feel each movement on herself. Christa shuddered at the thought and took a deep breath. The snake turned again and this time she couldn't help it and stepped back. One movement and it hit out at lightning speed.

Christa opened her eyes. It was gone. She still stood, she had felt it like a slap on her boot, she had kicked her leg up, trying to ... she didn't know what, ...trying to defend herself? She was too scared to look, where was it, what happened now, should she move? The thoughts were as fast as the snake strike. She looked down, she felt no pain, there was no blood seeping through her jeans, and she suddenly realised, it had missed! Christa was careful now, she didn't want to put her hand down in case the snake was still there, hiding, waiting to bite her somewhere closer to her heart. She swivelled on one foot and raised the other one onto the bull bar. Checking the ground around her again, on the count of three in her head, she pulled herself up and scrambled onto the bonnet. Sitting on the roof with her legs splayed across the windscreen Christa pulled up the leg of her jeans to survey the damage. Every scenario had already run through her head, she knew its strike had missed her, but just in case she was wrong, her mind was already setting a plan into place, even one up until her last breath. Christa ran her hand up and down her leg and pulled off her boot to see if there was even a mark but there wasn't. She started to pant, her body reacting automatically to calm her. She put her hand to her chest, blowing the breaths out to consciously slow herself down. She had survived, it had missed. Her mind replayed it over and over, she had closed her eyes to block the impact and her leg went out, it was seconds, no, milliseconds ... milliseconds which had worked in her favour. Maybe because it had turned away, moved just a little bit away so it was just a fraction too far, maybe her kick was just perfect timing, maybe, maybe. Whatever it was, it was unbelievable, no, she thought, bloody incredible. Christa promptly burst into tears and drawing up her legs she circled them with her arms as she sobbed.

A whistle from above made her look up as a hawk soared overhead. What are you doing, it seemed to call, and Christa realised she had to make a move, she wasn't sure now how long she had been here, but it felt like hours. Her whole body seemed to be aching, and she realised it was just the after-effect of the adrenaline making her feel this way as if it was draining out of her limbs. Christa also felt slightly lightheaded, she steadied herself as she turned onto her knees, and then pushed herself up so she was now standing on the roof. She searched the ground for the snake even though the sensible side of her brain was telling her it would be long gone, the other side filled her with stories of them winding themselves up on the chassis waiting to spring out at you next time you stopped. Christa linked her hands on top of her head and blew out a breath so loud she was sure the trees in the distance would sway. Climbing into the back she splashed some water on her hands in case by touching her boots she had picked up some venom. She rubbed her face, then scolded herself and washed both her hands, and face again. The radio crackled in the ute and a male voice spoke.

'Copy Christa.'

'Copy Christa, are you there?

Christa knew if she didn't respond all hell would break loose, so she slid one leg around the backboard and into the driver's window. Swinging her bum out she awkwardly managed to manoeuvre her other leg in and releasing one hand at a time slid in the window onto the seat. Her heart was pumping wildly again, and she paused for a moment as it took her breath away. The radio crackled again.

'Copy Christa, do you have a copy?'

'Yes, yes, I'm here, over,' she said breathlessly, then had to repeat it as she remembered to hold the button in on the side as she spoke.

'Where are you, Luv, thought I'd be seeing your dust by now. Over.'

'I just had a bit of a delay, I'm on my way again now, I'm sorry, I will get there as soon as I can.'

'No worries don't break your neck, just try to get here before dark and concentrate as the last bit can get confusing. You alright? Over.'

'Yes, all good now.' Christa spoke with a confidence she didn't quite feel. 'I'll see you soon, I think I'm about an hour out. Over.'

'Ok. See you then, if you get lost just give me a call or lay on the horn and I'll come to you. Don't leave the vehicle, will you? Over.'

'Thanks, Johnno, I won't.'

'And watch out for snakes, I saw the biggest mother of one today.'

'Ok, thanks Johnno. Over and out.'

Christa was still sitting awkwardly across the seats and felt like she was all legs as she twisted back into driving position. She turned the key and as the engine roared to life she spoke aloud to herself.

'Watch out for snakes. Check! I've certainly ticked it off the list today.' Straightening in the seat she glanced in the mirror as she moved forward, secretly hoping the snake would be curled up there behind her, so she would never have to wonder where it was. The track behind looked the same as the one ahead and her shoulders slumped as she realised the snake would probably visit her many times from now on, in her dreams.

Chapter 6

Christa managed to negotiate the maze of tracks in the earth and more by luck, chose the right one and saw Johnno's ute in the distance. The last hour was a bit of a blur as she let the ute follow the wheel ruts and had just poked along, willing herself to think about the possibility Johnno had called on Drew to come and help him. Christa still could not figure out why it mattered so much if the cattle damaged the turkey's nest, maybe it was a protected species or something, but surely a bird could share the bore water with the cattle? Christa decided to wait until it became obvious what the problem was as she had been the butt of jokes before, and it did still chip away at her confidence even though she laughed along with everyone else. A curl of smoke went up as she stopped, and Johnno's head appeared from behind the ute.

'There you are. I just got the fire going and I hope you brought a swag because there is no way I'll let you drive back in the dark.'

'Yes, the boss put in everything I might need, it's not too busy in the kitchen so he said to have a look around but be back by tomorrow night. I think the first lot from the north paddock will be in by then or close at least. Sorry I'm late Johnno.'

'No trouble Luv, I had other things to catch up on anyway, just glad you were alright is all. Did you do a tyre?' Johnno was puzzled as he didn't think this scrap of a girl would be capable of changing one, yet he did get a sense she could hold her own if she had to. Christa launched into her story about the snake and then stood looking out to the last rays of sunlight as she waited for him to tell her everything she had done wrong.

'Good on you, I hate the things, I would've still been there shaking in my boots. Trouble with me is, I don't think I could fit through the window.' He laughed loudly and Christa took in his broad shoulders and solid stature, even his hands were three times the size of hers, and Christa had never thought of herself as small. She laughed along with him as images of Johnno stuck in the window bounced through their heads.

'I'll tell you a secret. I always sleep in the back of the ute or zipped up in a tent, those cowboys rolling their swags out on the ground, well, they can have it for a joke eh? I don't care what they say but I not sleeping down there with the wigglers about, no way. Come on let's rustle up some grub, are you hungry?'

Christa realised she was hungry and was also happy to show Johnno the stew Cookie had sent, along with the slabs of apple pie for a treat. Johnno rubbed his hands in delight and quickly had it heating up on the fire. Christa didn't know when she had ever felt such peace. The glow of the fire reached up and dissipated into harmless sparks as it rose and twirled with the smoke toward the heavens, disappearing and becoming one with the twinkling stars in the sky. Christa did not think there could ever be this many stars and Johnno told her to wait until it was properly dark, as there would be a million more. He showed her a damper he had baking in the camp oven and stirred the stew slowly whilst pointing out distant satellites as they raced across the sky.

'Won't see them later, be too many stars, and it seems it must just be the right tilt of the earth and the angle of the sun, which catches them at this time of day. Hard to imagine what it would be like up there isn't it, but I think I'm quite happy down here with these two big hoofs of mine in the dirt, solid, it's what I like. What about you Christa, where do you think you'll end up?'

Christa leaned back in the camp chair and for a moment she couldn't answer, no one had ever asked what her dream was, and to be honest she wasn't sure. To dream was something she had pushed aside as a child, as they never came true, but out here, it seemed anything and everything was possible. Somehow this endless sky made dreams seem possible.

'I don't know Johnno, I've had a rough sort of an upbringing and until I met Emily and Drew, I never had anyone I could rely on. They are sort of like my family now, and I've just been enjoying those feelings for now. We are all just trying to find where we fit in.'

Johnno turned the damper out onto a tin plate and Christa watched as the heavy fragrant steam rose from it. He tore a piece off, lashing it with butter before handing it to her.

'It's what God has for breakfast I reckon. Of course, he probably cooks it on the sun and smothers it in cocky's joy, but just as good with butter and the perfect thing to soak up stew.'

Christa was a bit confused, but as soon as the soft scone-like bread melted in her mouth she did think she had never tasted anything better in her entire life. Johnno handed her a bowl of the hot stew and again Christa felt like this food was not only nutritious but an experience as well. The simplicity of it was taking her on a journey through her taste buds. Johnno handed her another chunk of damper.

'Now wipe this around the bowl and soak up the gravy in the bottom. Makes me think of my dear old mum this does. She must have cooked stew twice a week when I was a kid, sometimes there was no meat in it, but she did her best she did, and it filled our bellies. Can't believe you've never had a stew before, or a damper. Cities, it's what I don't like about them, people are forgetting the old ways. Old ways aren't bad ways Christa, a meal like this can't be bought in a shop, it's full of love see. Cookie sent this out because he knew I'd be getting low on supplies and probably a bit sick of cooking too, he knew it would make me think of my mum and he knew it would fill my belly, both our bellies in fact, then he sent the pie as well, just because he's a mate and one of the best blokes I know. He sent me a meal, but he sent me a handshake and a gidday as well, can you see what I mean Christa?'

Christa nodded relishing the taste of the stew and damper together. She liked how Johnno explained things, and as Cookie did, he made her wonder if this is what fathers were like, the good ones, who taught you things, and told you tales but spoke to you with respect for what you did know and encouragement for what you didn't.

'You picked a good station to come to, my girl, salt of the earth these people, every single one of them. If you ever need a hand again, you can always come back here. People out here, they'll look after you. I've heard how hard you work and always with a smile, those things don't go unnoticed and even if you decide to move on you will always be welcome back.'

'Thanks, Johnno, everyone is so nice, and even though I'm not much good at anything, I've learned a lot, but I do need to learn one more thing.' He gave her an enquiring look.

'How to make damper, it's delicious!'

Johnno laughed and spent the next half an hour telling her about the tricks with the camp oven, don't get it too hot or it will burn, a bit of ash on the top before the coals just backs off the heat, a bit as well as some ash on the hot coal underneath.

'This is why it's called damper because you damper the fire with ash to get the right temperature. It's not a slow cooker girlie,' he said, 'think of it as a normal oven where you adjust the temp.'

Then there were the different dampers you could make, walnut and date ones, pesto ones, cheese ones, herb ones, or everything thrown in and mixed ones, even pizza ones! Sweet or savoury, if you have flour and water, or beer he said and winked at her, and a match, you can make a meal in the bush.

Christa now knew what contentment was, her belly was full, and she had to admit her eyes did sparkle as they overfilled themselves with Cookie's delicious apple pie. The steady gentle tone of Johnno's voice and the deep dark blue of the sky as the billions of stars tried to twinkle and outshine it, gave her a sense of something she could not quite find a name for yet. It would come to her, and she knew it would be a special name, a big word that would encompass everything she was feeling inside at this moment and close to the place she was searching for. It came to her then, it was not a big word, just a small one with four tiny letters yet it was how this country made her feel, home.

Chapter 7

The rattling of the billy woke her in the morning. Christa could not believe how comfortable the swag had been, she had slept like a log. Johnno had stoked the fire and welcomed her with a big smile. For a man who was so comfortable in his own company, Christa knew he had enjoyed having her here last night and she had loved hearing his stories and learned so much from not only the content but the way he told them. Johnno had an almost deliberate way of speaking, not slow but each word held meaning and had its place, he never wasted one.

'Well, another beautiful day, not a cloud in the sky. When she comes she'll come in a hurry, and we'll be wishing we could have another day like today. Never happy are we?'

'Who's coming?' Christa questioned in a puzzled tone as she looked around for signs of dust in the distance.

'Rain. When she comes she'll play her game, sometimes too much and sometimes never enough, but even a teardrop would be welcome at the moment it's been so dry. At least we don't have the mice, hate them worse than the snakes, actually it's when you want a few snakes around to eat the buggers. After a mice plague you get the cats, they breed like mice they do when there is plenty of food around, and a year later you see them dying in the paddock. In a bad year, the mice die off then the cats do too. Stinky blighters they are, saw one take on an eagle once over some roadkill. Just trying to survive like us all but makes it a hard life out here.'

Johnno was off again, and Christa knew he was loving it, they toasted the leftover damper on the fire, and she thought the golden syrup he handed her might be the cocky's joy he had spoken about last night. Christa knew he wouldn't think her silly for asking.

'Johnno, we came through the cane fields over near Bowen and I didn't see any cockatoos, not like further south where the farmers were always chasing them off.'

'Not cockatoo's Christa, cocky like a cocky farmer, it's what we'd call the landowner, and this syrup always came in a tin see. In the old days, we didn't have a fridge in the car like we do now, so anything that kept well and tasted good became a staple. Cookie would order it by the barrel.' He laughed and Christa saw a memory flash across his face before he continued. 'Just had to scrape some ants out sometimes if you didn't push the lid right down, but they never hurt anyone.'

The radio crackled and then the satellite phone rang. As Johnno answered Christa looked at her phone for the time, it was the only thing it was good for out here and she wondered who would call this early with the sun barely over the horizon. Except for meals, time did not matter out here, if the sun was up it was time for work and when it set it was time for rest. The hours in between were always productive, and your pace was tuned to the weather or the task at hand. It was a way of life not just a job. Christa zoned back in to listen to Johnno.

'Yep, no problem, at least she can hold a piece of wire for me, and she's willing to learn. Yep, we'll get it done no worries.'

'The boss requested, if it was ok, for you to stay here to give me a hand, some jokers fell asleep on the job, and they will have to do some backtracking so he can't send anyone to help. I told him you'd do just fine.'

'Oh yes please, I was just feeling a bit sorry I'd have to go back, as long as you don't mind I'm fairly useless.'

'We weren't all born with skills girl, just some learn things earlier than others. I'm sure you'll teach me a thing or two one day, so let's get cracking then, if you tidy up camp I'll get the tools we need, and we'll have this job done in no time. I'm glad you're staying Christa, you are good company, have no backchat, and are willing to learn, it's what I told the boss too. You'll do alright.'

Christa blushed and turned away, she had never had much praise, and it brought tears to her eyes, she was happy to be staying. Johnno was a top bloke, and she liked how he made her feel worthwhile. Ducking her head, she rinsed the few dishes and pushed the few coals apart so the fire wouldn't burn as tall, breaking off a bit of saltbush she swept the ground around their chairs to scatter any crumbs that might attract the ants. Next, she rolled her swag and put it on the roof of the cab so they would not be pushing it aside each time they needed something. Pulling on her hat so it was low on her brow she walked with purpose to the bore to give Johnno a hand.

'Keep an eye out for snakes as it warms up. They love the frogs and insects you get around the turkey's nest and they need to drink too. If you don't come when I call, I'll just figure you will have to wait a moment for one to cross your path. Hope for a black, because then we'll be fairly safe there is not one of those other buggers about.'

'Why, don't' they like each other?'

'A black will hunt down and kill a tiger or a brown, just don't trust the theory a hundred percent of the time though. The bastards, them and mice bloody upset me something fierce, give me a wild charging bull any day. Come on let's get this part in first and then we'll work on the fence. They worked solidly until the sun was high in the sky. Christa mostly went back and forth for tools and finally learned the turkey's nest was the pool of water that was pumped up from the bore. Like an above-ground dam, the sides had been built up to form the dam and the water came up through the pipe into the nest and then was pumped out to the troughs for the cattle to drink. If the nest got too full, it overflowed to the burrow pit which was outside the fence. This burrow pit was just a cracked dusty shallow in the earth but there was still some greenery around it, straggling weeds that came and went no matter the season, and the cattle had not been here yet, to trample them down due to the bore's lack of water, Christa thought it would look like an oasis once the water was refilled. The nest had a bit of muddy sludge in the bottom and Johnno said there were probably some creatures buried in the mud until the water returned.

Johnno was pleased with the progress they were making, he didn't talk much while he was working but he was happy to answer any question she had and to explain the procedure. Although Christa didn't think she would ever be able to remember, she was learning you never know when you need to dig some obscure fact out of your brain and knowledge could sometimes get you by, even if your skills didn't match the task. Johnno set Christa to clean the troughs when he didn't need her close. A few of the troughs were set away to avoid a crush of cattle in close but with the pump broken, Johnno had explained it was probably why the fence was pushed down as the cattle smelt the water in the nest and pushed their way through trampling anything in their path. Add the kangaroos, and probably some wild dogs or dingoes pushing their way in and out, and it had ended up a right mess with parts of the dam lip pushed in as they went further and further in to get a drink as the water decreased. Johnno had shown her tracks left in the cracking mud and explained which was which. The dingoes had a smaller track and usually, he said, a mixed breed wild dog had a wider print even though they were often mistaken as dingoes as they seemed to retain the colouring which blended into the landscape. There was a long slide track Christa had mistaken for a snake and was shocked at how many there were, and how wide they were until Johnno pointed out they were from the kangaroo's tail sliding slowly as it searched the earth with its nose for the water or a meagre blade of grass to eat. You will know a snake track when you see it, he had said, once the kangaroo stands up to hop away its track changes but a snake, especially a big one will go side to side, and you can almost see the ripples made as it slid by. You'll know once you see it he said.

Christa wanted to impress Johnno and was chuffed when he said he couldn't have done a better job himself. They started on the fence after lunch, and she learned about tying off and straining the wires before twitching them to the post. This was a skill she knew she was learning from an expert, yet he still took the time to show her over and over again until she got it right.

'I've been doing this since I was a boy, could do it blindfolded I reckon but it might end up a bit of a crooked fence if I did.' He chuckled. 'Learn how to tension a fence properly and you can get a job anywhere. Told my old man there was a fence down one day, I was only a kid and never did again, the sheep got through in the night, and we lost half the mob. Carried a pair of pliers with me ever since and mended, best as I could, any fence I ever saw. The next was a poor winter and I felt guilty every night we sat down for tea, and I watched Mum's worried face. It was punishment enough and you know, Dad never said a word but just showed me how to mend the fence and went about his day. He trusted me to know it would never happen again, at least not on my watch. Good man my dad, yes, a good man.' Christa watched his face soften as he remembered his family.

Christa was already feeling muscles she didn't know she had and thought tomorrow she would feel them more. Each job was mentally ticked off the list until the last and using the shovels they cleaned out a bit of the nest and used some of the thick mud to reinforce the top of the bank as best as they could. Johnno ran the pump, and the turkey's nest began to refill. Birds seemed to know by instinct and appeared out of nowhere to get their fill.

'Let's call it a day. You've done well Christa, you're not useless, even with an experienced hand here we wouldn't have got it done much quicker. We can take the time to enjoy the sunset, and I'll show you another hobby of mine. There is enough stew left for tonight and you can make the damper while I set up the easel. You can even have a bath in the trough tonight, though you'd probably prefer to have that young fella of yours here instead.'

'How do you know about Drew and me?'

'Fastest thing in the world is gossip in the outback.' Christa shook her head and asked what the easel was for.

'You'll see, a little hobby I picked up from my mum, now remember what I said and don't be precious about amounts just get what you think is the right consistency and the proof will be in the eating. I threw a log on before, so I'll get the coals ready and heat the camp oven.'

Christa mixed the dough and by the time she was finished Johnno had the coals and oven ready and the rest of the fire stoked up with their chairs out ready for later. A rough but large easel was placed at the back of his ute with paint spread out on a tarp on the tailgate. The lowering sun was starting to colour the sky and even though they had another hour or so until it was finally set the taller objects in the distance were already becoming silhouettes.

'There are a couple behind the seat if you want to have a look. I've been told they're pretty good and I've sold a few, but I just like doing it.'

Christa pulled the lever on the seat and carefully removed the covered paintings. She gasped in delight at their beauty and raising her eyes looked across the landscape then back again at his work. It was as if she was holding the view in her hands, he had captured it beautifully.

'Oh Johnno, these are fantastic, wow, you are so talented. This must be at another bore, but I already feel like I'm there. You know I love to paint too. I did it at school but, I've never had the money or the courage to try again. I wish you could teach me this, but I think it is a gift, not something I could learn.' The colours he had captured were so true and as Christa placed each one down she marvelled at the way he had made the cattle seem like they were moving or a moment of stillness as a stockman and his horse waited at the yards as others stirred up dust in the distance.

'The painting back at the homestead, it's yours, I saw it there, it's a big one, and there is another one in the mess. You are a dark horse,' she joked and wondered where she had picked up the saying.

'Yeah, I gave one to the boss and his missus loves it. I must say I do feel a bit proud whenever I see it. You can have a go on this small one here. Don't paint what you see, paint what you feel and see how it turns out. I often paint a memory not always what is in front of me. You certainly can't tell the cattle to hold still for you, so you take it all in, absorb it, and then when you paint, the picture is in your head.'

Christa and Johnno worked quietly then until the last rays slipped away over the horizon. Christa could see how his shoulders relaxed, and he had let the peace of the twilight steep into his body, allowing any tension from the day to slip away leaving him almost cleansed by each stroke of the brush. Johnno moved back to survey her work, and she blushed at his reaction.

'So, did a bit at school eh? I must say I'm flattered, and I think you've made me better looking than I am but, my goodness girl I think you could do this for a living. The detail in this short time, it's incredible.'

Christa blushed even more, it felt good, and she could see how her feelings for this man had influenced her portrait.

'I'm glad you like it. I'll finish it tomorrow, I thought I might continue these lines down here and extend the fence, so it gives a bit more depth. What do you think?' Christa did not realise how wrapped up she was in what she was saying and suddenly stopped when she realised Johnno hadn't replied. He was staring at her with a look she couldn't read.

'I think you just found you, Christa, and I must say I'm honoured to witness it. You have a real talent girl and how you have survived without a paintbrush in your hand I don't know because I have a feeling this is something you won't be able to live without. Have you thought about going to art school, they could give you a few more techniques, and an audience of people to help you.'

Christa looked back at her work. She had only painted what she had seen today. Johnno's kind lined face, his enormous hand clutching the wire as he had held it up to explain something to her. It was a close-up, a portrait where the background didn't have to be clear or busy, just an indication of where he was. Once the paint hit the brush it was as if she had been in another world, only pausing to pick up a stick and use it to deepen the lines of his face. Christa did think it was pretty good but had never really taken in any praise she had been given at school, or if there had been an encouraging teacher, it was not long before Christa was moved both homes and schools and the link was gone. Christa moved across to look at Johnno's. The sky was quite dark now and the glow of the fire highlighted the colours he had used in his, it was the silhouette of a girl standing at a trough as the sun set behind her.

'Looks like we have a mutual admiration society going on here,' Johnno chuckled, as Christa realised the figure was her. 'I can do cattle and horses, scenery, but people up close like you did, I could never do it. You have a unique talent, Christa, be proud and don't waste it, a lot of people would get joy from your talent, maybe it is something you should think about doing seriously.' Christa felt quite chuffed at his praise but had to smile when he continued.

'Now how about we see if you can cook too? I bet it'll be the best damn damper I've ever tasted. Come on, before I ruin it and burn it on the bottom.'

As Johnno shuffled off to check on dinner, Christa packed away the paints, washed the brushes, and placed each of the canvases carefully on the front seat of the ute to shield them from the night air. She turned to take in the scene. A brilliant sky, overfull of stars, the glow of the fire and the hue of the colours it created lighting up their campsite, Johnno bent over, ladling the stew into bowls as her, not quite perfect, damper balanced on a board at his feet, the steam from it rising and curling like a wayward cloud. Christa realised, as if another piece of her had just fallen into place, this man, so kind and nurturing, this setting, the release her muscles felt after a good day's work, the satisfaction of knowing she had done her best would stay with her forever. One day, she didn't know when all those pieces would come together and then she would be home, her mosaic complete, but for tonight she would relish this piece today and everything Johnno had taught her as it was part of her now. Christa felt a happiness she had not felt before. To have this time here with Johnno, was something she would never forget and would always be grateful for. Of this, she was very sure.

Chapter 8

The trip back had been uneventful, Johnno had shown her how to double-check the pump and the water levels then the troughs. Everything was working perfectly and with a last check of the fence they had packed up their camp ready to move on. Christa could not help but voice her wonder at the variety of birds which somehow all seemed to have been told there was now plenty of water here. Johnno said the bush telegraph was not only for humans. The tiny finches and wrens seemed to be dancing with glee and flitted and bounced around the troughs, some even diving in for a wash in their joy to have the water returned. It certainly was the lifeblood of the land. Christa knew she would be glad of a shower when she returned, the quick splashes she'd had each night were not the same and her hair was letting her know the time had come for a refresh. Bundling her hair up under her hat, Christa turned sadly to say goodbye. Johnno looked awkward and without hesitation, Christa hugged him.

'I'll never forget this time out here with you Johnno, you have taught me so much these last few days, I'll never forget it.'

'Well, I've enjoyed your company too and I will be telling the boss I'd be happy to work with you any day.'

Christa hid the tears as they welled up in her eyes, she thought Johnno did too as he turned away and started to fuss around her vehicle giving her a million and one instructions for her return trip.

'I'll see you in about a week anyways and tell Cookie thanks for the stew, it hit the spot. Look after yourself Christa and if you ever need a hand, you just come to me, that's what mates are for.' With a wave of his hand, he turned away and Christa started the engine and headed off down the track. As she turned the first bend she looked back to see Johnno standing watching her depart and could have sworn he raised a finger to wipe away a tear as it fell from his eyes.

The trip back seemed to take half the time. Christa had kept up a steady speed only slowing through the creek beds and the snake section as she now called it. Afterward, she felt silly, but she had crawled past, then realising what she was doing, had sped up as if the snake had suddenly appeared and was chasing her. The cattle yards with their tall loading ramp loomed up in the distance and Christa felt like she was coming home. It was a strange feeling for her and not one she had ever felt with such warmth attached. This land did something to her and it was hard to describe. It filled her, made her feel safe and needed, here she felt part of a team, a cog in a wheel that without her would not turn as smoothly. Christa understood now why some never left, here the land made you family no matter your blood relationship, she tied you to her in a way so no matter where you were, she could always pull you back.

Even the sight of the kitchen excited her, she had so much to tell Cookie, and the dust, never quite getting a chance to settle as leather boots marched in and out, hung suspended at the door as if it was no longer worth the effort to fall. All the activity also meant the herds were getting closer, slowly moving in an ever-decreasing circle toward the homestead. Christa leaned forward clutching the top of the steering wheel as she strained her eyes hoping for a glimpse of a stride she thought she would recognise in an instant. Pulling around the back of the bunkhouse, she quickly unloaded her things and hurried to the cookhouse to lend a hand.

'Christa! Welcome back, I've missed you girlie.'

Cookie's broad smile warmed her heart and Christa had to resist the urge to fling her arms around him like he was long-lost kin. Christa grinned as she realised Cookie too had felt the same but now they both felt awkward for not showing their affection.

'How did you get on with Johnno? Top bloke he is, do anything for you.' Christa only had to nod and smile as Cookie continued. 'Did you want to tidy up or can you give us a hand now, those taters in the oven need turning and the dirty dishes are piled higher than a fence post at the moment.'

Christa washed her hands and set to work. The heat of the oven as she pulled out the trays of browning potatoes flushed her cheeks and made her tummy rumble.

'I'll just grab a bite and then tackle the sink if it's ok with you Cookie. I can shower later, I did change my shirt so I wouldn't completely cover you with dust.'

'No worries, these boys eat dust all day, what do you think I make the gravy out of.' They both laughed and Christa relished the ease with which she slid back into her role. Between loads as she carried the now clean plates back to their shelf, sorted cutlery into its matching drawer, and swept, stirred, or wiped whichever surface caught her eye, the banter continued and Cookie in his usual style distracted her thoughts with questions about her big adventure. Christa could see he was glad she had liked Johnno so much, and when she told him how Johnno had said the stew was like a handshake sent from a mate, Christa thought she saw a glistening tear come to his eye. Christa knew she had made him happy, and it too, warmed her inside.

As the sun descended in the western sky, a few station hands wandered in sniffing about for a bite to eat before the dinner bell rang. Cookie shooed them away with a scowl, telling them he would see them when their beards were trimmed, and the remnants of the cattle yards had been firmly stomped off their boots. Christa jumped each time the door banged, hoping against hope Drew would be the next one in the door, close enough to be sent in for a feed as the supplies from the roundup dwindled. She felt Cookie's eyes on her.

'Don't pin all your hopes on him, Christa.' Christa blushed.

'Lots of things happen out on the plains, especially now the women go out the same as the men, not being sexist but wasn't always like it. Once there were only the jackaroos and maybe the Missus from the house if they were short. Now it's all mixed, nothing wrong with it, but give a lonely man a swag, an open sky and a willing jillaroo, and you never know what will happen.'

Christa was puzzled.

'Not my Drew and anyway there is only Emily, Sarah and Kate, and I sort of think it would not be the men they were interested in if you get what I mean.' Cookie was silent and seemed to be slicing the carrots with a vigour meant for herbs.

'What is it, please Cookie, I'm the butt of jokes enough without having a bit of pre-warning of something bigger.'

'Just a rumour Luv, but your friend Emily doesn't seem to be the kind of friend you can trust and Drew, well the boys may all slap him on the back, but we all saw the look on your face when he left. I'm just saying he may come in full of bravado, or with his tail between his legs. Either way, he could have made a better decision if you ask me.' Christa felt like stone, her legs were heavy and though she wanted to run they wouldn't move.

'No, they wouldn't, would they? They're my friends.' Christa's gaze searched the kitchen for answers.

'Like I said, just a rumour, but at least when they come in you'll be aware there may have been a shift.'

Christa's eyes were large and when she raised them to look Cookie in the face, she could see the sympathy and the truth written there. It was no rumour, he had heard it from a reliable source. Nothing happened on the station without Cookie being made aware in a very short amount of time.

'I'm sorry Christa.'

'Thanks, Cookie, I appreciate it, I might just go and take my shower now, before the rush. Ok?'

'No problem, take your time, I'll sort it here.' The tears blurred Christa's eyes as she turned away and she stumbled to the door, peeking out to make sure the coast was clear of everyone before she made her exit.

'Christa.' Christa turned and allowed the tears to spill over. 'Should I let anyone know where you are or just act dumb for a bit.'

'If you could Cookie. Thank you, for everything, I'll never forget a moment.' Cookie nodded.

'You ever need me, this is where I'll be.' Christa nodded then fled to her quarters. From the corner of her eye Christa noticed one of the cattle trucks almost ready to go, the driver doing a last check around his vehicle. If she hurried she thought as she could feel the panic and anguish taking over and making her feel breathless. If she hurried she would not have to face any of them.

No, they wouldn't, would they? Yes, she could see it if she looked deep enough. Emily would not think twice, she would just laugh it off, it wouldn't matter to her, just part of her game another scalp in her belt she would close the door on before moving on to the next, but with Drew, when there were so many others, why would she deliberately hurt her like this. Drew, her Drew, a few days ago had become everything she had ever dreamed. Christa thought what they had was special, her feelings all these months, had they been a lie? How could he be so, and the only word she could think of was cruel. As the thoughts raged in her head, her hands had been busy throwing her few belongings into the backpack, A tiny chain Drew had given her, won at a fair or sideshow in a town now almost forgotten except for it and the memory of his smile as he clipped it on her wrist, lay on the drawers beside the bed. As her hand reached for it she heard the truck start and grabbing her hat, raced out the door and across the clearing. Dodging between utes parked at side angles, four-wheel motorbikes and horses, still saddled and weary tied along the rails, she rounded the front of the truck and reached high to open the door as the front wheel started to roll.

'What's this then.' The surprised driver reached over to pull her bag in.

'Sorry, can you give me a lift?'

'Sure, does the boss know or ...'

'Cookie will let him know, is it ok?'

'Ok with me, throw the bag here and I'll chuck it in the back. Ready? Good to go then?' Christa nodded as she pulled the door closed. The truck moved forward, its heavy engine growled, and the driver seemed to have changed three gears before the wheels had done a full turn. She glanced in the mirror. Drew was at the back of the truck, even from here she could see the guilt, she turned away and saw a figure sitting on the top rail of the yards as they rumbled past. Emily raised her hand to the driver and as they went by her mouth dropped when she realised Christa was in the passenger seat.

'Friend of yours?'

'No. Just someone I used to know.'

Chapter 9

The driver's name was Tom, he didn't talk much which suited Christa. Out here she had learned the men had few words, but when they did, you listened. The flow of idle chatter in the city made it noisy even in the quietest space and it was the inner stillness of everything out here which had captured her heart, even walking was adjusted to the pace of the temperature of the day, a conserving of energy for the task ahead, meals were demolished yet no-one ever rushed them, jobs were completed because there was no idle chatter to make them pause. The talk was saved for town, for direction, or for reminiscing after tea.

Christa watched the ball of dust the truck threw up in the side mirror, it curled and rose in a fury, a myriad of colours billowing out to settle on the mallee grass turning it a dirty yellowish red. Christa felt tired, she wasn't angry, not yet, and wasn't sure if it was worth the effort to go there. It was not her fault, it had been their decision, a decision which, if it had been her, Christa was sure she would not have made. Emily was like a sister to her, or so she had thought, and no matter what, it takes two to consent. Christa knew in her heart once Emily had set her sights, Drew would not have stood a chance. She had hoped he would have been stronger.

'Where you headed?' Tom's voice brought her out of her stupor.

'Isa I suppose. I'm, um, not sure, I packed up in a bit of a hurry.'

'Does Cookie know you've left.'

'Yes, I feel bad I'm letting him down, but he seemed to know before I did I was going.'

'No need to explain. There was a bit of talk in the yards something might cause a stir now the stragglers were in. Not worth it luv, plenty of fish in the sea and plenty of tumbleweeds in the outback. Just have to pick one with stronger roots is all.' Christa forced a smile and turned away and Tom left her to her thoughts.

The radio played a sad country song and Christa drifted off for a while, rocked by the truck as it rolled over the ruts in the road. Dreams came and went, some troubled, some kind, mixed to make no sense of reality. When she woke the lights of Mount Isa formed a halo in the distance, the road was smooth, and Tom crooned to another sad cowboy song.

'Have you got somewhere to stay?'

'No, but there is a backpacker's lodge I might be able to get a room at.'

'Look I have to drop these off at the yards and tomorrow they're off to the territory once they're fed and watered. You can camp in the truck tonight if you want, I've got my missus here, so I won't be using it. You'll be safe as houses, then if you are moving west I can hook you up with a ride.' Christa wanted to cry.

'You'd be fine, I know these blokes, they'll treat you like a lady. I hear they're looking for workers around Mataranka, a good place for young ones to have a bit of fun then I'd head to Darwin if I were you, dry seasons coming and it's a good place to disappear for a while. Lots to do too.' Tom added.

'Thank you, Tom, I'd appreciate it. I'll roll out my swag so as not to mess up your sheets. Thank you.'

'It's settled then. No worries, you'll be right, and look this is my card, if you ever need a hand, or a lift, give me a call and I'll find you one.' Tom stretched out his hand and clasped Christa's gently. 'My first wife cheated, and it nearly killed me it did, I took her back and she's the one I'll sleep with tonight. Still hurts sometimes, but people make mistakes, it's how they act after that tells you what kind of a person they are. Don't carry it, pain is something to deal with and to move on from, if you carry it, it keeps hurting.'

Christa put her other hand on his.

'Thank you, Tom. I'm so grateful for all the people I've met, I hope I will be as generous to others.'

'You will be, now lock the doors like this and there is a shower and toilet over there, a couple of trucks might come in later but except for the cattle and a few blokes watching over them, it should be quiet. I'll be back about six-thirty to pick up my load for the morrow and will talk to the fellas about who's headed where. Last resort you can keep my lady company for a few days until I can sort it.'

'Thanks, Tom. I can give you a hand to unload if you like, I've not done it before, I only worked in the kitchen at the station, but if you need help...'

'I'll be right, once I back up you go have a shower while I'm here and I'll get the missus to pick you up some grub at the roadhouse when she comes to pick me up.'

'So, you don't take the truck home?'

'Nah, easier to leave it here seeing I'll be gone again in the morning. I have you to look after it now anyway.' Tom grinned and Christa could only feel blessed for the kindness.

Tom's turn had come, and he deftly backed up to the ramp, he moved with skill and Christa exited the truck and hurried to the showers so as not to hold him up. It was one frequented more by men than women, but Christa welcomed the warm water and rinsed her hair as well wanting to wash the earlier part of the day completely away. Slipping back into her boots with her damp towel over her shoulder she dodged a few incoming bdoubles, found Tom's, and pulled herself back into it. She just had her things sorted, her swag rolled out across the sleeper and pulled back when he banged on the door. Christa slid out and was surprised by the petite woman who held out a bag, full it appeared of delicious-smelling food.

'Thank you so much, what do I owe you?

'Not a thing Honey, Tom said it was on the house. Is there anything else you need?' Her big sympathetic eyes were nearly Christa's undoing, and she visibly gulped.

'I'm fine truly, thank you so much, this is way more than I expected, I truly am grateful.' The woman smiled.

'We all run from something at some stage, as long as you don't need medical help ...' Christa interrupted her quickly.

'No, no I'm fine just a boy who I thought was mine found himself someone else to play with and I wasn't going to hang around to watch.'

'We all make mistakes, it's a lesson I've learned well, but when you find the right one it'll all fall into place, whether it's him or another, you'll know when it's right.'

'Trouble is,' Christa said, 'I thought it was.'

The girl reached out to hug her. 'Maybe it is, and he just has some growing to do. You go live your life and let the rest fall into place. Tom says you'll always be welcome and the same goes for me. Good luck honey.'

Christa returned the hug, she marvelled again at these people, salt of the earth they called it, and Christa couldn't think of any words that would suit them more. Tom came to say goodnight and made sure Christa was locked in before he strode away. Christa laid out the meal on the dash, a wooden knife and fork slid easily through the roast lamb dinner and the second foam container contained a big slice of apple pie and custard. Although they had been too generous, Christa surprised herself by demolishing it all. Contentedly she lay back on the swag, it felt so familiar after her nights out at the bore. Her thoughts led her back over the day, and it was with a great amount of resolve she decided Tom's wife was right, better to move on and see what the universe had in store for her, she would miss Drew and Emily, they were the most family she had ever had and maybe, just maybe, one day they could all be friends again, deep down Christa hoped so. The waves of emotion would come but Christa held them back as her inbuilt survival mode kicked in to what had to be done before she felt safe enough to release them. The long day helped her eyes to close and allow the sleep she needed to rest herself for the lonely journey ahead.

Christa was ready when Tom tapped on the door as the sun peeked over the horizon.

'Morning Christa, how'd you sleep, no trouble?' He didn't give her time to answer the first question before he launched into the next. 'Breakfast? Thought I'd pick you up first and then I can introduce you to Mac. If it's alright with you then we can head to the roadhouse, was dinner alright?' Christa nodded and it made her smile the way he looked so gruff on the outside but the minute he spoke you could see the teddy bear inside. Handing him the keys she followed him to an old ute, the dust, even at this time of day, scuffed up from their boots and coated their legs clinging to any drop of moisture on their bodies. Sweat was already forming on her brow, and they small-talked on the short drive about the temperature the day may reach.

'I've got a half day and then a couple of runs this afternoon and back out to the station tomorrow. Are you sure don't want to go back?'

Christa shook her head.

'Alright then, here's Mac, he's a good bloke and has a load to Darwin. Now you understand he has to take breaks, but he could drop you anywhere, Mataranka, Katherine, though Darwin would be my pick, you're still going into the wet, so she'll be hot, but you soon adapt. Plenty to do there too, and lots of young ones. Yeah,' he paused and looked thoughtful, 'if it was me I'd head straight to the top.'

It seemed introductions were only just done when a huge plate of bacon, eggs, and sausages arrived, Christa's eyes widened as she wondered if her stomach was big enough for the feed. Men and women dressed in the uniform of denim jeans, work boots, collared work shirts, and Akubra hats gave the door a constant swing as they came and went. Some stopped for a 'Gidday', while others tipped their brim in acknowledgement as they strode out. Christa liked Mac, or Macca as he said to call him, he was similar to Tom and Cookie, even Johnno, each sharing the special quality of taking people as they found them and treating them like family from the word go. It made Christa feel warm inside and gave her the confidence to think, no matter what, there were people out there who would help her if it was ever needed, she would be ok. Tom slid back his chair and balanced it back on two legs.

'So, do you think you'll be fine, Christa?'

'Yes Tom, thank you so much, I'll never forget your kindness.'

'Don't have to forget it, just pass it on, it's how it works out here, we all look after each other. You've had a bad start, but you'll see, your friends will realise their mistake and when they do, how they act will tell you the type of people they are. You're just a quicker learner.' Christa knew it was a big speech for Tom and she understood his point. Next time she saw Emily or Drew it would be their actions on which she must judge them, to forgive and move on, or forgive and let them back into her life. For now, she would have to leave it to the celestial motion of time to determine her future. Even this morning when she woke, her first thoughts had been of Drew and her body had longed for his touch and her mind wished they could talk it out. Tom's offer to go back though, was too soon, she needed to find herself, grow some more, and next time enter a relationship with a maturity she had not had a few weeks ago.

Tom drove her back to the truck and helped carry her swag and backpack to Macca's rig. The truck looked huge, bigger than Tom's and Christa could see the pride he took in it as the sun shone off the gleaming metal. The cattle were protesting another journey and the stockmen's voices were raised as they urged them up the ramp and into the different compartments. Both trailers were on now and the rear gate slid closed with a clang. Wide-brimmed hats turned away to the next pen for the process to start again, instructions and orders were called, and the noise of the cattle and men rose like the dust across the yards only interrupted by the roar of an engine as it rolled away.

Tom threw her swag up and turned to embrace her. Christa again felt tears rise, these men of the outback would always hold a special place in her heart.

'Look after yourself Christa, you'll be right, the world might be a scary place but out here, you'll be as right as rain. Don't forget, if you ever need anything, don't hesitate, it would be the same at the station too, a good worker like you would always be welcome back. Good luck.' Christa swung up into the truck, and Macca checked both mirrors before pulling away. Christa knew the drill, he would be quiet at first, he would let her settle, find her peace, and would know when she was ready to talk, or just ready to listen. The truck pulled slowly out on the highway, this was her last chance and Macca glanced at her as if he knew her thoughts.

'Here we go lass, one thing about this trip is we don't need a map, we go to the end of this road and then turn right and drive until we see the ocean. It's just the sixteen hundred kilometres in between which might bore you.' Macca laughed as he said it. Christa stared out at the barren rugged surroundings. Part of her was sad, well most of her really, and another part was a bit nervous, Emily had been the one to make all the decisions and plan their course, now it was up to her and a tiny voice in the back of her head reassured her she had survived worse.

Macca was right, only broken by two tiny settlements at Camooweal and then the Barkly homestead roadhouse, the Barkly highway was long, and the white lines were the only thing to splinter the barren landscape in two as it stretched out across the vast tablelands. Macca told her campers often were confused here, waking up and following the sun, only to realise an hour or so in they were headed back to where they had come, the bleak landscape giving no clear landmark to guide their way. He laughed but Christa could see how it was done, they had followed the sun west and it would seem to them the only point of reference out here as their minds numbed to the endless white line, in the morning, with the sun rising in the east, it would seem almost natural to turn toward it. Christa shivered, you could get lost out here, so lost no one would ever find you, she was grateful for Macca and his truck, it made her feel safe. Christa knew she would have to get smarter, people may not always be this nice nor would she always feel this protected.

'I haven't had the best life.' Christa hesitated, it was so unlike her to be so open.

'No worries luv, whatever you tell me won't go any further, let me tell you this though, even with a bad start, things can turn around. It's how you look at it is all, a bad start has taught you things you probably don't realise yet and you seem alright to me, treat people as you find them I say and you're alright girl, don't you worry.'

Christa smiled broadly, for quiet men Macca, Cookie and even Johnno were hard to stop once they got started.

'Thanks, Macca, it's just I had grown to rely on my friends, Tom told you didn't he.' It was more a statement than a question.

'Yeah, he did, but look at him and his missus, he was cut I can tell you, cut really bad but they have pulled it back together and to be honest I've never seen him happier or her, some people are made to be together, and a bit of honesty and forgiveness can go a long way.'

'I just thought they were like my family.' A tear rolled to the edge of her cheek, balanced not ready to fall. 'I had never been with anyone before, and I thought what we had was special, I thought he loved me, you know, in a special way. Emily ...' Christa's voice trailed off and she again turned to stare out at the bleak landscape in an attempt to hide her tears.

'What he does now will show you. Sometimes first loves last forever, others well,' he paused, 'others you just have to be careful they don't leave a scar in case you miss when your soulmate does come along.'

'Sounds like experience talking there.'

'Could be you know, it could be.' Christa stayed quiet as the tyres rolled and the kilometres sped by, Macca had said a lot without saying much at all and Christa could see him reflecting on his past. Again, unlike herself, Christa decided to pursue the conversation as to be locked in this small space with a father figure was something she felt she should make the most of and knew she would value his advice.

'Are you married Macca?'

'Yes I am, married to the love of my life, thing was though at first, I thought she had caught me on the rebound and I'm ashamed to say I punished her for it for quite a while.' He paused as if choosing his words. 'I thought I'd married her to hurt another, make my first love realise what she had lost, I am a bit of a trophy as you can see.' Macca gave her a wink as she took in his middle-age spread and cheeky grin. 'My girl knew though, and she stuck it out. As I watched who I had thought was my only love spiral out of control, I realised how she had tried to drag me down with her, it was only then I took stock and realised how deeply I loved my wife. She is my rock, and you know, she never said anything, but she accepted me for not giving her all of myself from the beginning, but each day I try to make up for it.' Christa saw his eyes glisten for a moment, and he adjusted his glasses in an awkward movement to cover his feelings. 'He will see it too and do something about it, otherwise Christa, he is not worth having.'

It seemed more like a statement for himself, so Christa remained quiet. Watching his Adam's apple bounce as he tried to gulp his emotions away, Christa realised how much he was revealing to her the vulnerability of men, as they allowed their layers to be peeled off and walls to be let down. Men had been absent from her life, only seen over a meagre breakfast or sneaking out long before the sun rose. There had been no interaction and probably, Christa now realised, many of them would have been unaware she was even there.

'She's a little beauty, my missus,' Macca seemed to have recovered, and a glow now crossed his face as he spoke. 'To think I nearly threw it all away because I was too immature to realise the truth. Truth is what it boils down to Christa, you will know the truth if you ever see him again, and if he is any kind of a man he will see it too and do something about it.'

'Thanks, Macca.' Christa felt a warm feeling inside, it was something she was learning to recognise, how friendship and family were a feeling which felt three dimensional like a solid object, yet soft and malleable, fitting in and finding a special place in her heart.

'What I'm trying to say is, don't close your heart because of this, open it more so you never miss out on someone loving you.' This time Christa reached out and touched his arm.

'Thank you' she whispered.

Again they drove in silence for a while, each reflecting on their new friendship and thinking about both their past and their futures. Christa napped only waking when Macca tapped her arm. In a daze, she realised they were at the Barkly Roadhouse, and they were almost five hundred kilometres from Mount Isa and even more from Drew and Emily.

Yawning loudly and stretching her arms wide, Christa could see Macca in the side mirror, already checking the load to make sure everything was in order. Opening the door, she marvelled at the steps which seemed to magically appear and scrambled down them only to feel a bit unsteady as her feet touched the ground, and the heat of the earth rose around her.

'Have a good stretch and a walk around, it can cramp you up a bit without your realising.' Macca said. 'I'm just off to the men's room then I'll meet you inside for a bite to eat. Tell the girls you're with me and they'll look after you.' Macca started to walk away, 'Oh and order whatever you want, I won't be long.' With a wave of his hand, he disappeared around the edge of the building.

Christa took her time, circling the truck several times to get the feelings back into her legs. So used to being on the go constantly these last few months, sitting still for the last several hours made her legs feel heavy and weak. Several trucks were parked up, Christa knew some would be snoozing in the sleeping compartment of their cab taking the required rest break for however far they had travelled. The numberplates seemed to be from every mainland state in Australia and Christa could see how this network was the backbone of the country. Cabins and accommodation buildings were nearby, and a few caravans could be seen parked up to stay overnight. Christa knew it would only be a few months, and they would outnumber the trucks by two to one as the talked about dry season approached. There was the odd single vehicle, some obviously from stations further out, their paint colour almost invisible under the dust they were covered in. Pushing open the door the cool air welcomed her in, and several truckies turned to watch her as she took in the surroundings. Feeling self-conscious Christa spied the sign for the ladies' room and made a quick skirt around to get to the door and away from prying eyes. Splashing water on her face she realised she would have to toughen up and try to act more confident even if every nerve was jumping under her skin, there was no Emma now to boldly ask for help or directions. The people she had met so far had all been so kind and welcoming and though she had to be wary, Christa also had to step away from her past just a bit and put some trust back out into the world around her. Giving herself a harsh stare in the mirror she pulled open the door and squared her shoulders. You can do this she thought, you have to, plus if your tummy grumbles any louder they will hear you coming like a freight train. With a smile she made her way to the counter, eyeing off the range in the souvenir section as she passed and admiring how clean the whole area was despite the dust and heat which must seep in through every nook and cranny.

'Christa, over here.' Macca waved his arm and pulled out a chair next to his. 'This is the young one I was telling you about, Christa, this is Baz, Goof and Wombat. This is Christa.' They all nodded, and Christa wondered if anyone from here on would have a proper name.

'Any of you know of work in Darwin for her? She's a good worker, happy to have a go at anything she is.'

'Nah,' Christa wasn't sure if it was Baz or Wombat, 'but there'll be plenty with the dry, you won't have a problem. Darwin's a melting pot of cultures and be lots of young ones same as yourself looking for work.'

'Would I be better staying back in Katherine then?'

'No I wouldn't. What do you reckon Goof, there'll be plenty of jobs. Tourist season is almost here, and the vans will be lined up like a caterpillar all the way there and the planes will be flying in from Melbourne, Sydney and the like. I reckon you'll pick up a job on day one, What do you reckon Goof.' The silent Goof nodded, and Christa had to suppress a giggle at their speech and mannerisms. Baz continued. 'Yeah you'll be right, if it is station work you want, then hang back in Katherine but if I was your age I'd be straight to the top. Darwin's a great place and it's where I'd go but move on before the next wet, too bloody hot then and the rain pours down at any time of day but the humidity before it, well, tougher men than me can take it but it melts me into the bitumen it does. The other three men nodded in agreement as he continued hardly drawing a breath.

'It should be starting to cool down a bit now though it'll still take you a few days to adjust. Those folks come off the plane straight from down south, open the airport doors, and POOF! Hits them like a brick wall it does, but at least by driving you are acclimatising a bit before you arrive. You'll be right Luv, I've got a cousin there, I'll give you his number, his kids are probably your age so if you need a hand give him a bell and they'll look after you, won't they Goof.' Again, a silent nod, and both men pushed back their chairs, Baz standing did not seem much taller from when he was sitting, and was probably just as wide, yet Goof rose, and Christa had to lean back to still see his face. Christa thanked them and Baz went to the counter to borrow a pen and returned having scribbled his cousin's contact number onto a serviette.

'Wouldn't give it to you if I didn't mean you to use it, he's a good fella and his wife, salt of the earth. You need help, give them a call, plenty of people in this world willing to help, you just have to learn how to pass it on later.' With a wink and a grin, he pulled a worn cap on his head and Goof with a shy smile dipped his brim at her as they turned away.

Steaming plates of roast beef and vegetables smothered in gravy were placed in front of them. Macca tucked in immediately and Christa thought roadhouses must always have a roast in the oven as it didn't matter what time of day it was it always seemed to be available. Wombat too took his leave in much the same manner as the others, happy for the company shared but committed to the job at hand and to the family waiting for his return.

'Eat up, there won't be a lot open by the time we turn north, and a sandwich will do us on the next stop. I saw Tom's wife order your roast last night so thought it was something you'd like. Tastes like home food doesn't it? They do a good job here.'

Christa nodded and let her taste buds take her on a journey, the meat melted in her mouth and the vegetables, all tasted fresh and full of goodness.

'Time to go, it was good to see the boys though, sometimes we pass in the night so good to have a chat. Like me, they mean every word, so don't be afraid to trust if things get tough.'

Christa knew she was getting a dad lecture, yet it was all said out of kindness. A part of her felt excited, Darwin sounded so exotic, and Christa hoped it would provide her with everything she needed, and hopefully a pathway to the future.

Chapter 10

Macca had been right, they had gone to the end of the road and turned right. The Stuart Highway disappeared into the distance in front of them and Christa felt more excited every kilometre they travelled. All it would take was courage and the rest would fall into place, ahead were new friends, hopefully, a decent job, and a whole lot of adventure. Christa was grateful, without Emily she would never have come this far, or envisioned she could. She pushed thoughts of Drew aside when they wormed their way in, dreaming of him every time she closed her eyes was enough to deal with as it was, time, keeping busy, and moving forward were the things she needed to learn while she nursed her broken heart.

Biting her bottom lip, Christa took in the changing scenery, some trees were taller here, rising above the scrub as hawks soared above searching for prey. Termite nests made from the red earth poked towards the sky and Christa laughed as some of them had been dressed up with beanies and t-shirts, it helped crumble the monotony. Macca explained about the birds and some of the trees, blackboys he called them, their blackened trunks and grassy heads standing out against the low-growing gums and drying grasses.

'It won't be long before they start burning off, they do it every year up here, to stop the wildfires.' Christa turned her attention back to listen. 'They sort of chequerboard it if you know what I mean, burn one section this year, another the next. I think it's every three years a patch gets redone. See how the trees all look the same height, part of it I reckon is the burning, everything kept at the same growth rate. Once you notice you can't unsee it, you get the odd one that stands tall but does it good too, to burn. The heat germinates the seeds, and a slow burn is always better for the animals, giving them a chance to escape. Wildfires take everything out and takes years to recover. Good thing I reckon, they should do it down south more, would save a lot of heartache.'

Christa could tell it was a passion of his, no matter the harshness of the land if you worked with it, it would give you just rewards.

'What kind are these?' Christa watched as birds soared, wings outstretched in the thermals overhead.

'I call the smaller one a fire hawk, smart birds those. I've seen them on the road, fire on one side and they wait for the vermin to run out across so they can have a feed. The clever thing is though, they'll then pick up a burning stick and drop it on the other side of the road so the rats and mice, or whatever, keep going to the next clear ground and they can just pick them off for dinner. Takeaway for birds.' Macca grinned. 'The big ones are probably pelicans, yes amazing. You thought they only lived near the ocean didn't you?' Christa nodded. 'They live anywhere those things, as long as there is water, in fact a big nesting area for them is at Lake Eyre in the middle of Australia.' Macca was still smiling at her amazement.

'It's true, I think it's the fourth biggest salt lake in the world, some years there is no water in it but when they get rain up at Isa, Longreach and down round the stations it all flows inland, amazing I reckon. Flows down to the lowest point in Australia to Lake Eyre, funny the lowest point is not near the ocean, does my head in a bit but once you get around and see things, nothing is a surprise really, just sometimes hard to work out.' Christa watched as the smiles and memories played across his face, he enjoyed sharing his knowledge and Christa thought he would miss her more than he knew on his return journey.

'You're going to see a lot of things in the Territory Christa, to survive up here you have to learn to adapt, just like the birds and even the termites, everything up here is out to survive, so listen and learn and you'll be just fine.'

'You love it, don't you.'

'Yeah, but I can see the time coming when I want more. I see a lot of country but don't get to look at it. I think I might turn into one of those grey nomads and get myself a wobble box so I can show my wife all the good bits of Australia.'

'What's a wobble box?'

'A caravan,' he laughed, 'they look like they wobble along the road like a wombat. Watch if we come up behind one and if a road train goes past you will wonder if the wind off it will push them over. I don't mind them, most let me pass, I'm working and they're not, there are idiots in all vehicles, even trucks, so as long as they stick to their speed I can work it out.'

'Where's all the kangaroos? I thought there would be heaps.'

'Everyone thinks the same, I mostly see the big reds in Queensland, more likely to see them down around Alice Springs as well as camels, thousands of them out in the deserts.'

'Camels?'

'Yep, more camels in Australia than any other place in the world someone told me, it's hard to believe. Of course you have your eastern greys and wallabies etc down south, ever been to the ACT? You can see thousands of kangaroos around Canberra, it certainly is our bush capital.'

Macca was on a roll now and Christa was happy to absorb his knowledge, she thought he too was quite enjoying having company for once.

'Once we get up here a bit you might see some donkeys. Too many of them there are as well, heeing and hawing in the night, scare you half to death they do, and then there are the curlews.'

'Curlews, what are they?'

'Murder birds I call them. They've got this cry, and you would swear someone was being attacked or in trouble, you hear it in the night, and it can make your blood run cold. Damn things, big round heads, long legs, and googly eyes, you'll see them, they're an odd one for sure.' Macca took a breath. 'Most people worry about snakes but just be careful, would be as many down south as up here, they don't worry me much but those crocodiles, you know not to swim up here unless it's safe.' He glanced at her for her acknowledgement.

A few places you can go, but always check first, they get them on the beach and take a whole lot out of the harbour each year.' Christa's mouth had dropped open as she tried to envisage the prehistoric creatures. 'Never underestimate them, I say, they've lived here for thousands of years and not only have survived, but they have thrived. You know how they say down south, always swim between the flags? Well, up here it's don't swim at all unless you've done a crocodile check. You'll see the signs.' Christa remained silent as she stored this important information away.

They passed through tiny settlements, some just a mark on a map, others trying to stay alive and catch the tourists with a feature or landmark to encourage them to stop and spend a dollar or two. Renner Springs, Elliott, Daly Waters, Larrimah with its giant pink panther, they all flashed by, and Christa could see how Macca's curiosity to explore them and take the time to stop and smell the roses, had grown over the years.

Shadows were lengthening and Macca discussed their sleeping arrangements. He had to take a longer break this time and even though he had offered Christa the sleeper cab, bed she knew he needed a restful sleep while she was able to doze at other times.

Pulling into a rest stop, Macca jumped out to again check his load and relieve himself. The lights of Katherine glistened, and Christa could see how it was a much larger town than the ones they had passed through. It seemed only seconds and Macca was snoring, having scoffed the sandwiches they had bought earlier. She sat with the door ajar, enjoying the coolness as the evening star lit the sky. Christa knew it was a planet, Mars or Venus, yes Venus she thought, was the first to show its face, and even as the Milky Way flung itself across the heavens it would still shine bright until they were all set in place before it would fade away until just before dawn. Her phone lit up and she quickly switched it to silent so as not to wake Macca. A glance brought all her heartache back in one fell swoop, Drew's name lay heavy across her screen and the vibrations as it rang were like knives piercing her heart. She clicked the power button and then held her breath to see if he would leave a message. Part wanted him to be the man she wanted and stand up to ask for her forgiveness. Part wanted him to give up, not try and show her how she had not misjudged him so her wall of protection could creep a bit higher. Christa stared out into the darkening sky and thought about the advice she had received. Cookie, Johnno, Tom, and Macca had all admitted mistakes, some had run away never resolving them, others like Tom and Macca had faced them and reaped the rewards of giving others a second chance, even themselves. Christa had a choice, she could hear him out and then make the decision or ignore the call and never know or be able to judge what he had to say. Truth, Macca had said, and the minute she thought it she knew what she had to do.

The phone buzzed again, and the voicemail loops had a number one next to them. If I think again I'll just delete it she thought. Pushing the door wider she clambered down the steps only resting the door closed so as not to wake Macca on her return, though with his loud snores, she thought it would take an earthquake to rouse him. The air was still warm, and Christa moved along the trailer a bit before leaning back against the tyres so they could hold her steady. Her hands were shaking, and she punched in her password three times before getting it correct. Pressing the tiny arrow, she closed her eyes and braced herself ready for the blow his words, she was sure, would bring.

'Christa, I'm sorry,' A pause, 'I'm an idiot, and Emily, I, I well, I can't undo it but when this job's done, I'm coming for you so we can talk it out, Tom said you were on your way to Darwin and as soon as I'm done ...' the time limit was up, and a tiny bit of her heart swelled. All the questions and answers listed themselves in her head.

He wants to talk, -it doesn't mean we will get back together.

He said her name, – will he bring her too?

If he cared he would come now – no, he won't let them down, and it is, what you would want him to do, finish the job.

He called! – He didn't have to.

Will I forgive him?

Don't jump the gun, Christa, she scolded herself, what will be will be, and as Macca said, leave yourself open for the opportunity as you never know where life will take you. Drew was her first love, but as yet she did not know if he would be her only love. Time would tell though his call had given her an inner strength to keep going. Christa considered her words and then typed quickly into her phone before turning it off. Letting things settle in her heart and mind was what she needed and if he called back she was still not sure if she wanted to have the conversation now. If Drew proved himself a man of his word then it would be a giant leap of faith for Christa. Until then she was determined to have fun and look towards every opportunity which came her way. As she pulled herself back up into the truck she felt more settled, no matter what happened in the future at least there had been communication so any awkward meetings in the future would not want to make her flee, at least now they would approach each other with a new maturity and respect. At least she hoped so.

The occasional rumble of a truck was the only thing that made her stir. Curled up in the seat, even Macca's snores seemed comforting, and Christa slept far better and longer than she had expected.

Chapter 11

Darwin was not what Christa expected, Macca had warned her it had a laid-back lifestyle, and walking down the main drag, Mitchell Street, Christa could feel how the city had a life and feelings all of its own. There was no hurrying here, her own pace had slowed, and the warm air filled her with a need she had not recognised before.

Several weeks had passed and the kindness of Macca still clung to her. After dropping his load at the depot, he had taken her to the backpacker's lodge, pushed a one hundred dollar note into her hand, and given her an awkward hug, which Christa had returned with much more enthusiasm, making the tears glitter in his eyes which he tried to hide by putting his sunglasses on. It had made Christa laugh as he still called out dad-like instructions as the motor roared and his truck started to pull away. The loud blast of his air horn resonated an empty sound in her ears as the tiny nervous thread of now being truly on her own hit her. Christa had waved until the last corner of the trailer rounded the bend and then taken a deep breath to give herself some courage. She could do this, she must do it. A tiny longing for Emily's energy and spirit had made her wistful. For a moment Christa had wished it had never happened and both Drew and Emily could be there with her now, firing up the fun and urging her to cut loose and enjoy whatever the future held. If nothing else she had decided, they taught me things work out, and if they don't I am the one to change it. With her thoughts resolved, Christa had thrown her backpack over her shoulder, stuffed the money Macca had refused to take back into her pocket, and marched, with more confidence than she had ever felt, into the hostel.

The dry season was fully here, Christa could feel the energy lift as tourist numbers rose and festival posters graced each shop window. She had found work easily enough, kitchen work mainly though she had her fingers crossed for a job as a tour assistant which would allow her to see the sites for free and get paid at the same time. Having no vehicle had never been an issue but up here the distances were vast and once the city sites were done the real earthy parts she wished to explore would cost her more than she could afford. People were nice and the other backpackers included her in their outings if she was free. Christa had contacted Baz's cousin, his daughter had been welcoming, though her dream was to head south, to Sydney and Melbourne, the places Christa had no desire to see again, they stayed in contact and Bella had asked her out several times to party with friends. Christa knew part of it was her fault, her walls were up to protect herself from any more emotional anguish, not willing yet to allow anyone to get too close in case they also betrayed her trust.

The sun on her face made her smile and it seemed the whole world was happy here. Locals were glad the rain and humidity of the wet season had departed, and the tourists on holidays were happy to be away from their southern winter, and all out enjoying the day just as Christa was. Today she was headed for the jetty, Stokes Hill Wharf was always alive with people enjoying the many alfresco eateries. Christa liked Cullen Bay better and would often sit on the beach there or in the little park, near the marina sketching as she sat on the grass while watching the antics of people taking their photos with the crocodile statue in the middle. It was her birthday and though no one else knew, Christa had decided to treat herself to lunch, it would just be a takeaway, it was all she could afford, but the joy of feeding the fish over the edge of the wharf, being a part of a crowd inconspicuously was something she desired, felt in need of today, to pretend they were all celebrating with her, were all joining her for lunch to celebrate this milestone which in reality Christa knew, even her mother would not remember. Christa's colourful bag, made of rags and old clothes she had worn out, rubbed gently against her thigh, her legs stretched out long and lean, tanned and strong from all the walking she did each day. A tune hummed in her head as she calculated her budget and decided an ice cream might be on the cards as well, just this once.

Christa was saving everything she could, the work was available now but once the tourists made their way south and the locals drifted back inside their air-conditioned homes to wait out the wet, the work would dry up and the humidity was something Christa did not think would be her cup of tea. She smiled at her expression, cup of tea was something Emily would have said, a homely term used in loving homes and one Emily had said often when being cagey, not wanting to offend. They had played in her thoughts lately, especially in her dreams, Drew would come to her, and the scenarios would play out. She missed him, all of him and although a few others had made advancements toward her, Christa knew it would take someone special to make her feel the way Drew had made her feel.

Cars circled the car park searching for a space, and the air was full of laughter and conversations. Families spread their fish and chips out on tables, the smell of the sea raising their hunger and increasing their delight as the salty food filled their bellies. Christa adjusted her hat, its wide brim protected her from the sun's harmful rays though it was still able to place freckled kisses across her nose no matter what precautions she took. She felt happy, carefree almost, and allowed her body to absorb the atmosphere. Browsing the food outlets, Christa carefully considered each menu and felt satisfied after choosing a mixture of calamari and prawns to go with some chips. Her water bottle would suffice as a beverage and Christa hung back against a wall clutching her order number while she waited for it to be called.

'Fifty-two, fifty-two.' The shop assistant lifted her chin, so her voice projected across the crowd. Christa stepped forward, raising her hand as her tummy rumbled in anticipation.

'Christa.'

Christa spun in her tracks, his voice felt as familiar as a warm blanket, and she froze. Every nerve in her body begged her to flee, while her feet felt like they were encased in cement and no matter how hard she tried they would not come free.

'Christa.' He was waving, weaving his way toward her, Christa's eyes were wide, and she could feel the panic rising.

'Fifty-two, is that you honey?' Christa turned to face the woman, 'Are you ok?' Christa nodded and gripping the box turned away hoping against all hope there would be a giant hole for her to fall through so she would never have to face what was to come. He was almost to her, she could feel the happiness in his voice, the relief, as if she was the treasure he had been searching for and here she was, ready and willing to be scooped up into his arms once more. Christa searched for an escape route, the crowd she had longed for today became her prison and she pushed against them in her bid to flee.

'Christa, wait.' He was here now, reaching out and Christa folded her arms in an act of defence.

'Christa, please wait.' Drew's touch felt like a sting and Christa flinched as the bolt of electricity charged through her body. He spun her around, holding her forearm in a firm grip.

'Christa, I'm so glad to see you. We've been searching for you, I'm so glad you are ok.' Christa's chin went up.

'Why shouldn't I be and will you please let go, you're hurting my arm.' A passer-by stopped.

'Are you ok love, is this fella bothering you?' Christa blinked as she realised the man in the Hawaiian shirt and thongs was just a tourist trying to do the right thing. Her mood softened at his kindness.

'Yes I'm good thank you, just a difference of opinion.'

'Alright then if you're sure, and you, young fella, keep your hands to yourself.' The man glared at Drew, and he loosened his grip. Christa almost giggled, the colour drained from Drew's face as he realised how it must look, he mumbled something, and the man retreated though Christa was sure he would be keeping an eye on her just in case.

'I just want to talk, will you listen? Christa? Please. It was all a mistake.'

Christa stood staring at him, every feature felt so familiar, and her heart melted as the feelings she had been trying to suppress rose toward the surface.

'Mistake Drew, I'm sure when you unzipped your pants it was not a mistake. I would call it a choice. Now if you will excuse me, my lunch is getting cold.'

As Christa stalked away, she heard snickers from the tables around them and knew Drew would be floundering as he processed her reply. Finding a seat on the edge of the wharf., Christa tried to give her full attention to the huge fish swimming below, eager for any morsel that fell their way. The food, she had been so looking forward to now tasted bland and the salt on her lips was irritating and hard. Christa knew she was only eating now to make herself look busy, to immerse herself in something to stave off her thoughts. Why was he here? Did this prove he was sorry? We have been searching for you, the words sprung to the surface, we! Was Emily here too? Had they come to flaunt it in front of her face? Christa adjusted her position, scanning the crowd while all the retorts she had ever envisioned coming out of her mouth, jumbled in her head vying to be the one she would use when she saw them together. Shoulders slumped and the sight of him filled her again, he had filled out, not much, just enough for her to notice, his eyes had twinkled until her reply had shaded them as he sought words to make it alright, the same as they were before. The very core of Christa longed for him and yet she was not ready to forgive. Gathering her rubbish, she shoved her water bottle back in her bag and rose to leave, her eyes were blurred, and her emotions stretched as they grappled with her decision. Should she give him a chance or just walk away, was it because she had never been loved? Was she scared to walk away, was she wanting to cling to someone simply because she needed to belong, a longing to belong to something, somewhere, or somebody? Darwin had been good to her, she had survived, coped with any challenges on her own, and grown more confident. I can do this without him her head argued as every pore on her body filled with the physical need for him. Christa's head was pounding as her mind raged trying to counterbalance both the anger and affection she felt for Drew.

Christa realised she had not moved, she scanned the area again, flicking past him at first then realising, doubled back to raise her eyes to meet his gaze. He was just standing, waiting, a look of longing on his face. A movement caught her eye and the girl, seated, reached up to tap his arm as she too realised, Christa was staring. Emily. Her face looked plain without her wide grin and infectious laughter bubbling around her, Christa knew it could come in an instant if she thought all was forgiven. She saw Drew push Emily's hand away, he seemed annoyed she had touched him. Why were they here, and together? Why would he bring Emily? Is he only seeking forgiveness, her head argued and then concluded that he was plain dumb sometimes. What seemed like a thousand memories flooded her mind as she remembered Drew's antics on their travels, his funny awkward gaffs and silly mistakes which had often led them on a crazy adventure or landed them in exactly the right spot at the right time for good things to happen, a job in an orchard or even the one on the station had been because he had kidded them into going out on the town. She knew he was sorry and yet the woman in her wanted him to suffer a bit more, show her he really meant it and it would never happen again. Flicking her eyes over with a look of disdain, Christa turned away and weaving through tables headed back along the wharf towards the city. If you mean this Drew, she thought, now is the time to man up and chase me.

Christa set herself quite a pace wanting to be clear of the crowd she had so craved and get to a more open space where, when he caught up, she would have more room to react. Run or stay her head argued, she knew deep down she loved him, he was her one, her dreams were still full of the dreams they had shared, the plans they had made for when they found the place they would want to stay. They had talked the night they had made love, wrapped around each other, their deepest desires expressed as if they were still one and always would be. Did he talk with Emily in the same way? Did they find dreams as well?

'Wait up Christa.' Emily's voice stabbed at her heart. 'Just stop will you? For goodness' sake, do you think your arse looks good when you walk like that, looks like you have a broomstick up there.' Emily grabbed her arm and swung her about. 'You are going to see us anyway, we are staying at the same hostel.'

Christa stopped. Looking into her friend's eyes was the hardest thing to bear, she searched for the remorse and felt cross when she could not find it. Emily had saved her, given her a life, taught her to dream, and even taught her to love, not only herself but others. Christa felt a guilt now as if she was the one who should forgive, thank them for all they had done. It all seemed too hard, and she longed for how it was before, before the muster, when life was fun, and her future had seemed trouble-free.

<h1 style="text-align: center;">Chapter 12</h1>

They walked in silence to the end of the wharf, past the convention centre and the wave pool, and onto the Peninsula Lawns. Several families were dotted about, picnic rugs spread as they enjoyed the sunshine. Christa could feel Drew as if he was still inside her. She could sense his emotions, his confusion at the silence, and knew he felt the spark of electricity between them when his arm accidentally brushed against hers. Christa knew he had thought he could fix this, turn up, say sorry and it would be done. Twelve months ago, she would have accepted it, it would have been enough. Now, since her body had shown her what a woman could feel, she wanted more, not his subservience, it was something else she couldn't describe, it would be something he would do or say. Even if it was only one word, she would know he felt the same as her and all they had shared had been their truth. Emily still bounced in her step though her face was grim, Christa could feel by their movements it had been nothing, a mistake, a conquest Emily regretted. Christa hoped she could now see the fallout from her actions and finally stop trying to be the boss all the time. Emily's survival skill had been to lead and dominate and when Drew and Christa had fallen for each other it must have triggered something inside her to show them she was still in control. Christa could see now it was fear, fear they would join together and leave her - just as her mother did, a fear to hang onto Drew so at least she would have one of them and a fear which would enable her to cut Christa away, or so she had thought, and it would not hurt. Christa had been to enough therapists in her life not to have picked up on how people thought, and she had done it herself at times, clung to one to forsake all others. Being moved on, she had been forced to realise she should accept all who wanted to be with her, the more friends the better. Drew and Emily had been all of it to her and more, they became her family. In this short walk, Christa realised this was something she did not want to lose.

Christa found a spot away from others and sank to the grass crossing her legs in front of her and indicating for them to do the same. Drew couldn't get his legs to tangle and ended up leaving one straight out in front of him to keep his balance. Emily sank with grace and her skirt settled around her as if it had been arranged. Christa wasn't sure if she should start.

'You got it wrong Christa.' Emily looked determined. 'He loves you, yes we made a mistake and yes I had been a bit miffed you two were so lovey-dovey, I'm glad for you I am, but I don't know, it annoyed me as well and I just wanted to ...'

'What! Spoil everything, the trip, our friendship. I thought you were my family Em, I trusted you. I trusted you both after all we have been through.'

'Jacko was being a, well you know, we got back, and you've buggered off and Cookie and everyone is angry because they all loved Christa. It was like I was ostracised so at dinner I stood on the table, didn't I Drew, and I told everyone what an a-hole Jacko had been just because I was a girl, I was being snickered about and I'd done my job just as good as them. They weren't talking about him the same way as they were me! Told them they could stick their job if they allowed women to not be treated with the same respect as the men.'

'So Em, you think making an equal rights stand makes it alright do you? Your latest flirt annoys you, so you throw me under the bus to make him jealous?' Emily at least looked guilty as if the truth rang true.

Drew was shaking his head.

'It's true, after, ...well you know what we did, we shouldn't have. Emily's my mate, nothing more, I don't like her like that, Jacko tipped his water bottle down her swag, and it was like he was trying to make trouble then one thing led to another because Emily was upset, and I had overslept. They saw Emily crawling out, then me and it went from there. No one said anything but the word spread fast as a tumbleweed blowing across the flat with no fence to stop it.'

Christa was amazed at his analogy, to Drew everything was simple, the complications of emotions were something he could not understand, it was simple, this is what happened, and it should be as plain as the dirt beneath your feet was how he thought.

'Boo Hoo,' Christa's lips were tight. 'Poor Emily, and if they hadn't seen her Drew, would you have told me?'

They glanced at each other, and Christa knew it had been discussed, probably the very day, before they knew it was too late, and the rumour mill was way ahead of them.

'I think I would have' he said at the same time as Emily shook her head.

A tear she couldn't stop rolled down her cheek and Drew reached out to take her hand.

'I'm sorry Christa, I want it to be like before, I made a big mistake, but I can't make it unhappen. I promise I will make it up to you, please.'

His puppy dog expression hit the well of sadness inside.

'I don't know, Drew. You hurt me a lot, both of you, but I've missed you both so much,' Christa sniffed and wiped her nose with the back of her hand. 'We can be friends but only friends nothing more.'

Christa couldn't look at him, she knew it hurt but time was what she needed, time and proof his words were true. Christa's self-defence guard was up, and she knew it would not come down too easily.

Emily jumped up and hopped around in a funny dance as she tried to shake out the pins and needles in her feet.

'Ow, ow, ow. So can we just hug it out now and get on with it, I'm hungry and could use a beer. Hey, it's your birthday! Happy Birthday!'

Christa nodded and Drew's hand tightened its grip as he helped her up.

'Happy birthday Christa.' Christa allowed herself to look into his eyes and could not stop a surge of longing filling her.

'Thank you' she whispered shyly and as he tried to draw her into an embrace she stretched out her hand for Emily to join.

'I'm sorry Christa, you know I am, it won't happen again.' Emily's voice was muffled.

'I promise it won't,' Drew said.

Emily pulled away, 'Truth be told it wasn't great, bloody awkward in a swag and to be completely honest the only thing we were both thinking about was you.'

Christa's mouth dropped open, and Emily turned, flouncing away as she did, moving on and making it all about herself. Christa looked at Drew and his eyes were wide, not knowing if he should be offended or not.

'She's right' he whispered, 'it wasn't great.'

Christa released her grip. 'Just friends Drew, I mean it.'

'For now.' His tone surprised her, and it was as if Christa could see him maturing in front of her and a tiny spiral of pleasure ran through her.

'Come on you two,' Emily called, 'First beers on me, you two start holding me up I'll find some new friends who do want to drink.'

Christa moved forward. Emily was back, bossing and pushing them to move on with life. For Emily it was already over, she never carried baggage for long. For Christa, what had happened would stay with her, though in this moment, it felt like a huge weight had fallen from her shoulders, she would never be like Emily, her mask was not as thin nor her feeling as shallow, yet this was something she had to learn, to forgive, even if she would never forget.

'Come on Drew, we had better pick up the pace, you know what she is like.' His eyes brightened at her inclusion. 'It is my birthday after all so if you two are paying, I might even go top shelf.'

It was a start Christa realised as they ran across the grass, a bit of give and take from each of them and although it would never again be like it was before, maybe it could be the start of something even better.

Chapter 13

The dry season was certainly an experience. Each day after their truce was reached, was filled with laughter and an almost heightened sense of joy. It was like old times though Christa still had her guard up if either of them got too close. The inbuilt protection mode she'd always had was in place though she wasn't sure if it was age or learning, which stopped her from fully withdrawing as she would have done in the past. The kitchen hand work was at least reliable, and she was able to pick up a few waitressing shifts as well to add to her savings. Emily wanted to pool their money and buy a vehicle as had been suggested in the past and although Christa had been firm in her reply, Emily still tried to chip away at her about it.

'How will we get to WA? We'll have to head south before the wet, there'll be no jobs up here then for our skills and it will be the same down the centre with all the tourists going home. It's best if we see a bit then head to Perth or Esperance for the summer. If we had wheels at least we would have a choice and built-in accommodation.'

Emily's summary was accurate, from now on buses and trains would not exist for travellers and it was certainly too far to walk. It made practical sense and yet Christa still hesitated, could she trust Emily at her word? Emily acted as if the whole adventure to the station had not happened, she skipped over it in conversations with others about their travels and Christa wondered at times if she had forgotten the whole affair. Drew was quieter than before, he always tried to be by Christa's side, irritating at times though she understood his pain. The thread between them was fractured yet had softened from the tightrope it had been. At times Christa longed to reach out and touch his hand, his sad eyes made her cry in the deep of the night as she wrangled about whether to give in and run with the feelings she couldn't deny. One touch or word from her would heal the rift but still, the chasm of hurt was there and whatever it was she was waiting for, from him, had not yet appeared. As August rolled into September and the first stormy clouds began to appear on the horizon, Christa knew she would have to decide, to travel with them was a no brainer but if anything happened she wanted to have her nest egg tucked away safely, not driving off in the distance abandoning her when Emily or Drew decided their plans had changed. It was Drew in the end who worked out a solution.

Sitting on Mindil Beach, the music and noise of the crowds at the markets behind them as they waited for the sun to set over Fannie Bay, Emily was flirting with her latest crush. The French backpacker was happy for the attention in his last few days in Australia, with no ties or commitments needed they were both enjoying the fun before they each moved off in separate directions. Christa had lost count of the boys Emily had attached herself to and it amazed her how swiftly they fell under her spell and also how easily Emily discarded them when she was done. As Christa listened to their banter, she acknowledged it was time to accept Emily for who she was, an outrageous flirt, with a kind heart and a broken soul who kept her life on a steady keel by being dominant and always on top, control was her family and without it, Emily did not know who she was, and her world fell apart. Christa hoped one day she would find the person who could share her burdens. Drew on the other hand was harder, she so wanted to forgive him and was almost desperate to. Even now as she watched him peel off his t-shirt, his muscles rippling across his back, her inner thighs became moist, and her body tingled with the memory. Christa had to admit some days, in unexpected moments, he would brush past or flash a rare smile and she would want to throw him down and have him right there no matter who could see.

'Christa' Drew's voice shook her from her daydream, and she turned to him with a softness in her voice as if they were lying naked in the aftermath of making love.

'Mm. Oh, sorry um, yes?'

'Christa, can we talk,' he nodded towards Emily and Louis.

'Sure.' Christa tried to readjust her thoughts as her body resisted the actions of her previous thoughts. Drew looked a bit taken aback and she knew everything confused him as he tried to understand the female mind and make amends.

'I was thinking,' he was keeping his voice low, 'I was thinking about the car thing. Louis's mate is going home back to France as well, and he has this van they bought in Sydney when they arrived. It has like, everything we'll need, you know cooking stuff and a bed. He wants to sell it as a job lot.'

'And?'

'Well, the thing is, I know Emily's been harping on at you about putting in for a car, but I thought, what if I buy it outright, and then there'll be no hassle, you know if something happens.'

'So, when something happens you just drive off and leave us on the side of the road somewhere?' Christa knew she had raised her voice.

'No, I wouldn't, not to you.'

'What about Emily, would you do it to her?' Christa saw a flash of exasperation cross his face.

'Of course not, we're mates. I would never leave either of you in the lurch I promise. I just thought if money, or lack of it, was the thing holding you back, then at least you can be reassured you have all your savings, and we can all stay together. I was just trying to help.'

Christa could see he was annoyed as his suggestion had come from a good place, how long would he hang around if she didn't give in a little?

'There are only so many times I can say sorry, Christa, I can't change it, and I want to keep travelling with you, find our place just like we talked about,' he took a breath and looked away searching the horizon as he chose his next word. It cut Christa to see his pain, it leaked from his pores and drained the colour from his cheeks, he had said sorry, she knew he was, and as he turned back to look deep into her eyes, Christa realised it was time to choose her path, one of regret and sorrow or one of chance and unseen promises. Her hand was on his knee before she realised and her eyes blurred as Drew welled up at her touch, hope in his eyes as he curled his fingers under her chin.

'Let's take it slow,' she whispered and closed her eyes at his touch.

'I'll take it any way you want, thank you Christa, I'll make it up to you, I promise, with all I am, I will.'

Christa raised her lashes as her heart filled with both desire and thanks. Thanks to this man who was promising to love her and take care of her. So much emotion filled his beautiful face, relief, love, and desire shone back at her and Christa knew, no matter how inexperienced she was, no man could ever make her feel like this. The crowd applauded as the sun did her daily job and sank below the horizon, Drew's lips brushed hers lightly, an apology and a promise for the future combined.

'Thank God! Finally!' Emily stood over them, hands on hips, a look of triumph on her face.

'You two, are a couple, no?' Louis' accent was both charming and inquisitive.

'Well, they were, and then I slept with Drew, and everyone got their knickers in a knot about it and Christa ran away. Blind Freddie could see they were meant to be together.' Christa and Drew both giggled as Louis tried to comprehend Emily's prattle.

'Knickers? A blind man had her knickers?' Emily looked at him as if he was a fool.

'No look let me explain ...'

'Come on, let's see if there is any food left.' Drew stood up, pulled his shirt back on, and reached down for Christa. She paused for a moment to take him in, he too hesitated, then raised his other hand to his hat and with two fingers dipped the front of it towards her. There it was, one action, a gentleman's acknowledgement to a lady, an age-old tradition of respect acknowledged by both without a word being spoken. Christa grasped his hand and laughter bubbled up as they stumbled, giddy with emotion along the sand. One tiny gesture was all it had taken to seal her fate and at this moment Christa knew he could not have chosen better.

Emily and Louis were disappearing into the crowded market space, Louis still shaking his head as Emily went to great lengths to explain her Australianisms, something Christa knew he would never understand. The crowd pushed in as the path off the beach narrowed, the feel of Drew's body brushing against her was almost overwhelming and her tiny daydream resurfaced and then tried to imagine what people would think if they dropped to the ground to go at it there and then. Drew's mouth brushed her ear.

'I'm not sure how long I can do this slow thing, I'm fighting every urge not to take you right now in front of everybody.'

Christa's insides nearly burst as her face blushed pink as if they could all hear her thoughts. Playfully she smacked him on the arm then slid her hand into his.

'Not on an empty stomach you won't, the growling of your belly is certainly not the romantic tune I had in mind.' Drew grinned and gripped her hand tighter. Come what may, Christa knew no matter the outcome, this was one chance she could not have let go by, only the future knew if they would make it or not, and for now, this was the only thing in the whole world she desired. As crazy as it felt her heart was not only singing a tune, but it was also doing a silly dance along with it.

The crowd was thinning as the air cooled slightly, the music died, and the stall holders packed their wares. Emily and Louis cruised one side of the food aisle while Drew and Christa did the other. All nationalities of young people mingled as the food stall owners thrust containers of leftovers onto their tables, some asked for a dollar or two yet when the request was rejected most just gave it away, preferring not to waste it and knowing for some, it may be the only food they would have eaten all day. Backpackers lived on the edge, picking up work where they could but often using their money to enjoy every moment of their adventure, food was often not a priority, alcohol higher up the list and their mother's three meals a day would be a welcome treat when they returned home but until then life was for living. Christa and Drew scored some kebabs, three pieces of chicken, and a fruit salad. Emily and Louis had fared better with four containers filled with meats and rice of varying flavours and some pastries. They gathered under a huge banyan tree, a distant streetlight throwing their shadows as they sat along its branches and balanced the feast between them. Passing the containers around they scooped the contents of rice, succulent meats, and noodles into their mouths with their fingers. Christa thought no food had ever tasted as good. Glancing around, the shadows distorted their faces, and Christa took a moment to recall how far they had come. Emily had taught her to dream and at this moment she was living it, their carefree lifestyle had given her freedom, a release from the past, and the ability to look towards the future. The backpackers with their sense of adventure, and their bravery to travel this vast land so different to their own, taught her to embrace it and rejoice in it. These lessons she had not expected. Drew, the steady rock, the one who, like her, knew it would end when they found their place, and their desire to move on would then dissipate, melt away as another dream rose and urged them to fulfil it. It made her excited, a bit nervous, and now, with Drew by her side, eager to move forward and face the unknown ahead of them whatever it may be.

Chapter 14

Christa had been sad to leave Darwin, the days had been filled since Drew had bought the van. Days off were turned into trips to see the sites further afield before they would have to move south. One trip to the Litchfield National Park would stay with her forever.

To swim across the plunge pool at Florence Falls took her breath away. As she swam under the falls, the cool water had felt sharp and charged every nerve as it tingled and vitalised her skin. Christa thought she had felt more alive in those moments than ever before. Wangi Falls, pronounced Won-guy by the locals, scared her as her eyes searched for a crocodile they said sometimes lurked there. While others had clambered near the edge to get their perfect photo, Christa had hung back, sure in her heart it would be her that an ancient beast would be most attracted to. The Buley Rockpools sang like her heart as they cascaded down. Sharing one with Drew, the cool water rolling over their shoulders, relaxing and massaging her skin, her physical desires for Drew had heightened as their bodies touched and even now the memory of the sensation still made her shiver. As his eyes had admired her figure in the skimpy swimsuit she had chosen for the day, it had made Christa more flirtatious, and she had known she was using her body to tease him in a very womanly way.

Emily had been called in for a shift and despite her protests, Drew had insisted they still go as planned.

'We can always go again, and you have already been with one of your little toy boys. I feel we are running out of time, and I don't want to miss it.' Pouting and sulking, and a lot of it they knew they would have to put up with on their return, Drew had said Emily would recover and it was the first time Christa had realised, she and Drew would be alone together for any length of time since their reunion. Remembering it all, Christa, just as it had been the first time, knew from the beginning it would be the day when they would no longer be able to hold back. With Emily out of the picture, it was like a light had turned green and there was no longer anything to stop them. The tension had built all day, and Christa had felt nervous with excitement. The last stop was at the giant termite mounds and as Drew snapped photos of Christa as she posed against them making funny expressions, their smiles had made passers-by hesitate for a moment as if wanting to capture some of their joy. With the red dust coating their feet on the way back to the van, Drew had seemed nervous and had stumbled over his words.

'Spit it out Drew, what's up?'

'I, um I.' Christa looked at him quizzically. 'I um, I wondered if maybe you would like to camp the night, you know, so we can test out all the gear.' Christa couldn't help but smirk, it seemed now after his false starts, he had developed verbal diarrhoea.

'We have enough food and like um, the sheets are clean, we would have to share but,' he had looked at her then with puppy dog eyes. 'Like, nothing has to happen, like, not if you don't want it to, I'll sleep in the driver's seat, whatever you want Christa, I just thought maybe we could move forward like, um, you know be together again.' Drew finally had stuttered, stammered and 'liked' through what he wanted to say.

'Sure.'

'Like it's whatever you want, I'll under... What?'

'Sure, I'd like that.'

'You would?'

'Sure.' She'd been grinning now at his awkward approach and blushing face as he'd tried to say the right words. It had only made him more endearing. Like a Christmas tree lighting up in sections as each light took a turn to sparkle bright and clear, his face had showed every emotion as he digested her reply. The worry lines on Drew's face erased as pockets of happiness had burst through making him glow.

'We can still take it slow Christa.' The whisper still harboured his fear of ruining it all. 'I never want to hurt you again in any way.' While his face had glowed, his eyes grew larger trying to hold back the excitement and convey his sincerity.

'I just wish you would start the car and get to wherever we are going because I'm not sure how much longer I can keep my hands off you.'

Drew flustered as he turned the key and as if the car knew they were in a hurry it revved with energy as Drew drove slightly faster than normal along the road. Christa thought they would blind the oncoming traffic with the beams of their smiles.

'What about Em? I'd better send her a message, so she won't worry.'

'Um yep, good idea.'

Christa had not been able to hide her surprise at their scheming as the penny dropped. 'She knows, doesn't she.' Drew tried to look a bit embarrassed at being caught out but could not hide the grin.

'Well, actually, I did mention we might do an all-nighter and so when the shift came up, Emily thought, you know, money-wise, she should take it.'

'You dirty devils,' Christa laughed. 'So the whole boo-hoo, whinge-whinge about having to work was all fake?' She shifted in her seat, 'And our conversation this morning about how she would get over it, was all fake too?'

From then on Christa hoped she would never forget a moment of the night. In all her dreams, as magical as the day had been it was the night that followed which wrapped around her heart and left her in no doubt about the man beside her.

Drew's grin widened as he tried to keep his eyes on the road and concentrate on driving. They fell silent for a while, glancing at each other shyly as their anticipation grew. Christa felt she could hardly contain her joy and hoped she would never again have to live through the anguish she could now see, they had both shared. Drew would never forget the pain his actions had caused and as her wise mentors had explained with their heartfelt stories and sharing of their feelings over the many kilometres, the sign of the man was in what he did next, and despite his mistakes, were what she should judge him on. In every way, this man beside her had shown her the man he was to become and the man in whom she could place her trust.

They pulled into the campground and after a brief word with the caretaker, chose a spot towards the back of the park. Drew fussed about, seemingly unsure about what to do now his plans were all in place. He produced two chairs, and a bottle of wine Christa knew was normally out of their price range. A small plate of biscuits, dip, and roughly cut cheese were set out on the smallest table Christa had ever seen but as tiny as it was it fitted in an awkward space in the van and did the job. Drew poured two glasses and turned away hoping she would not see the grimace as the sharp flavour assaulted his tastebuds.

'Would you prefer a beer?'

'No, all good, the first mouthful is always a heart starter,' he replied.

'Thank you for all this, you have gone to a lot of trouble, and I am grateful, truly I am.'

'No problem, I just wanted to make you happy, make it special.' Drew said it with such pride, Christa knew even the fanciest restaurant or motel in the world could not outshine the picture right in front of her. Her life with Drew would never be fancy or over the top, their tastes were simple, and the joys of little things would far outweigh a fancy car or mansion overlooking the water somewhere.

'How about,' she said leaning over to remove the glass from his hand. 'How about you grab us a beer, and I will finish this later over dinner.'

'I've only got snags, we could walk to the pub if you want to, but I thought, you know, simple might be the key.'

'It's perfect Drew, don't worry, now get the beer and relax, I'm not going anywhere, and snags is great. Is there bread too or are we eating them off a stick?' Christa felt cheeky having the joke at his expense.

'No, I have a salad, it's just in a bag from the supermarket, but it has dressing and everything. It looks good though and I got some of the fancy bread you like as well.'

'Sourdough?'

'Yep, the sour stuff.' He looked so pleased with himself Christa's heart melted all over again and she could have cried a whirlpool of happy tears.

Beer stubbies firmly in hand they clicked glass for cheers and settled back to enjoy the view. Wild birds flew in and their flashes of colour were like miniature rainbows across the sky.

'They feed them here, for the tourists, we can go look if you like, there'll be lorikeets and galahs, those funny pigeon things we hear everywhere cooing in the mornings.'

'All good Drew, I'm enjoying just being us, it has been the most perfect day and I'm excited to be camping out in our little home on wheels.' Drew beamed and Christa realised what she had said. Home. A small word with a big meaning for both of them.

As the sun set and cast her colours across the sky, Drew cooked the sausages on a gas stove and tipped the contents of the salad bag into a bowl carefully reading the instructions before applying the dressing. Each movement he made Christa realised, was thought about to make sure she was the focus, and it made her feel like a queen because of it. To another, the dusty camp, rough chairs, paper plates, and plain food would be looked down on, but to Christa, it was like a banquet he was preparing in the grandest dining room in the world.

After sharing the cleaning up they settled again to watch the stars and wonder at the beauty of it all. Christa told him of her time with Johnno, watching the satellites, making damper, and discovering her inner artist in the outback. He had laughed at her antics after the snake and listened intently to Johnno's stories she relayed about the bores, turkey nests, and life in the outback. He in turn told her about the aftermath of when she left, how Cookie had torn strips off him, and the way some had looked sheepish when Emily made her grand speech. Everyone he said had told him she was missed. The boss had shaken their hand when they left, Emily had wanted to leave straight away but Drew had put his foot down, said Christa would need some time, and they had made a promise to the boss they must keep. He hoped she had understood. Once the cattle were all sorted, marked, and taken back they had given their notice The squeeze of a hand helped them both through the hard parts of their stories.

'How did you know where to find me?'

Drew told her about the men she had come to admire. Each of them had sussed him out and asked his intentions if they told him what they knew. Emily had fared the worst he said, and many a night had broken down as she felt she was being blamed for it all. Siting her at the jetty had been by chance though they knew she was close, and it would only be a matter of time.

'The day we saw you was the first time I saw her snap back to her old self. She knows what she did was wrong, I can't say she is sorry, it is Emily, but she can see hurt now and I think would think twice another time.' Drew shrugged and they let it go, neither of them wanted Emily to be a part of this night.

The silence of the night seemed to smother the past. Christa stretched out her arms as the peace descended, they had needed this time, this time to reconnect on a different level, their hesitations dropping away so what to come was met with a maturity and passion neither of them would have felt before.

'Time for a shower I think,' she said, 'and to christen our little home, maybe we should give her a name.' Even in the dark, she thought he blushed and together they gathered their toiletries and walked to the amenities. There was a contentment between them which had not existed before and as Christa washed the day from her body she wondered if life could ever be better than this. There would be short-term highs and hopefully shorter time lows, but this sense of contentment could be her daily life, and she hoped it would.

Chapter 15

It was like there was a constant bubble of happiness around them. The look on Emily's face, when they returned, was classic, it was as if it was her achievement, look how happy she had made them by helping set this plan in place.

'Now the gangs all here again, really here. Nothing like a good, well you know what, to get things back on track.'

Christa had blushed as those around them giggled, it was obvious Emily had told everyone in the hostel about the whole situation. It was funny Christa thought, Emily was so open about her part in it, yet no one called her to task, some even seemed to admire she had admitted it and taken steps to make amends, all the while remaining best friends with both of them. Weirdly, she felt a kind of admiration for the friend who had hurt her so deeply.

In Darwin during the dry season the sun shines in a clear sky every day, and yet somehow after their camping trip, it seemed to shine brighter, just as the grass was greener and the bougainvillea more colourful. Christa struggled to keep her hands off Drew in the daylight hours and leaving him to go to work each day was almost painful. To see him waiting at the end of the day was the biggest high any drug could ever make her feel Their night out at Batchelor had been so much more than she could ever have imagined. Drew had taken it slow, and together they had explored every detail of each other's bodies. It had felt new, different from the first time, their deeper feelings bringing them a sense of comfort and pleasure that had been missing in the past. His tenderness and care had her rise to heights she had never felt before. The softness of his skin as he ran his fingers over her and then moulded his body to hers, the scent of the aftershave she knew he had splashed on nervously beforehand was now embedded with the memory of the night. It had been everything she had hoped for and more, so much more. The look on his face in the final moments, the way he had held her, stroked her hair, and looked into her eyes after they were done, as the pale light of the moon shone in the window throwing patterns across his face. Each minute she hung on to, each second was one she would never forget. The term making love was one she now understood, it was not the act, the chemistry, the actions, it was much more, so very much. As for Drew, she thought he could see nothing else, any moment she turned, his eyes were on her, it was not possessive, just a constant need to have her in his sight, protect her, and convey feelings he could not deny.

Since the day they returned hand in hand, neither one wanting to break the physical touch they had shared, they had explored each other in every way. Walks on the beach were for the long and constant conversations they wanted to share, it seemed there was so much to say and even though they had all the time in the world they both felt the need to lay out their past so together they could work toward a future. Nights were for loving and sharing the hidden desires and dreams for their life ahead. To Christa this time was precious, as they whispered their secrets and spoke as if they were one.

Emily often butted in, bored between her latest conquest and the next, she sought them out to demand some attention. As happy as she was for them she still teased them mercifully making her hard to ignore. Mostly it was fun, they were living the life, seeing Australia, experiencing new lifestyles, plus meeting and making lots of friends. Along with the happiness they shared, they also had food in their bellies, money in the bank, and wheels for travel, Christa's life was perfect., or closer to it than ever before. Laughter filled her days and contentment filled her body.

Plans were made and they had a leave date. Each of them had a healthy balance in their accounts as well as survival money for the next leg. Emily was torn, her latest love was leaving a mark she had never expected, both Drew and Christa were amused by her willingness to bend to him in ways she never had before. In the end, it was decided he would travel with them to Broome in the west before scooting south to return to his regular life in Perth, whatever happened between here and there it would be Emily's decision if she would like to go with him.

They decided to spend their last night at the markets and splurge on their own choice of food. Drew said they could always do the rounds as well and put it in the fridge for the following day. Christa knew it was his dream to buy some land of his own and he was determined to put as much away as possible to fulfil it. They wandered the stalls for an hour or so until the surging crowd brushed their arms, and their personal space felt invaded. Pushing their way through they spied Emily and Matt dancing on the grass, swaying to the music, lost in their private world, and even as the band changed tune, their rhythm never increased.

'She is smitten,' Christa voiced her observation.

'I know, I think, even if she stays with us it won't be long before she moves ahead. She even asked me to do something without bossing,' he laughed.

'I like him, he's kind and I think he sees Em for who she truly is, keeps her on an even keel.' The crowd was changing direction, the imminent sunset saw them fan out along the beach, phones raised to capture the photo of the day as a yacht sailed on the horizon, its silhouette surrounded by the rich array of colours, the perfect circle of the sun sinking faster as if to frame it, giving them all the perfect holiday shot to show their friends at home.

The sun was now a handspan above the horizon, they found a spot and snuggled together to watch as it dropped, or seemed to, into the ocean before throwing up its last fingers of colour as it bade farewell.

'Drew!' 'Drew, it is you.'

Drew's head shot up and he jumped up so quickly Christa felt she had been thrust aside and put out a hand to stop herself from falling.

Drew grabbed the girl and swung her high, her long tanned legs just missing a passerby. People were looking and smiling at their delight as their laughter rippled the air around them. Christa could only stare and her head was calculating how long she and Drew had been apart, for him to know a girl this well. The green finger of jealousy stretched out to scratch at her heart. Just when I thought I could trust him again, she thought as the steam inside began to rise. Christa rose and stood awkwardly not knowing how to play this out, confront him on the spot, and get it done her head demanded. The girl was pretty, tall, and lanky like Drew and had a smile that could rival Emily's. Drew released her and it seemed neither of them were aware of the world around them, nor had Christa ever seen him so animated and excited. Not willing to burst their bubble she turned away to gather her bag.

'Christa, wait, look who it is, please.' His eyes were pleading, confused. 'I can't wait for you to meet her.' Drew was behind, tugging her arm and Christa was confused by the range of emotions inside.

'Old flame is she?' Christa could not keep the cutting edge from her tone. Drew pulled her straight holding both her forearms steady. The glint in his eye told her he was pleased by the jealousy, and he struggled to keep a straight face at her glare.

'Don't be silly, come on, come and meet my sister.' Christa wished a hole would open up so she could disappear into it. Drew's sister was smiling in the background but moved forward quickly to hug her and help shield her embarrassment. Christa knew she liked her already and the relief of dismissing all the arguments in her head had her sink into an embrace and return it with enthusiasm.

'It is so good to meet you,' the girl stepped back to hug her brother again and examine Christa more intently. 'I have never seen Drew so happy, goodness he can't take his eyes off you.' She reached back and a blonde good-looking boy stepped up to take her hand. 'Don't worry he was as confused as you, I couldn't believe my eyes, I just ran. Now tell me, tell me everything.' The girl took Christa's hand, and the question was to her, not Drew.

Sarah was more outgoing than her brother, and she had the gift of making you feel included, part of her family, or like a best friend almost immediately. Looping her arm up to her elbow Christa felt herself guided by Sarah back into the throng of the market, she glanced back once to see Drew and Sarah's boyfriend in deep conversation following them yet so engrossed, they were oblivious to their surroundings. Sarah talked endlessly, not like Emily, Emily's every thought blurted out to be considered by all whereas Sarah chatted, drawing snippets of information at a pace that she had surmised was comfortable for the teller. Christa blushed as she realised how much of her feelings she had revealed in such a short space of time and hoped Sarah was going to be someone she could trust. As if she had read her mind Sarah paused causing people around them to readjust their pace as they sidestepped around them.

'You can trust me,' she said looking deep into Christa's eyes. 'Drew is the only family I have, and I would do anything for him. 'I know I ran off and left him, but I couldn't take it anymore, our

Dad, well, he was cruel to us both but to Drew, I couldn't stand to watch how he tried to make him the person he thought he should be, not let him be who he was. I bolted and I'm never going back.'

'He has told me some, and I hope one day he will tell me more, but he talks the most about you. I think he has been worried, he will be so glad to see how happy you are.'

'Same, you make him happy I can see it in his face, he is a good person Christa, and he deserves the best. You can trust me and in return, I think I already trust you to look after him.'

Christa felt tears well and nodded. Another tiny crack could be felt inside as a tiny mosaic piece fell away to find its place, loneliness breaking off as Christa realised there was another person to care for her, and Drew, someone they could rely on and call at times, who would be there for them both no questions asked. Grabbing Sarah's hand, she beamed.

'I'm so glad you are here and are not some random ex. Are you hungry? Let's grab some food, the boys and some beer to celebrate.' Christa stopped, she sounded like Emily, and it amused her. 'You'll have to meet our friend Emily as well, we've all travelled together since the group home, you'll like her, everyone does.' Sarah grinned and it seemed to cement their friendship.

'Group home?'

'Yes, where Drew went after your father threw him out.'

'What! Seems we have a lot to catch up on.' Together they turned back and extracted the boys from the throng, their eyes lit up at the suggestion of food and they all pushed their way down to the food aisle picking up Emily and Matt on the way. Suddenly it felt like a party and Christa's contentment as she looked at each of them could not be described. Each of them was making her world a bigger and better place, it scared her a bit too, as she never wanted this bubble to burst.

Chapter 16

Christa knew the ball in her stomach would fade. Each time they had moved on to a new job, a new town, it had been there, she was always wary of the unknown. It was smaller though and she could feel how her confidence had grown. Making her way to Darwin, sorting both a job and accommodation on her own had made her realise that whatever happened, she could continue. Eventually things would, and could come together and as she learned more, matured and trusted in herself, Christa realised anything was possible. Being back with Drew and Emily, plus now Matt as well, her nerves steadied before they had even reached the outskirts of Darwin on the road heading south. As they reached the Humpty Doo turnoff, Drew stretched out his hand to take hers.

'Funny we know where all these places are now, a year ago I would have thought it was a joke there was a place called Humpty Doo.'

Christa nodded. Humpty Doo, Noonamah, Rum Jungle, were places she had never heard of and if it had not been for Emily, neither of them would ever have ventured out to find them either. As they passed the one hundred and thirty kilometre-an-hour signs they both laughed, the van was comfy and reliable, but they would certainly not be going at any great speed, instead hanging back with the grey nomads Drew had said. Emily and Matt were strapped in the seats at the little table in the back, it folded down as part of the bed, so it had been a shuffle to fit everything in with the bed having to be packed up each day out of their way. The boys in the end had fitted roof racks and their swags were then strapped up there which made daytime stops easier to manage. Christa and Drew were to share the bed while Emily and Matt had bought a tent for privacy and were going to use their swags as well. Christa couldn't wipe the smile off her face. Emily sang along to random tunes, Matt looked up points of interest and Drew, Drew looked as relaxed and happy as she had ever seen him. He had his van, he had his girl, and he had the whole world in front of him.

The kilometres melted away. They had a quick stop in Katherine at the hot springs for a swim and to heat the leftovers they had saved from the markets. When they turned west, Christa just had to look back at Emily and her smile did say it all, it was everything she had ever dreamed of and more. Christa saw her squeeze Matt's hand as the emotions played across her face. Looking straight at Christa they both silently acknowledged it all, their friendship, the past, their love for the family they had become, and their excitement for the future.

'First stop Timber Creek, next stop the world.' Drew yelled in delight, making it sound like Timber Creek was a must-see on everyone's calendar. They all whooped in delight and Drew turned up the radio until the static hurt their ears and they were deafened by the sound of their voices. The changing landscape lulled them, and Christa rested her head against the window, remembering it all and allowing her mind to drift. She wasn't sleepy just content. At last, her world felt even, balanced in a way it never had been before, she liked it. The ball of anxiety in her belly had disappeared, hopefully never to return. By turning west it seemed they had all finally found the right road, it suited them and unexpectedly settled upon each of them. Christa felt more mature in a single turn, and had a growing confidence everything would work out, it had so far and even when things had not gone to plan, they, together, had worked it out.

Ahead was Western Australia, the largest state and one Christa was sure would be full of opportunity. Drew had already made enquiries about jobs at mining sites and though he would prefer farm or station work it would be a way to make some big money in a short space of time. They were both a bit scared of daily life consuming them and worried moving to a town would quell their dreams until they forgot who they were as conventional life took over. Especially for herself and Drew, the new sense of family was something they put above all else, they both knew how precious it was.

The van shook as huge road trains rumbled by, blowing their horn in thanks for Drew slowing after they pulled out lessening the time frame they spent on the wrong side of the road. Caravans wobbled in front of them and towards them, each occupant waving hello showing their joy at seeing another traveller in these wide-open spaces. The drone of the motor made Christa's eyes heavy, and she shuffled in her seat readjusting her head against the window hoping to not wake with a tell-tale sign of drool on her face.

Christa woke to the sound of Drew's raised voice.

'Just wait Em. We can pull over up here and have a break and you can get it then.'

'But I'm thirsty now.'

Christa turned to see Emily unstrapping her seat belt and bum walking sideways on the seat allowing her fingers to reach a few more centimetres to the tiny fridge. It swung open as she felt the crash. Emily's mouth was open though no sound could be heard, and the last Christa saw was her feet lift off the floor and her head angle awkwardly as it hit the roof. It was as if the world stopped, Emily, her head was shouting, EMILY. Why would no one listen and get her down, she was just hanging, not caught, just suspended in the air, where was Matt why didn't he help her? Christa reached out, frustrated at being restrained by the seat belt, the air felt thick and heavy, and she couldn't reach, it was taking all her effort as her body twisted and her fingers stretched trying to catch her friend before the world began to turn again and Emily would fall. Grey clouds descended blocking her brain, Christa fought back and tried to think, she sensed a movement, and as Drew's head slumped forward the seconds caught the minutes and time moved forward at a faster pace to catch up for its loss. The memory buried itself deep within her brain as the white noise faded and a single light glowed urging her to follow.

Noise crashed in her ears again, it was overwhelming, and she wanted it to stop, Christa opened her eyes for a moment, but light beams were flashing like lightning across the blue sky so jagged and piecing they stabbed at her pupils stinging them like needles, again she faded away to the safety of the single glow. At times she heard voices, some a distant chatter, others close, directly in her ear, urging her to come back though an unseen force pushed against her making it feel easier to move the other way. Time was an empty space and strange people tried to block her way, Christa was moving without walking yet the scenery flashed by. Some she recognised while some felt jumbled and confused. There was a kangaroo in a wardrobe hitting its nose on a light, a city street full of snakes who slid over broken toys and out of empty food cans. Emily came but faded away as Christa tried to run towards her, yet her heart felt full to see her friend safe and well. Christa called for Drew, but he never came and when she did, it was only Matt's voice she heard. Christa was tired, confused and the core of her told her to stop, rest, float with the current, and lift with the breeze as unseen fingers guided and motioned her to a better place, one where worry would no longer exist, and safety was guaranteed. The voice in her ear urged her to turn back, fight again as she had always had to do, find her strength, you can do this Christa, it called, you must, he needs you it whispered, and it was then she turned.

It was night when she woke, the corridor light spilled across the room to only leave shadows in the furthest corners, the smell told her where she was, and flickers of the accident taunted her brain. A shadow moved and she closed her eyes again not willing as yet to hear the truth. The nurse hummed a tune as she moved about quietly and gently ran her hand along Christa's arm, her eyes flickered again, and the nurse squeezed her hand.

'There, there, hello, take your time, you are in the hospital.' Christa tried to focus and mutter a few words though her voice felt scratchy and her throat raw. 'Take your time, you are a very lucky girl. The doctor will come and talk to you soon, it is good you are waking up, take it slow and I'll be right here with you. Sleep is a good thing, but I will wake you when he comes.

Christa felt herself drift away, it was different this time, the dreams had gone, and her body just felt heavy as if she had worked a long hard day and her muscles were complaining from overuse. When the nurse shook her awake, her head felt lighter, and her eyes adjusted quickly to the dawn light filtering through the now uncovered windows. The doctor looked stern, a deep crease across his brow as he studied the notes on a clipboard and quietly questioned the nurse on the sidenotes made there. Christa tried to raise her head, and the nurse took her hand as he spoke.

'How are you feeling?'

Christa stared at him with wide eyes, the gentle tone made tears well, and her throat choked so she just nodded, and half shrugged her shoulders in reply. He moved closer.

'You have been very lucky considering, a few cuts and bruises and your left arm is broken. It was a clean break so will mend with time. Do you remember anything about what happened?'

'Some,' she croaked. 'My friends, Drew and Emily. Matt. Are they ok?'

The nurse's grip tightened slightly, and Christa turned to study her face.

'I'm sorry Christa, but Emily is gone, we did everything we could to keep her with us. I know the police are waiting to speak with you so they can contact her...'

Christa did not hear the rest, it couldn't be true, Emily was her rock, her sister, her dearest friend, no, no, no, her head screamed.

'No, it's not true, where is she, where is she?' Christa struggled to sit up and the nurse wrapped her arms around her to help her into position and also hold her close.

'Will I give you some time, you must still try to remain calm and rest your body and your mind. The nurse here will give you something to relax.'

'Drew, and Matt, where are they?' She held her breath and then whispered, 'They didn't' She couldn't bring herself to say it, 'they ... are they ok?'

The doctor moved then to the side of the bed and Christa's heart sank, she tried to raise her hands to block her ears, she had asked the question but now did not want to know the answer.

'Your friend Matt' the doctor cleared his throat, and she knew the answer without the words being spoken, again the looks cast between them were all she needed. 'I'm sorry,' was all she heard as he moved forward quickly as if time was pressing, and somewhere inside Christa acknowledged the ache he must feel at conveying news like this over his lifetime. 'Drew is still in ICU, I won't lie to you, he is in a serious condition and his family are on their way to be with him.'

'Sarah's coming?' she felt relieved. 'Can I see him?'

'Sarah? No, his parents are coming, and no not yet, just family for now.' Christa felt confused, his parents, he would hate they had been called she thought, did Sarah know, of course, she would, their parents were on their way. Emily, my poor Emily how will I live without you, and Matt, was it good they were now together? The tears welled and the first large drop rolled down her face. The doctor backed away nodding to the nurse and, re-placing the clipboard murmured 'I'll pop back later.' Christa felt him leave more than saw him do it, her chest felt tight, her body almost refusing to release the buckets of tears and emotions it held inside, it would be too much to bear all at once and as silent sobs shook her shoulders and the nurse fussed and put tissues in reach, stroked her hair murmuring condolences, and making soothing noises so alien to Christa, it broke her will and opened the doors for the tears to fall.

Exhausted she leaned back, a head popped around the corner and with a reassuring pat the nurse left her to tend to other pa-tients' needs. The sky was grey, and Christa was glad, as it was not a day she wanted the sun to shine brightly. A tea lady rattled in and fussed about moving a table within reach and placing a magazine to the side 'For when you feel up to it' she said kindly before patting the bed. Christa turned away and the woman slid out as silently as she could. Breakfast came and went, nurses did their observations and departed leaving her feeling relieved yet lonely for someone to share their space with her. Part of her wanted to talk, to tell them of her lively friend, of her smile and the way she made them laugh no matter the situation. Christa wanted to share, to share Emily so she would never be forgot-ten, to make her real, not just a memory to fade away. She would be with her mum now and sadly it made Christa glad, glad her friend was safe and with someone who loved her. Christa's face felt dry, the salt from her tears staining her cheeks with rivets as the tears fell. There would be more, many more, but for now, Christa had only released as many as she could bear.

Chapter 17

The police allowed Christa to sift through the contents they had taken from the van, her few clothes, wallet and hat were all she had. Christa had taken a shirt Emily had almost worn out as it was her favourite and her camera full of photos of the times they had shared. The police were none the wiser and sympathetic towards her task. Anything they had needed as evidence had been taken and Christa's crushed phone was no good to anyone as it was shattered beyond repair. The policewoman offered a pocket watch, looks like a family heirloom she had said, and Christa had pounced, my grandfather's she had replied and taken it with such genuine amazement on her face it did not look unbelievable. Drew's grandfather's watch and something he had valued. One day Christa hoped it would lead her back to him, a link she knew he would seek out if he could, though the doctors had indicated it may only be a grave. As Christa had tried to heal and claw her way from her bed, they had taken him at night, a special flight to Perth where his father had made decisions for his ongoing recovery if there was to be one. Everyone was sympathetic, they could see her pain, her confusion at times as her head tried to settle back into a sequence she could understand. The officers who had pulled her free, the paramedics who had fought for their lives as they lay on the road in a tangle of metal reassured her, yet they could not break their rules. Drew had family who had responded, they had come to take care of their own, it was their legal right of which she had none, and they were sorry, they all were, even the receptionist at the hospital in Perth. Information for family only, sorry, maybe if you would contact them ... and a few weeks later, I'm sorry there is no patient with that name. Christa had cried then, holed up in a hotel room she could ill afford, Drew was gone and all avenues she had tried became dead ends, he had talked so little about his past. Sarah had given her more information than Drew ever had, but she was gone too, her phone number embedded in the road beneath her crushed phone. The few contacts of Christa's life vanished into a world that no longer wrote numbers down or made them traceable to mere mortals. The time had come for her to make decisions, Kununurra was not big enough to hide from the emotions she felt, it was time to move on, continue their plan, make a life she had dreamed and talked about long into so many nights with Emily. It was now her job to live enough for two of them as she knew Emily would want her to do.

Christa left her new number with the hotel, watching as the clerk taped it in the book on the page next to the date she left before giving her a satisfied smile.

'It should be right there, it's where I'd look if I was searching for you, the day you arrived and the day you left. You've been through a lot, maybe you should head home and spend some time with family?' Christa knew he meant well, they all did, they had family, someone who cared and probably could never imagine being alone in the world. In moments her life had been reduced back to one, it felt familiar but so much sadder than before. Now Christa knew what it was like to be loved, sought out, and have someone to rely on and now it was back to only her. It would take a mountain to hold back all the self-doubts she knew would return. Take all you've learned, she whispered.

'What's that luv?' Christa realised she was still standing at the check-in desk.

'Nothing sorry, thanks for the advice.' The warm air hit her as the door closed behind her and she took a deep breath. To go east would only be to live in the past, one day she would go back, back to the station to hug Cookie and Johnno, back to Isa to thank Tom and Macca again for their kindness, show them she had made it, survived and moved forward with the strengths they had encouraged her to use. Darwin too, one day she would go back and sit on the sand at Mindil Beach, to relive the joy when Drew had told her he loved her. Back, to when all their futures had looked so bright. Emily flashed across her vision, well get on with it, it's no good moping around here there is a whole world to see out there she pushed, and Christa felt comforted to know she would always be by her side.

The bus station was more like a tin shed and Christa was surprised she was not the only one about to take this journey. There was only one number recorded on her new phone, Christa had written hers in so she wouldn't forget it, details seemed to allude her now and the doctor felt time would be the healer of the pockets of her memory which were now blank. Part of her wished she still had Emily's number so she could call to hear her voicemail message one more time and yet was glad, as it may have been her undoing. Drew's number too, gone in a digital age where there was no need to remember anyone's details until the device was gone and the consequences of the loss were revealed. Christa wished she could remember details, clues about his home, suburb, something which might lead her to him or his family if all else failed. Their conversations had been about the future and Drew had been reluctant to talk about his past.

Christa also wished it had been other memories that had vanished, the ones she wanted taken from her childhood could have easily disappeared with no need for them ever to return. Time heals many things the doctor had said, so allow it to do its job Christa, to force it might only delay them returning. Time was all she had, and she hoped good luck would pass her way leaving a small trail to follow.

To go west was to find Sarah Christa had decided, convinced now Sarah didn't know about the crash, otherwise, she was sure she would have come back. Christa could not help but wonder if Drew's parents had come out of a sense of duty or if they finally had realised the love they had cast aside and come to redeem themselves and make amends. Drew's passing would be their karma, snatching back their child just as they discovered how much they wanted him to return to the fold. Surely they would seek out Sarah too, let her know, and allow her to find comfort as a family. Christa leaned her head against the bus window and stared vacantly at the empty landscape beyond, perhaps I'll never know she thought, perhaps Drew was sent to show me what to hold out for in the future, anything less will never be enough. The rumble of the engine tried to lull her to sleep as memories of the day, the one on which she had not known they had to say goodbye, crowded her thoughts and dared her to close her eyes to witness the dreams they held.

Chapter 18

Drew

The world and the doctors had scoffed at his choice but once he had found the papers, the paper trail of his hospital visits, the lies of his parents had shown themselves, and the confrontation had been emotional. It was his mother who had broken, confessing yes he had not been travelling alone, yes there had been survivors, no his sister's whereabouts were unknown but she had made calls to his phone before they had cancelled, no, not continued with his pre-payments. Drew's father had become aggressive, his face looking inflamed as he condemned his son as a no-good has-been who would now, again, be of no significance in their lives. After all they had done, flying across the country, paying all the bills, putting food into his ungrateful mouth ... the list had gone on and the tangle of Drew's brain told him he had stood here before and heard the same words. The endless months of therapy had made him bide his time but deep inside the pull of the outback was there and he wished he could remember how it had been able to sink into every pore. Flashes came sometimes, unexpectedly scenes that felt familiar and true. Big smiles and lowered eyes, lashes, holding the droplets of tears he felt had been his fault curled around his brain as he tried to piece together the mosaic that they caused in his head. The unseen force of nature and his father's evil heart were the push and the pull he needed to pack his bag and leave. As he had carefully latched the garden gate and a truck rumbled its way down the street behind him blocking some of the noise in his head, he had only paused for a second to look at the house he had been raised in and knew it was a place to which he would never return.

Drew had caught a bus to Adelaide, his nest egg, untouched by his parents, encouraged him to not be wasteful. The back-pack felt familiar and the further he went the more at home he felt. The barren Nullabour flashed past as he hopped from the cab of one semitrailer to another in a bid to save money and hopeful of a jolt that might tell him where he had been. There was a pull in his chest, he had flashes of her face but somehow he felt it would be the tilt of her head or the touch of a hand which would tell him he had found her.

At the crossroad at Norseman he had to make a choice, should he head straight to the top and retrace their steps, or search here thinking they, like others, would have moved south? The work up north would have dried up and Drew wanted to find Sarah as somehow he knew she would be able to fill in some blanks, their time shared in the womb alone was a bond that would never break. It was hard to decide as the months had flown by without his knowledge and the timeline blurred in his head as to what decisions he would have made before this all happened. Hyden lay straight ahead but a ride would be hard to find along the dirt track. He could go north towards Kalgoorlie then cut across to Perth, or south to Esperance and search the beaches for Sarah. The beach was what made his decision, it was one place he knew Sarah would not stray far from and therefore cut out a whole lot of country he would have to cover. His heart told him she would still be in the west, it was probably now as close as she would want to be to their creators.

Esperance for all its beauty was unfamiliar and even though he could have gone north to Queensland and then across, his decision to come the opposite way had been based on the trucking routes and transport availability. If he got to the Kimberleys and had no success he would go east and retrace with whatever clues he could find. His memory was improving as the doctors had said it would, it would take time but Drew was too impatient to wait. He had already, through no fault of his own, forgotten the look of her and he had to find her before she could forget him. Deep down in his dreams, he knew she never would, for although he could not see her face he could feel her touch, the softness of her skin, and the silkiness of her hair as she lay with him in his dreams.

'Hey kid, this is as far as I go.' Drew jolted out of his daydream.

'No worries, thanks, I appreciate it.'

'Listen if I hear any of the blokes talking I'll give you a call. Good luck son.' Drew shook his hand and grabbing his backback, paused to get his bearings.

'The beach is that way.' Drew nodded his thanks and set off. He had told every driver his story hoping against hope they too had picked up someone with a story that matched. The accident was the key that might stay in someone's head, and as these truckies transversed the country both ways Drew hoped the story of anyone involved may move along the grapevine until it hit someone he had met along the way. With each goodbye, he had passed on his number and the sincerity of each handshake let him know if they heard even a thread, they would be in touch. At this time, it was all he had.

Drew's jeans and western shirt were a contrast to the scantily clad beach goers and as a few glanced his way he sat down and removed his boots to try and blend in more to the scene. It was a bit late in the day for the surfers who seemed to prefer the early morning breaks, but there were still a few out on their boards waiting patiently as they rose and fell with the swell of the ocean. Drew had scanned the carpark trying hard to recall the make or even colour of Sarah's car. He knew he had seen it but it was mixed up in the blur of his memory somewhere, the only advantage was he knew he had seen her since the first time he had left their parents' house, and now. Somehow Drew knew she would know what to do or fingers crossed could at least catch up on some of the missing pieces. As his eyes scanned the waves searching for a flow of blonde hair he could almost feel it, he was getting closer he just knew it, a memory of himself and Sarah playing a game when they were little where one of them had to find something and the other would say cold, colder, warm, warmer and then hot, hotter, and when they got so close yet still could not see the hidden prize one of them would be squealing with the anticipation yelling hot, hot, burning, ...on fire, until the reward was found and it would start all over again. Drew watched as one boardrider rode in and he walked down the beach to once again tell his tale. A warmth filled his body and again he recalled the game, he was getting warmer he just knew it, and the more people he asked the more his story would spread instead of being one lone soul. Drew felt like he was building an army who were spreading out across the state to help him in his quest. The surfer had shaken his hair and was pulling his arms out of his wetsuit by the time Drew got to him.

'Gidday, hey do you mind if we have a word.' Drew stopped a couple of metres out to not crowd his space.

'Sure dude what's up?'

'Look I'm searching for someone, my sister, she's a surfer and we lost contact.' Drew swayed a little and felt for a moment as if he too were on the rolling waves and not standing on terra firma.

'You all right.' The surfer stepped forward and grabbed his arm to steady him and help Drew sink to the sand.

'All good sorry, I was in an accident and yes I'm am good, thanks. As I said I'm looking for my sister, I truly am, my phone was crushed in the crash and we've lost contact, it's a long story but I am genuine,' he grinned, 'not some freak stalker.' The guy had sat down as well his elbows resting on raised knees, he glanced at Drew and grinned before turning back to scan the waves and his buddies who were still out there.

'No worries, I've got time if you need to talk, now what does she look like and don't say blonde, blue-eyed, and a nice tan,' he turned to smile again, 'cause if that's the case it would be like looking for a grain of sand on these beaches.'

Drew reached for his wallet. ' Here's her picture it's a few years ago and here's one of when we were little, to prove I'm for real ... we're twins and she's all I have. I had a car accident and they flew me to Sydney, I was out of it for a while and now ... now I need to find her and tell her what happened, she's the only family I have.' The surfer studied the photos.

'So twins, yes I can see the likeness.'

Drew had hung his head thinking this was another dead end though none of them would be in vain. He felt more than saw him reach out to return the photos.

'Well she is blonde and blue-eyed but no one could ever call Sarah a grain of sand, that smile of hers lights up every beach.' Drew's head shot up.

'You know her? Is she here?' his eyes scanned the beach and the waves.

'No they were heading north, top chick your sister, never told me she was a twin but there was something about parents.'

Drew looked like he had been caught out but was glad he was testing him to judge his sincerity. 'Yes our parents are in Sydney, that's why they sent me there but I can tell you they are not people Sarah and I call family, not anymore.' A nod of acknowledgment and Drew knew he had passed the test. The ball in his stomach tightened as he waited for this half-clad, dread-locked surfer to feed him his link, not only to his past but also to his future. Drew wondered if he would ever understand the significance of what he was about to reveal. 'If you don't want to say, I understand but if you have her number I will give you mine and you can pass it on.' Drew was on his knees now and his heart was pounding in disbelief. To be dropped off here, for him to pick this one surfer who just happened to be exiting the water as he walked on the beach, it felt like a scene from a movie and all Drew could hope was it would have a happy ending.

'She was up at Injidup the day before yesterday and said they were going to catch some waves at Smith's and The Quarries, then slowly head back up the coast. If I were you I'd head straight up through Nannup then up the 104, and chances are you'll run straight into them.' Drew felt a surge of energy at his words and turned as if to run there now and his heart told him he would be there by dark, impossible, but Sarah was his key, his link to the gaps in his brain and the only family he had in the world, surely she would know where he had been and who he had been with. Drew tuned back into his surroundings, the surfer was grinning as if he had won the lotto and others had gathered wondering who the hell this country boy was on their beach.

'Anyone going up to the Quarries?' One voice piped up from the back.

'Yeah, but I'm not doing the coast road if that's what you need.'

'Nah perfect, can you give ...' he paused looking at Drew.

'Drew, my name's Drew.'

'Can you give him a lift a lift, he's Sarah's brother and he needs to catch up with her.'

Drew stuck out his hand and the teenager returned the shake.

'If you can wait while I grab a bite then we can head off.'

Drew could not believe his luck and again something un-locked inside telling him things would work out, though part of him hoped his share of it would not run out too soon. The swag and duffle in the back of the ute as he threw his in, made Drew realise his world was not so far apart from these beach lovers, they were all chasing a dream, a chance at happiness in a some-times troubled world. A wave, a beach, an outback station, the dreams were all the same, good people seeking out good people in whatever environment they felt comfortable in. His heart was racing in anticipation and he hoped the kilometres would rush by.

It was a scream which brought back a thousand memories, the same girl ran towards him but he seemed to instinctively turn back so as not to leave someone behind. The gesture filled in her hair, her height, a shy smile, and the glow in his heart ex-panded as he waited for her eyes and her whole face to come together. It was like looking in a river that only wanted to give him a rippled reflection.

'Drew!' His sister grabbed him and the hug filled all the crevices of his memories of them both until they were full. 'I've been trying to call you. Where's Christa?' Her eyes searched the beach as Sarah gave him back her name. Christa. The name filled in her eyes and as the warmth of her returned he knew the doctors had been right, the memories would come back when he, and they were ready.

'That's what I've come to find out, didn't Mum and Dad tell you what happened.' Sarah almost smirked.

'As if,' she replied quizzically. Drew looked around, the boy who had given him a lift looked relieved Drew had told him the truth, and as the sun lengthened her rays others had come in carrying their boards but slowing their pace to make sure Sarah was OK.

'Let's go up to the cars, so I can get my swag and I'll start from the beginning.' As Sarah seemed to skip all around him in her excitement, Drew could not help but hope Christa too was not far away.

Sarah couldn't believe it, tears flowed. Are they even alive, she'd asked and Drew said he could only trust his gut they were. Sarah scanned her phone, but no one answered the numbers she had, and the next few days were spent consoling, releasing the tears, and clinging to the bond between them. Sarah wanted him to stay but she knew he had to go, his need to move faster, search wider try to evaluate their movements, and check in with hospitals hoping against hope he would strike someone who would leak him a clue. Australia was vast and without a phone number to start Sarah thought his task almost impossible though she knew he would never give in. The way her brother had looked at Christa had been enough for her, and a small part sadly hoped Emily had found a new path. Even though Christa would be lonely Sarah knew she would be working just as hard to find Drew. In Emily, Sarah had sensed an envy she did well to hide, and although it had only been a glimpse, no more than a millisecond, she knew Emily had seen her recognise it and had quickly stored it behind her wide smile. Sometimes moments lingered longer than hours.

Drew was getting restless, the beach held no appeal, Sarah's taste of habitat was opposite to his own. The people, the salt and the sand he could tolerate for a short time but the wide open spaces had fed his soul and settled into the pores of his skin. Thoughts plagued his mind, should he go back to the start and retrace their steps, should he search the country or the cities, he wished they had all been more interested in social media but they had only had themselves and few other people to know, neither of them had seen the point. To be honest he thought, none of us wanted to be found. More memories drifted back each day, her smile had expanded and her eyes now glittered, he remembered her body, her touch and he ached to feel it again. He remembered Emily too, the mistake they had made, and how he had felt it was deliberate not some random moment when they had both lost control. Clouds surrounded some things still and Drew would have to wait and allow his feelings to tell him the truth.

Sarah would be sticking to the coast, heading north again for winter, and assured Drew if either of the girls were looking for him she would be a link they could search for, and if, like for him, she was the only clue, they would be sticking to and searching out the coast and would eventually find her. Closer to cities would be harder but she would put the word out to contact her if anyone asked. Drew felt more settled with the plan, this gave him a smaller search range in this gigantic state but lack of habitation and deserts further east would rule a big strip of country out. It was with sadness but confidence he said goodbye and shook all the surfers' hands as they wished him luck and he was happy his sister had found her tribe, a family of people who chose to be together and who all looked out for each other. The plan was in place, first a search in Perth but only around hospitals first then hostels and backpacker accommodation where even though time had passed, he didn't think the girls would be forking out for anything more expensive. It was in these places he could also spread the word and as it was all he had, people may be the superpower he would need to find them.

Perth made him jumpy, it was the noise of the roadworks and the hum of conversation which filled his ears and confused his mind. Drew had tried all the hospitals, rehabilitation centres, and even a few doctor's surgeries in desperation. The hostels and cheap hotels were next and even as his mind cleared more rapidly, every day the throng of people wore him out as he searched each turned face for a hint of recognition. His mother had rung and he wondered why he had even left his number, guilt he supposed and they had at least nourished him back to health although the verbal degradation had continued as if he had never been away. His father was unwell, though he would never go back he felt sorry for her and knew once she had to make decisions of her own she would stagger and fail, too long being bullied into his beliefs. Between sobs she said she would be in touch and Drew knew he hoped it would be, for her, bad news when she did, any feelings for either of them seemed to have disappeared into thin air, just like Christa and Emily. He would never forgive them for not checking in on his friends, not touching base with Sarah, or leaving a contact for any of them. The last straw had been laid on his back and he intended to never let it fall.

Drew had walked the banks of the Swan from the stadium past the casino and the many parks along the way. Although people mingled in different sections it gave him some space and time with his thoughts. He turned away from the lovers on the grass, their rugs laid out beside baskets full of wine and cheese and with eyes for no one except each other. They made you want to stare, soak it in, wish it upon oneself as you might try on a warm coat, but it was something he was not ready to feel yet, too big an emotion to release, and even when he saw her, he knew it would have to be held in check so as not to overwhelm.

It was like the tinkling of a bell, the laugh, ringing slightly higher than the rest as he was about to turn back but it had made him turn, a birdsong on a breeze which had drifted his way. Black swans were scrambling for bread with the ducks as the cranky drake tried to chase away the competition, the girl's laugh rippled above the squabble, and it shot through him like a spear, a spear of the pain of longing he'd endured, a spear of hope and an overwhelming sense of joy rushed through him.

Three male figures blocked his view of two girls, one throwing the bread and the other laying out on the grass, her flowered skirt hitched up as if sunning her legs. Drew moved closer, wanting to rush in and call out but also unsure, was he just clinging to hopes and dreams? Was it only wishful thinking he could be this lucky?

One boy sat down reaching out to the girl on the grass to tuck her hair behind her ear. The gesture brought Drew up short, it made his heart flip and his groin tingle, he remained in the shadows watching hating his body's reaction yet longing to rush in and feel the bond again. As he skirted a small bush, the other girl turned, seeming to glance at him whilst dismissing him and moving on within the same look. His heart sank, he had only found one. He knew her face now and her touch had returned to him in his dreams, and although he felt relieved to see Emily alive and sparkling as she always did, he still took a moment to compose his feelings. The sun moved behind a cloud and as Drew stepped forward to reveal himself, the other girl spoke.

'Come on Christa, you have a turn, if I keep feeding them I'm scared they will follow me home.' Drew recoiled. Christa! This was Emily, he was confused, had he got it wrong, was his body telling him something his heart had not yet worked out? He stepped back as the sun came out slightly blinding him in his confusion and he stumbled almost losing his balance.

'You right mate.' A hand reached out to help as his vision cleared and he saw the look of astonishment on Emily's face.

'Drew.' It was barely a whisper, but the colour drained from her face. Drew felt torn as to what he should say. Should he keep up her facade until they could talk, or blurt it out only to be rejected and have to face the boy who would automatically step in to protect her? He saw her swallow, eyes darting at her friends as they watched a scene they didn't understand play out. Drew had already realised Emily, this girl in front of him, was the only one who knew what was going on. Drew stepped forward.

'Drew' she said again as she rose off the grass automatically sweeping her hands down her legs to rid the creases in her skin of the squashed blades. Emily's eyes never left his face and as the boy shot glances between them both and moved closer in protection mode, she turned and fled across the park her short skirt lifting with the speed and the smile for once, completely wiped from her face. Drew felt frozen and the young men closed ranks barring his way as the other called to her with a name he knew didn't belong. Emily, her name escaped his lips as the love-struck boyfriend pushed his shoulder in a sign of aggression.

'I don't know who you are mate but clearly she doesn't want to see you, so why don't you just piss off back to wherever it is you came from.'

'Yeah and her name's not even Emily so wrong call mate!' One of the others decided he had something worthwhile to say and Drew backed off hands defensively held in front of him. He didn't want a fight, but he did need information.

'All good, I don't want an argument but, whoever you think she is, she did know who I was so, maybe that might give you a clue I'm legit.'

The boyfriend looked puzzled as if weighing up the truth of the information. Drew decided to sidestep him and target the girl who seemed distressed and unsure of what to do.

'Can you go and make sure she is alright and look, if I give you my number it will then be up to her to call me.' The girl nodded as if this now gave her a plan of action, passing her phone so he could key it in. Drew knew once the shock wore off she too would want to delve into her friend's mysterious past. 'Tell her I'll answer no matter what time of day and tell her,' he fought for the right words so she would respond. 'Tell her I remember it all now and I just need to find her.'

If Emily knew where Christa was, he knew she would not be able to stay silent, and if she didn't, the guilt of using her identity and now knowing someone could call her out on it would eat away until she could smooth it over or make it go away. Drew returned the phone and backed away as the girl turned and fled in the direction Emily had disappeared. The three men stood shoulder to shoulder, fierce protective looks on their faces making sure he did not follow the girls. Until he edged around the bush and was fully covered in the shade of a eucalypt he did not turn but felt certain they would follow for a bit so kept a clean line and strode away with purpose in the direction he had come. The sleuth in him wanted to lose them and skirt back around to follow but he also knew if caught, it may fully close the walls around them all. Once they got to wondering, it may be him they turned to for information as he was sure the girl would not discard his number once she passed it on. Emily now had two clear choices, to call or to flee, and whatever her reasons for telling them her name was Christa, may be damaged if she chose the second. All he had now was hope and his best call was to hang around the area and try to spot any of the four new faces he had catalogued for future use. Drew felt tense and torn as to what to do, he decided to walk off the restlessness but caught himself constantly checking his phone to make sure he had plenty of battery and service though this close to the city reality told him he was safe. The city streets swallowed him up and his stomach made him stop at a bar for food, though he resisted the alcohol which beckoned to him as a way to de-stress. Hope had risen and also crashed as his mind tossed all the scenarios around. Emily was alive, so Christa could be too, every part of his body told him she was, even though he could not feel her close. Maybe it was the dreamer in him who told him he would know, and they would be drawn together like magnets. Once close, it would be a force so strong they would not be able to resist. His head told him this was a story, a fairytale or a movie scene, but his heart told him to hang on to it, it was true, when love was deep, and souls collided.

The nightlife crowds irritated but his need to seek them out overrode the desire to flee, somewhere here Emily was hiding, and she was the link, without even knowing she could be holding the key which would lead him back to Christa. Why did she run? Why wasn't she Emily? What and who was she hiding from? All the questions Emily could answer gave room for more and Drew stretched his memory for all the moments, the pieces of time when he had caught Emily out, pensive in her thoughts for a fraction of a second then covered with a smile so big it cleared not only her own but the minds of all those around her.

She had talked that night, the night in the swag when her body was warm and a trickle of sweat coursed down between her breasts from their exertion. They had talked of Christa, but that had been at the end when guilt stole in to make them turn away. He knew some of it, mostly by an instinct of living on the streets and it had occurred to him there were some untruths in her story, her mother dying seemed not to be the catalyst for her turn in life and her arrival in theirs. Something was missing and as she emerged from the cloak of physical intimacy she had quickly covered her tracks and tried to wash her comments away with talk of Christa. He had known then who he chose, the man in him finally standing up to know the right from the wrong he had just committed, leaving the boy behind as he should have long ago. He had known he would have to face the music and when Christa had fled to Darwin his loyalty to the job had been the only thing which had kept him there. After Christa fled he had watched as Emily flirted and batted her eyelids at every stockman in camp, in guilt he had thought at first, but one night when she slipped into his room he had known it was to make him jealous. Drew had thought himself a man but looking back he saw how cloudy his judgement had been because of his youth. The accident had made him older, and wiser about what he wanted from life, and he needed to get there now and start a future. The time for finding his feet had passed, he was ready to put down roots and move towards a life he had only dreamed of. Drew's boots told him it was time to rest and as he closed his eyes blotting out the stained ceiling of the cheap boarding house, his phone gave one 'ting' and a message he could read without opening his phone lit the darkness.

Tomorrow, 10 am, Toast café.

Drew closed his eyes in relief, it was a step forward and all he could hope was Emily wouldn't run like a scared rabbit again. Tomorrow at ten, a smile twinged his lips as he drifted off, tomorrow he might find her.

Drew was there at nine-thirty, the decision to wait outside so he could follow if she ran, or to find a table and appear casual as if unaware of her approach was the hardest. Glances from the staff guilted him to a table and an order for coffee and cake. The memories had haunted him all morning, the hotdogs and donuts they had consumed in towns that had seemed like cities after the farms and properties they had worked on, it seemed so long ago but also like it was yesterday. Their whole lives had changed, they had been changing and now each of them could be a different shade of who they had been in the past. How young they had been, so full of hope and fun, and now reality loomed lacking the confidence it had always had before. She was there now, sliding into the seat opposite, her eyes wide but the smile not so much, questions in her eyes and hiding at the back, secrets she may not be ready to tell.

Emily reached for him, it was instinctive, a reassurance of his presence and their shared past. Her smile came, the cover one, and he knew she would at first try to blindside him and he was not going to let her.

'Christa?'

'Drew, I'm sorry.'

'Sorry Em, sorry for what, not being her or for lying and pretending you are?'

The guilt washed over her then but even as it flooded her face she glanced around checking who was within hearing range and also it was no one she knew. Drew accepted her actions now his thoughts had settled, he knew none of them would surprise him.

'I thought you were dead, it was such a shock, truly, I thought I was seeing a ghost. Oh, Drew, I'm so happy you are here.' Emily reached over to portray her anguish as if seeking some kind of support. 'I just ran, it was the shock. I'm so sorry, it was a lot to take in.'

'Where is she?'

'I'm sorry Drew.' It was a statement, and the tears welled in her eyes, and he could see there were words she did not want to say. The air left his body. He had been so sure she was alive, he could feel her, and yet suddenly it was like a heavy weight was on his chest and a black mist was settling below it. 'I left the hospital, I hate them, people die there, and you were both dying, they said it was touch and go, and Matt, Matt was already dead.' All the words tumbled out, falling onto each other into a pile that Drew heard but did not want to recognise. The tears spilled over and rolled down Emily's cheeks, balancing on the edge of her jaw before falling silently onto the table. Drew felt he had been too tough on her. 'I just wanted to be someone else, not feel the pain, not be Emily anymore because everyone around her dies. At least being Christa I felt closer to you, and I thought you would look for her first.'

'Then why did you run? Why didn't you stay? We were a family, and you left us, left me, and Christa too.' Drew couldn't keep the hurt out of his voice, but it hid the surprise of how much he cared. Emily brushed the dampness from her face and they both took awkward sips of the lukewarm coffee., clutching the cups as some kind of life support. Drew's insides felt like a block of cement, solid, holding in the grief to come but once cracked, he knew it would shatter and then nothing would be able to hold it back. Stabbing pains in his stomach were making him feel nauseous and his eyes felt dry but swollen from the yet unshed tears. In private Drew would have ranted, cried, and fired a million questions at her, but here, in public, his restrained actions felt awkward while he struggled to suppress his feelings so as not to draw attention. Emily was glancing around the room, and as if a light flicked off and then on again, a new Emily emerged.

'Can we start again,' a smile touched her lips. 'I've missed you and what did happen, happened. How did you find me?' The Emily of old had jumped in. Like two sides of a coin she flipped onto the next moment, burying the past for another day. Drew hoped for her sake the emotions she suppressed would never catch up, too much was buried there, and he feared the outcome when, and if it did.

'Are you kidding me Em? I have to go, I need to be alone. I loved her you know, I told you that.' Drew pushed back away from the table 'I have to go.' He could feel the tears forming as the shock and realisation set in and hoped he had time to get somewhere quiet and allow the process to begin. Turning right he was almost running by the time he hit the end of the street. He could see some tall trees in the distance and headed toward them.

The park was small, but the canopy blocked out the sun. Drew wanted it to be as dark as he now felt inside, no longer wanting the sun to shine today. Gone, she was gone, and he did not know how he would live without her, the future looked empty, and the plans they had made now forgotten dreams. A park bench beckoned, and he sank onto it as his shoulders shook and the process of grief began. Head in his hands the waves of grief felt too much to bear and the arm that slid along his back was both comforting and irritating. Giving in to the anguish he turned sobbing into her shoulder as if the world had ended and there would not be a tomorrow.

Chapter 19

'Whoa, one question at a time. It was chance, pure chance.' Drew wanted to talk about the past, about Christa and felt Emily, though probably trying to distract him from his grief, was again directing every question so she would be a part of the answer. 'I'd given up for the day, too many people, the traffic, along with the disappointment and then, that crazy laugh of yours hit me like a tornado. All night I wondered what if you hadn't laughed at that moment, ships in the night they say and now I think I understand it. As for number two, my parents came and had me flown to Perth then Sydney, at Perth I was conscious enough to protest but not enough to stop them. Even now I wonder why they did. Things certainly hadn't changed in that house.'

They sat close, their knees lightly touching. The couch's threadbare cushions, covered with a colourful rug, was the only seating in her tiny bedsit. After the park they had come here, emotions too heavy to speak about and unwilling to lose sight of each other. Emily had encouraged him to stay and eventually, when Drew's eyes could no longer stay open, he had agreed. Together they had curled up on her bed to sleep, comforted by the familiarity of each other's touch.

'And then?'

'Then I came here, I told them to shove it thanks very much but even unwell my memories wouldn't let me forgive them. I already have enough scars on my body from him.' I remember them she said and traced a finger across his ribs, Drew shivered but continued talking trying not to let her see he did not want her affection. Could she not see it was too soon for even a hint of what the touch implied? Drew shifted his position trying to inch away and hoping she would take the hint. 'I didn't have to take it anymore. I didn't know where to start, my rehabilitation had taken so long and by the time I felt able enough to leave, all traces of you were gone. I tried all the hospitals down here and even in Darwin in case they had flown you east. I rang the station thinking one of you might have touched base with Cookie but nothing.' Drew put his hands out in despair. 'I don't even know what happened to our stuff, not that it would be much good now but there were a couple of things I would have liked to have. I suppose everything was destroyed in the crash or they would have contacted me.'

'No there was nothing, well nothing worth saving anyway. I left it all and was glad of our savings as my wallet was about all I had. Nothing worse than having to get new identity documents.' Drew felt taken aback and some of his anger returned as he lashed out.

'So who's wallet was it, yours or Christa's? Is that how you were getting away with pretending to be her?' Emily fumbled over her excuse and Drew wasn't sure he fully believed her.

'It was mine Drew, I lost things too, my camera, all our memories were on it and now they are gone. It's probably still smashed on the side of the road along with the inside of Matt's head.' Emily burst into tears and Drew knew they had to stop, stop doing the blame game dance and try to deal with the here and now. Wrapping his arms around her Drew too, let the emotions flow until neither of them had anymore to give.

Chapter 20

Pity, grief, loneliness, and despair, had all gathered and sat within him. Each day when he woke, Emily's body curved against his, her hair spread out across the pillow. He had regrets, not many, but a few. It seemed so long ago now, another lifetime when they were young, carefree and they had been three. Drew knew he had never recovered from losing Christa, the right to say goodbye properly may have helped and on days like today before the sun rose in the sky and the fences called to be mended, the troughs to be checked, and the calves to be marked, he knew he should be grateful, grateful for the life they had made and for the deep friendship they shared.

Moving on had meant functioning each day until the pain became so familiar it was barely acknowledged, and it blended and wove its way to be a part of him. Everyday Emily's smile still beamed, he thought he had given her a contentment, a solidness she had longed for, a base. As each year slipped away she was moulding into the person she always thought she wanted to be. Taking up this pastoral lease had been a gamble and although Emily had wanted to finish the circuit and see all the states, the north had beckoned to him and the chance to be his own man, make a mark on this land, and leave one behind, had been too strong a pull. He'd had a lot to learn, he had known that, but the time in between finding her and now he had spent learning from the best. As they moved from one station to the next, and with pride, he could say earning a reputation as a cattleman worthy of those who had shown him the ropes. Drew loved it all, the smell of the yards, the long hours, the hardship, and the triumphs had all been shared but he had longed for it to be his own, his cattle, his decisions, and even if need be, his despair. The red dirt and arid landscape lived within his soul, and some nights as he stood staring out across the saltbush, he wondered how he had ever been born outside of it. Thinking back to the city of lights and sadness made him understand better the restlessness and anguish he had felt, and how lucky he had been to find this. This was the one thing for which he owed Emily his deepest gratitude. Without her prompting and pushing, he may have never found out the sense of emptiness he had always felt inside, was only a big hole waiting to be filled with red dirt and outback sand.

Emily had, in a fashion, followed wherever he led. At first he thought it was to escape the embarrassment once her friends found out she was not exactly who she claimed to be. It had not been her finest hour but in true Emily style whatever the tale she spun them, all had been forgiven as her smile wrapped them up and she moved them all past the moment. Working casually at a retail outlet had not tied her to Perth and although at times she stayed back in a town, while he worked remotely on a station, they were never far apart. Neither of them had forgotten their goals. Knowledge as well as the paycheque were Drew's, and Emily, as much as she loved to party, never wavered from her savings routine. It had been nearly a year before they slept together. Drew had resisted. The accident sat in his brain as punishment for his betrayal of Christa. Reality told him it was not true, but deep inside, on days when his eyes still scanned a deserted street wishing she would appear, he could still feel it nagging there.

Months rolled into another year and Drew felt the distance from their youth measured further than it had been because of their loss. Matt was never forgotten in their thoughts but for Drew the feeling was less, and it was only when Emily reflected on a memory did he stop to consider she had lost more than him. It wasn't often now they spoke of her and had both adopted a way of recalling a funny moment or a task leaving Christa in the shadows so as not to expose their feelings. Drew knew he hid his well.

Sarah kept in contact and although he knew his opinion of Emily was not high, she could never pinpoint her distrust and on the few times they'd caught up had acted with a friendly though guarded manner. Sarah herself had moved on, a corporate job had replaced her hours in the surf and a husband along with two children filled her life. Their parents both passed away within months of each other and the inheritance they had deemed good enough for their offspring to inherit had been enough to set them both up on the path of their choosing.

The move here had been awkward, and the timber unfinished house was not all Emily had imagined. The verandah was wide but still the heat encroached taking away the majority of coolness it provided and in the end, only being a barrier from the sun above. Every few months it got the better of her and she scuttled away to the south, meeting people none of whom Drew would ever meet and it was not as if he was asked to, the names changed, and he suspected the lies flowed but she always came back full of life and adrenaline which slowly ebbed away as the weeks dragged on and the monotony of the station dragged her down. He was happy for her and their time apart was good for both of them, he had no interest in asking after a trip on her return, and as months and then another year rolled by, she no longer felt the need to tell. As much as Emily wanted him to declare his undying love they were words he would never let cross his lips and he had often wondered why she stayed. The feelings he had for her he kept to himself, she was company and though it sounded harsh, the sexual attraction they had was all that held them together. In another life, Drew thought their friendship would have drifted apart, coming down to the occasional call or a card on a birthday. It was Christa who held them together still, her loss had scarred them both and as two people who had always blocked or hidden their feelings, she had been the one thing they could never hide away from, and so they clung to each other for the tiny past they shared.

On lonely days as he scanned the horizon, the sun would play tricks with his eyes. The silhouette of a girl would blind his view and for just a moment he could feel her again before a blink wiped her away and another drop of sadness trickled into his heart. Drew wondered if it would ever go away. On days when Emily was gone, he explored the thousands of square kilometres he could now call his own, the long lease part of the system up here and financially one which suited him. Some nights he would camp out without a care in the world, the Milky Way arching across the night sky as his entertainment and the buzz of insects the only sound until they too went quiet, and in the absence of sound still felt like he could hear them. Some days were slow as he navigated territory he was sure only aboriginal people had crossed in a far distant time. The saltbush which would sustain the cattle in harder times hedged itself around the ghost gums and the camel trees. Bushes with names he could not recall, and Barley Mitchell grass brushed the doors and left seeds in the tyres to be transported along the way. Drew admired the spinifex, curling in circles in places or making letter shapes in the sand. If he were to light it up it would send curling black smoke spiralling into the air and was a sign of help needed for anyone who could see it, and they would come, and know exactly where to find him by tracing back the burn. Alone out here meant hundreds of kilometres of no one, but a community would always come together if needed. Out here you relied on your neighbours, when trouble came they would all be there to help no matter how far apart you were. This was something he had seen in every part of the country, distance did not define how close a community could be. Camels stood on the sandhills their ability to survive the harsh conditions had them breeding out of control and Drew knew a cull would be on the cards once permission was granted.

The cattle he'd purchased mixed and the rogue ones he had found in his search, hidden away from musters of the past, their rangy horns allowing him to judge how wily they had been, and for how long. They would add to his returns and as soon as he straightened out the camps he hoped to do a full muster and start to hire some hands to help him. It would have to be seasonal at first but one day he hoped he would run a station like the one he'd been on in Isa. With quarters, a cook, and the best darn hands he could find, young or old he knew they would each bring a different experience with them so he would never discriminate on age, or gender, Christa would never forgive him if he did.

Drew slammed on the brake, Christa. He had made a mistake. Emily, he was with Emily now, was his mind confusing the two. Why couldn't he finally accept what had happened and move forward completely, he knew he never would, or could see her again. Drew was living his dream, not all of it, but the part he was missing, was someone he could never get back. Drew realised he still had his foot hard on the brake and releasing it eased some of the tension he felt, it was time, time to let her go, time for them both to move on in the worlds they were now in and accept all the good he did have.

A rocky outcrop rose ahead, and he could see birds circling the sky and knew a water source was close. He drove as far as he could and as the rolling spinifex faded away the snappy gums thickened along its banks clambering for space before thinning out as the spring disappeared beneath the earth, until the wet returned. Exploring on foot now, Drew hoped he would not have to scratch down far to find water if he needed it. As he made his way along the bank a string of billabongs stretched out ahead and he could hear the water running further up between the rocks. The gorge lay on his boundary and from this angle, he could see it was bigger than the maps had suggested as its steep sides rose vertically from the ground only leaving a narrow path for him to navigate without getting wet. A curve blocked his view of the inner gorge, and he had to concentrate to not stumble as the path almost disappeared and the way forward became only rough foot holes in the red jasper walls. Once past the curve the temperature dropped, and the walls above curled in to leave a narrow opening blocking out the sun's rays at this time of day. He shivered but not with the coolness.

Drew had heard people talk about places, Uluru and such, where they felt a deep sense of belonging, a peace that settled within them just by being there. Drew now knew what they meant, it settled on him, and in him, a feeling of oneness with the earth and satisfaction with oneself. Whatever spirits lived here he felt they had been waiting for him to arrive and it was as if all that had gone before, was now in its rightful place. Drew paused, not wanting to break the spell it had cast, before sliding sideways along, his back against the wall, and his fingers spread to get the widest grip he could on the surface until he had enough space for both his feet to fit comfortably together without fear of falling. A tranquil pool of water, dammed by some boulders and the narrowing of the gorge, looked inviting. Lush ferns of different varieties and sizes grew in abundance, their every shade of green a contrast to the drying paddocks on the other side of the walls. Drew edged back to find a way down to the floor of the Gap, jumping across lower downstream and then winding through the growth to a large flat outcrop on which were two flat topped rocks that looked as if they had been placed there on purpose. It was the perfect spot to sit to take in the peace of the surroundings. Drew stripped off and lowered himself down into the cool water. Dust from his body floated in a ring around him and he ducked under rubbing his hair while pushing away from the edge then slowly rising back up to the surface to turn on his back and take in the serenity. Thoughts tried to invade but he shut them off as his body relaxed and he allowed his mind to find some peace.

Part Two

Chapter 21

Christa

The street was wide and straight, a thin strip of tar in the middle mostly covered with a coating of dust that hid any visible lines underneath. Some of the houses lining it were boarded up, while others stood neglected, abandoned as if the person had left intending to return but then never had. Screen doors hung down at crooked angles, some flapped slowly open and closed on the rare occasion there was a breeze and the gardens were non-existent. Dry hard earth yards which even the hardiest of weeds could not penetrate were surrounded by decaying, paint peeling fences that no longer stopped anything from getting in or out. It was a far cry from when Christa had first arrived, the busy street had been full of young mums and children whose noisy chatter filled the air each day as they ran from one house to the next. It had been a town of growth and false wealth as the mine paid a premium for workers to come and then stay in this desolate landscape. As each section of the mine closed down the population dwindled, each promising to keep in touch, but she knew it wouldn't happen. As their new lives caught them up they would move on from town to town, mine to mine, following their men as they chased the top money. Each of them would repeat the spiel saying it would give them a good start, one day they would go back to their old life, buy a house and settle down. Christa suspected they never did, their money frittered away by the costs of living in remote Australia and the online shopping for useless goods to relieve the boredom.

Christa stood in the empty street. Only five residents remained, crazy it seemed, but the others didn't know how to leave, like Josh, they had found their place, and even though it brought them no joy, it gave them a sense of belonging they had not found elsewhere. Josh was out at the mine as caretaker, there was much to do, as dry as the land is, the ground water still had to be managed, recorded, and pumped out, machinery checked along with fuel and chemical storage. When the commodity prices rose and the next boom hit it would reopen, another company would step in, rework the tailings, extract the unseen metals with new technology, and the town would again come to life. Until then he was happy to look after it, start the generators, keep the access roads and airstrip clear, maintain the buildings and make sure no one trespassed on company ground. He occasionally had to entertain an engineer or geologist who came to fill in their forms and report back to their boss who in turn reported to shareholders, urging them, she thought, to hang in there, reassure their investment was safe as the company did the deals to pass it on.

Christa knew he liked the isolation, and at times she thought he considered it his baby, his place. Initially, he had done turnabout with Jimmy, but Jimmy had moved on and so Josh had to sleep out there every week now, sometimes five nights in a room off the workshop, a satellite TV, and study books his only companions. The generators ran all night to keep it lit and deter those who thought it may be unattended. He didn't have much trouble, the odd prospector trying their luck with a detector, feigning they didn't know it was private land or aboriginal people wanting access through to cultural grounds.

Christa lifted her hair off her neck and let it fall again, her hand immediately sticky from the sweat gathering there. The heat was endless, unrelenting. The dust puffed around her feet as she headed back into the house. It didn't look much different to the other houses in the street, the same peeling paint and cracked dry yard. At least the wide verandah gave some relief from the heat, its slow fans turning trying to push it away but in reality only achieved in moving it from one spot to another.

Christa's days were solitary, she attempted to keep the house clean, but it seemed as soon as she finished the dust found a way in, unseen, to settle on everything again. She didn't bother much now only doing a quick run around the mornings before he returned. She ate when she was hungry and whatever she felt like, if it was cereal for dinner, or ice cream at breakfast she didn't think it mattered and only cooked if it was a means to fill in time or if he was there.

The week stretched before her, empty as it usually was, but today there was an impatience, a ripple in her belly which made her agitated and unable to settle. Not even her painting could soothe her. Maybe she could walk down to the roadhouse and have a chat with Hilda, though the conversation would not be any different from their last. A few caravans or trucks called in to slice up the day, but it was only Hilda was now too old to leave and had nowhere to go, or anyone to take over, that the shop was still open. At least it was a drop-off point for more remote stations though they too were hundreds of kilometres away and often flew in now, landing on the strip at the mine to pick up their goods from there. Christa often thought Hilda's husband saw more of Josh than she did as he backed his old utility out and took whatever mechanical part had turned up or the odd supply out there to meet them. Every six months the stations would order big, restocking pantries in case the big wet came at last. Often the wives would come in too, by road to help cart back the goods and have a day away, speak to another woman, not on a two-way radio but face to face, a rare event in these parts. At times Hilda had asked her to help out and it broke up the week sorting and labelling the supplies which, for the recipients, was precious cargo. As she sorted, Christa would listen to their conversations as Hilda filled them in on the news of the month, it made her feel like there was still a community out here, not a visible one but still there in times of need.

Christa's supplies and mail were dropped here as well. She never got letters but liked to order her paints and personal items by post as they came in sealed bags hiding their contents inside and giving Christa a bit of privacy in the tiny town. Receiving a parcel was big news and gave the others a few days of gossip speculating the contents. Apart from Hilda and her husband, the only other resident was Jed. Jed lived about a kilometre out in a house he had decided he liked. Christa didn't think he owned it but then nobody probably did anymore. He was harmless, a drifter who had drifted in one day and never drifted out, finding in this tired godforsaken town whatever it was he needed. Jed didn't say much so most of her knowledge of him came from Hilda. It seemed he had found his bed and was happy to lie in it, funded Christa thought by the government. His presence didn't worry her, and Christa never thought of him. If you had asked her what he looked like she couldn't say, he was just there, someone to glimpse in the distance so you knew there was life out away from these four walls.

The idea popped into her head it seemed out of nowhere as the heat seeped thick across the shadows of the verandah and the temperature rose towards its peak of the day. The Gap! I could go out to the Gap for a swim. Christa had never ventured there by herself. In the early days when the population was greater they would occasionally have picnics and barbecues out there in the long summer months. After they had all gone, the few times Christa and Josh had been out there it had been partly dried up with a rim of thick rank mud. Christa couldn't think when the last time had been, at least it would be cooler as the sun only seemed to penetrate the gorge as it lowered in the sky ready to say goodbye to the day. Christa hoped the few storms they'd had pass over had at least left a pool for her to cool her feet even if they were not enough to break this endless season.

Christa gathered a few things together, driven now by the thrill of doing something different with the day. Water, a thick slice of fruit cake and a piece of fruit were placed in a basket and a threadbare towel was thrown across the top. Hat, sunnies, keys, a book, and a small first aid kit thrown in at the last minute, Christa had a moment of self-doubt but brushed it away with the flies as she stepped out the door. The station wagon had seen better days but it was all she needed to get around, it was full of fuel so no need to venture down and have to explain her movements to the township. She turned west and stuck to the centre of the road, the ride smooth until she turned off onto the track towards the Gap. Christa slowed as the corrugations shook the vehicle and she tried to negotiate the shrubby edge to ease the pain. Again doubts flooded in but she'd come this far now and with the window down and the air circulating the car she felt a freedom she hadn't felt in a long time. Another turn known only to locals took her along a dry creek bed. The she-oaks hung their branches down brushing the sides of the car and dropping their woody cones as the vehicle wobbled from side to side over the smooth stones and knocked them free. Christa felt confident, this wasn't so hard, a few more turns then a rise up the hill and she would be there. The car growled as it turned and the tyres dragged over the bank and up the hill. A lone tree stood at the top, showing its defiance of the condi-tions it dealt with. A chatter of budgerigars rose, annoyed she had disturbed their peace and she heard the call of the black cockatoos as they settled again in the she-oaks below.

Christa pulled the car up as far as she could beneath the sparse limbed tree, then set the sunshield across the windscreen hoping it would keep some of the heat out for her return trip. Taking the basket she made her way, following the track as it descended between the walls of the gorge cleverly hiding the entrance from her parking space above. Eyes alert for snakes lurking close to the water she could gratefully see, glistening below. Christa felt the tension of the journey ease away. Eager now to have a swim and cool down, the sweat beaded across her forehead and she again flicked her hair to release some heat. The Gap rose above her, its steep walls so close together at the top overhung the cool deep pool at its feet. It wasn't very long but the bend in the middle shielded the pool from the sun's glare and held in the cool air above it. Tiny birds flittered in and out of the water, taking sips or just cooling their wings, she wasn't sure. They all stopped for a minute, considering this new arrival as they balanced on blades of grass calling to each other to just wait a second to assess the danger.

Christa took a deep breath, the water beckoned and she placed the basket on a smooth rock ledge, slipped her loose shift over her head, and slid in. She shivered slightly as the heat of her body dissipated in the cold water. She lowered her face and rubbed it washing the dust from her pores a faint swirl of colour dirtying the water around her. Pushing out from the edge in a slow breaststroke Christa felt her body adjust to the temperature and relax. Today she was the only person in the world, she could be and do whatever she wanted. Today was a day away from the world she had chosen, chosen because she'd had nowhere else to go.

She loved him, Josh, he had given her stability and routine, the things she had craved. It was not a passionate love, more a grateful one, and for him too Christa knew, if he was pushed, he would admit the same. They had both had a hole to be filled, a void neither had wanted to crawl out from and had not known how. Somehow they had just melded together, trying to fade out the crevasses they could no longer bear to think about. Days when he came they may exchange a kiss or a small hug, on low days they consoled each other and used sex to divert their thoughts to a different place. They were comfortable with each other, understood each other, and both would be happy if the other could find their new course in life. By accident, they had met and convenience had joined them, lost souls seeking something neither of them could put their finger on but in need of a safety blanket to tie themselves to and give them purpose. Neither wanted their past to define them and both knew when they found the means to cope, is when one of them would leave. Until then, and always after Christa thought, they would feel bound to make sure the other was in a good place, this love would never die, it would just fade and change to fit in with each of them.

Christa knew she had to move forward, not without Drew and Emily, as they were part of her and who she had become, but with them in a new and different form, sharing their memories and including their love in the future. The days Christa thought she could share them were still followed by too many she could not and time was not always a friend she could rely on, it moved too fast away from when she had last felt their presence and yet lingered slowly giving her hope one day she would find Drew's resting place and be able to say goodbye.

Today Christa felt her insides reaching out, her sensuality heightened by the remoteness of where she was. She turned back towards the bank, slipping her straps off then reaching back and undoing her bra, releasing her breasts from its confines. Throwing it on the bank towards the basket, she slipped her panties off and tossed them in the same direction. The feeling of freedom intensified as the water swirled and touched her inner thighs. Christa couldn't believe how she felt, the Gap was casting its magic as she floated. Turning on her back to stare up at the rich, warm colours of the rock walls overhead a noise startled her and she flicked over quickly searching for movement along the banks. Finding nothing she again reached her arms forward and slowly swept them back in a circular motion propelling herself forward towards the bank where she had left her belongings. The rock was cool against her skin and she hugged the thin towel around her body. It would only take a few minutes to adjust again and she shivered slightly then rubbed her skin harshly to warm it through. Standing on the ledge she swung her hair around to one side and rubbing it coarsely gazed out along the billabong. The reflections were now motionless in the water except where the birds, accepting of her presence, made tiny waves that rippled out forming ever-increasing circles across the surface until they dissipated and disappeared. It was good here. It gave her peace, she would bring her paints and easel next time to try and capture the beauty. Maybe she could stay overnight to watch the sun as it crept its way up the Gap trying its hardest to stretch out its fingers of light into the darkest corners before it dropped below the horizon to light the other side of the world. It would be safe enough, she could sleep in the car, high up away from snakes and dingoes, and could light a fire, watch the falling stars and marvel at the beauty of the Milky Way. Josh could join her, but then a part of her wanted the freedom of her own company. It had been a good choice today, it had lifted her and restored a bit of her soul. Christa had no idea of the time and hungrily ate the cake and then slowed as she munched on the apple, it wasn't crisp. It was something she missed, a fresh crisp apple that called out to you at the first bite, its juice causing you to suck inwards before dragging the bite away and twisting it in your mouth for your taste buds to enjoy. She pushed the book aside, there was too much to take in today but she would leave it in the basket for future days when her mind had absorbed the beauty and she could pull her eyes from it and relax leaving the world behind.

Christa saw the first finger of bright light poke around the bend and she did not want to dally today. As her confidence grew she would stay longer and take a chance on the light but for today she would leave, get to know the road better, and travel in daylight. Slipping her dress over her head, she threw her underwear in the basket and made her way back up the path only turning back once to again search the banks, and silently voice her leave.

The heat in the car was stifling, such a contrast to where she had been. Christa didn't mind, it made it like two worlds in her brain, the line of the shadows creating a deep contrast between the two, the one she had to live in and the one she had chosen today, her dream world. The corrugations did not improve on the return trip but the rewards of the day overrode the minor hardships to get there. Christa felt good, tomorrow she would be more prepared, could leave earlier and spend more time. She smiled to herself, today was a day she had felt closer to Drew than she had for a long time, and the pain of his loss had mellowed slightly as she swam. The water had cleansed her pores and her mind so only the good remained forever embedded and the rest now felt lighter and easier to bear. Today she had found a snippet of joy and she wanted more of it, so much more.

Chapter 22

He watched her from the shadows of the Gap, the crevasses in the walls allowing him to remain unseen. His loins stirred when she released her breasts and floated on her back, her breasts rising cooled by the water, her nipples erect. Her hair floated out around her head and he leaned forward to take in her whole body. A twig snapped beneath his feet and he pulled back flattening himself against the hard surface behind him It seemed she looked right at him but then she turned making her way to the edge, pulling herself out and stretching her body, drying it with a towel, hugging it to warm up then tipping her head to the side, to dry her hair, her body shaking as she rubbed it with vigour. His body betrayed him as he stared and for a moment forgot he had meant to hide. The rock wall seemed to clutch him from behind holding him back even though moments before he had felt like a clinging vine unable to let go. He watched her walk up the path, her thin shift clinging to her slightly damp body. My god! He had not felt like this for a long time. His desire to chase her and hold her down offended the gentleman's side of his brain, but he could not deny the thoughts were there.

Chapter 23

Christa

Christa returned every day she could. At the Gap, she felt free, free from the heat, free from the loneliness which of late had wrapped around her. She had always been a loner but it was the steadiness of the nothingness around her which was scratching at her skin and seeping into the sores. As she floated in the cool water she wondered if it was time to move on, was it the travel bug telling her she had remained too long in this place, or the comfort of a steady companion keeping her here?

Kununura and Broome seemed so long ago. The bars, the shops, the ice creamery where she had scooped copious amounts of mango ice cream into cones for tourists and passed them over with a smile that never reached her eyes. Loneliness still clung to her like a cloak, there was not a day since the accident she could remember flinging it aside to laugh aloud and accept the things she could not change. Sarah had never been found. As Christa moved from one dusty town to another and along the coastal fringe, enjoying the freedom of the life she had chosen, she had searched. Each surfboard was examined as it lay on the sand, and each blonde head that bobbed in the ocean was studied until a movement or a glance dismissed it could be her. Christa had hoped her number at the hotel would be searched for and news of Drew's passing would be confirmed so she could move forward at a brisker pace. Part of her dreamed he was out there searching for her, fully recovered and desperate to find her. There had been times when these feelings were so strong, so real, she had wanted to fly to Darwin and sit on the beach knowing it would be one of the first places he would look.

Seasonal work became scarce and the further she moved south the slower it became in the tiny towns dotted along the coast. Karratha held no appeal though the work would have been well paid. Christa had felt the need to keep moving for now, searching, not only for Sarah but also for herself, she was lost and as much as she called to Emily for support, there was only so much she could give. Exmouth, Carnarvon with its outer space tracking dish dominating the hillside, Geraldton though slightly bigger was winding down, as all the towns did when the grey nomads scurried home to enjoy the warmer months down south and escape the humidity in the north.

Meeting Josh who was travelling on his gap year had saved her. He was trying to find who he wanted to be and the marks he wished to leave, but had never imagined the hardships, nor the loneliness at times as he struggled to find a place he belonged. Together in their friendship they had found a plateau for their emotions to balance on, for Christa it was the longing for what she'd had and for Josh, someone to support him as, for the first time in his life, he was making decisions on his own.

Family had called him home early, the hold he had tried so hard to escape, was now the security he craved. Josh had offered her accommodation in his home if she drifted close and the hardship of finding lifts or buses had worn her down making Christa too, scurry towards the south not too many weeks after he had left. The swag had lost its appeal and at times she had felt vulnerable on her own. Dongara, Cervantes, and Lancelin all slid by, their natural beauty not enough to hold her in a tiny place where everyone would want to know her business. It was still too raw and Christa again felt the loss of family, someone to lean on, even though it was a feeling she had never really known. Her lonely past and detached childhood had let her head dream of feelings she saw in others and some days it was all she had to hang on to. She would find it, she had found it and now it was lost but out there somewhere there must be more. Christa just hoped one day she would find it again.

The first year had slipped away and as she moved into the second Josh had called and invited her to join him here. They had conversed a lot at first, he was after all the only person Christa knew in the entire world, the only person who knew a snippet of her past.

Josh had buried himself in a course and when Christa had arrived in Perth she had approached all the hospitals begging for information which was now buried deep in a file somewhere. They were always sorry, they couldn't help her, maybe if she went back to the police, it may be the way the information she wanted could be obtained. Christa had searched for Drew's parents' phone number, the few with landline phones listed in the Sydney metropolitan area resulted in dead ends and Christa as a last resort scanned the internet for funeral details. Josh had told her to stop, there was no point, they were gone and nothing Christa did would change the facts, then he had held her as she cried and she had slept with him for the comfort of it and felt guilty afterward.

For a time she had worked in a gallery, the owner rejoicing in her judgement and skills. Again though, Christa kept her past to herself and pulled on an invisible mask each day to cover her feelings and focus on the sales she was employed to make. Again another piece of mosaic fell into place as her desire to paint returned and her interest in other techniques was fulfilled. Talking to artists about their work slotted the neglected piece into its spot just like a piece from a jigsaw puzzle and she realised how important it was to her whole being to pursue her talent. The money had been good and staying at Josh's parent's home was cheap, though his mother was not short in voicing her disapproval, her son's involvement with a drifter as she liked to call her, had placed a barrier between them which Christa knew would never be chipped down. A frantic call from Joan the gallery owner one morning had seen her throw a few of her canvases in the car and with her paints and easel hurry to work to try and relieve the crisis. Joan had been speechless as Christa set up her art station in the very place the working artist of the day had been scheduled to be.

'What's this? Are they coming now, was it some kind of fool's prank to say they wouldn't be here?' Joan's questions left no room for answers as Christa produced a few of her finished works and scattered them around the space in a casual style then placed a small gallery table with assorted tumblers of water and paints next to the easel. For Joan the penny started to drop. Pulling on an old paint shirt Christa smiled as Joan realised Christa was saving her day, and reputation by being the artist for her spotlight event. Her astonishment turned to admiration as she took in Christa's work, one of Johnno catching her eye.

'You did this?' Christa had hung her head embarrassed now at the lead she had taken and at putting tickets on herself she would be good enough to be displayed here.

'Sorry, when you called, it was all I could think of to save the day, I'll pack it up, I was foolish to even think it.' Joan had put out her arm to prevent Christa from moving.

'Just leave them right there' Looking at Christa and clapping her hands in delight she said. 'Brilliant, simply brilliant, you are a dark horse aren't you, my goodness these will be gone in a heartbeat, have you more at home we could bring in.' Christa had nodded dumbfounded while Joan grinned from ear to ear.

Christa had blushed a deep red at the attention but Joan had quickly assessed the situation and moved into business mode. Pensively holding her finger across her lips she had eyed Christa and blown her away when she spoke at last.

'Seeing you have saved the day, and you can sell as you work, and display your skills I'll reduce the commission to thirty percent,' she had raised one eyebrow and felt a crack in her own frosty-covered heart at the look on Christa's face. Not waiting for her reply she continued. 'They are raw but for this today, wow it will add to the feature, unknown artist debut. This one here I might make a few calls about, I'll see what I can do but I'm estimating six thousand for this one here, now if it was a series...' Joan had gone off in her little world while Christa, still to this day could not remember what had happened in those next few minutes as the shock of Joan's statement seeped through her body and the weight of just existing financially eased. The day had been a huge success, people had loved the idea of watching an artist at their work and had reached deep into their pockets to purchase not only one of Christa's in their raw state but also some of the many others Joan had on display in her collections.

Since the accident, art had saved her emotionally and the financial freedom now saved her physically. It put food on the table and still gave her the freedom to live each day as she chose. Yet still, the Gap gave her more. The spell it cast on her the first day became a drug she could not survive without, once the wet season came she would not be able to drive the creek bed and as the days went on a new form of grief, for the future, began to form.

Josh's stint at the mine had been to earn the final funds for his study and when it closed he still hung back unwilling to be pulled back into the stranglehold of his mother's love and yet craving the life he believed he had been brought up to have. Although he enjoyed the isolation Christa could see his doubts about living this no man's land existence. Josh had driven back to Perth for Christmas and Christa, already aware of his mother's latest disapproval had elected to stay. She had told him of her visits to the Gap and knew he could feel the change in her. The lifting of some of the guilt, the pressure of why them, and why not me, had made a shift to where it belonged in the past. He understood and while he cautioned her to be careful, he also encouraged her visits. Christa knew he felt responsible for her and yet did not want him to carry her weight or for it to block his way into the future. When he left, she knew it was goodbye, and somehow the loneliness of that thought did not sit with her in any kind of disagreeable form. It was time and there was nothing she could do about it nor wanted to. The shift the Gap was making in her was redirecting her anyway, into a new direction and hopefully a new way of life.

Christmas Eve had dawned sticky and hot from the first light. Christa had already packed the car and was gathering some last-minute items when her phone buzzed. The urge to get to the Gap and set up her little campsite almost made her ignore the call but impulse made her pick it up and answer.

'Christa, Joan Armatige,' Christa bit her lip. 'Look I know it's Christmas but my friend I told you about just got back today and Christa, he was blown away by your work and is keen to speak with you.'

'Sure, no problem, thanks, Joan. Look I'm away for a few days …'

'Christa, he is an agent and works with a lot of government agencies and wants to talk with you about doing some commissions, word on the street has it the National Library is after several pieces, anyway I told him I'd call you and pass on his number.'

Christa was dumbfounded. 'My goodness Joan, thank you so much, I can't believe it.'

'Happy to help, I loved your work from the minute I laid eyes on it my dear and we both know I've done well from it too. The more people who see your work, the more who will come to my studio to buy, a win-win I'd say. I'll let you go but I'll text you his number, he is genuine. I told him you were very busy and he must give me a break over the holidays before he starts to annoy me about you. Making them wait has always been my policy, it will make him want you more, mark my words.'

Christa was still in shock, this could be the break she needed to be able to live independently wherever she chose. Commissions put her name into bigger circles and would move her in a direction she now realised she had been searching for. Christa had been lucky, her art had paid her way. Tiny canvasses depicting outback scenes, the tired creases lining the stockmen's faces held an appeal that reached into the soles of ordinary Australians no matter where they lived. It was in these places she painted Christa wanted to live, the places she and Drew had talked about, the places they had wanted to call home.

Along with Joan, the internet had helped Christa's income and it was always with Johnno's invisible encouraging hand on her shoulder she posted each original out to her clients. Joan's voice drifted in and out until Christa realised she was saying goodbye and would be in touch again soon to see how she got on. Mumbling her thanks it was with a renewed warmth Christa felt at the kindness of strangers, so many of whom had eased her way.

The fans whirled as the heat curled its way in, and the warm glow she felt was not from the heat of the relentless sunshine, but from the anticipation of the days ahead. Freedom came to others in different ways, the isolation seemed to give Christa back her strength and courage to move forward. Behind it all was hope, it lay there always, hope she would find the truth, slighter hope she would again find Drew, in whatever form, so she could finally lay him to rest over her heart.

The one CD in the car played over and Christa left the windows down, relishing in the warm breeze created by her speed. Somehow she wanted her body to be hot and so sticky with sweat that at her first plunge, she would feel the layer of it peeling away, a fresh skin to leave her clean, raw, vulnerable, and open to the freedom on offer. Somewhere deep inside she felt today was leading her to something greater, something which would set her soul to rest and finally her heart to peace. Drew had never felt closer and as Christa turned onto the dry creek bed tears welled as she felt his love envelop her and she knew it must be some form of goodbye.

The sole tree still stood firm, its mottley leaves not casting enough shade to warrant parking beneath it. The tiny budgerigars chattered as they flew yet only circled as if knowing she would do them no harm and they would be safe to come back in to land. Christa felt impatient to enter the Gap yet knew it would be best to set up her tiny table and stove, cover her windows, and leave it all prepared for the night ahead. She had considered lighting a fire later but did not want it to get away. Her camping experience was not enough to cope with anything going amiss, not when she was here on her own, and not in this dry heat. Stepping back she felt satisfied with her accommodation set up, a shade across the back of the car covered a mosquito net which she had strung up as best as she could. The bedroll was made up across the folded-down back seat and she had placed items along the wheel arch. A torch, insect spray, and toilet paper would all be within reach if needed in the night. Grabbing her basket Christa filled it with the sketch pad and watercolours, a sandwich, her fruit, cake, and the thermos before covering them all with a Turkish towel which would act as a picnic rug as well. Sighing with satisfaction she picked up the basket and a small esky she had packed and intended to leave in the shady surrounds on the edge of the water. Christmas is here she thought and the joyful anticipation of the day, and the season added a spring to her descent. The cool walls closed in above her and a chill ran down her spine at the change in the air now the sun could no longer crinkle its way across her skin. The path seemed more worn, padded down by her previous visits perhaps, crushed grasses on the edge browning off from the pressure of her steps. The water shimmered and beckoned below and Christa knew this had been the right choice, no Josh's mother bitching and barking, his dad looking guilty in the background yet not willing to call out his wife's behaviour. Josh, unseeing of the tension he had learned to think of as normal and with his studies complete and savings safely tucked away he would be looking ahead to start his future. Christa was glad, there would never be ill feeling between them and the Gap was the best Christmas gift she could have given herself. Every single day since she started coming here she had felt herself inch away from him being her future.

The rock was smooth and clean as if it had prepared itself for her arrival. Settling the esky in a cool spot she laid out the towel placing the basket on top to hold it down. Her stomach growled its displeasure but she knew the water would win as her skin ached for its freshness to cleanse her both inside and out. Pulling her dress over her head, Christa released the halter strap on her bikini and dropped it, and her panties down. Stepping out of them she crouched down letting her fingers drift in the ripples they made before sitting and slowly edging her naked body into the water. The coolness made her shiver and again she felt the allure and sexuality of the spell this place cast upon her. The water caressed her breasts as she pushed away from the side and breaststroked slowly forward, enjoying as each part of her opened and stretched, the water searching for her warm hidden crevasses, soothing and healing as the layers slid away, sinking to lay in the hidden depths below. Rolling on her back the rough walls seemed to dance with colours overhead, deep reds and rich browns were broken only by a range of green shades of the hardy plants which clung precariously to the steep but jagged cracks in the rock. It was not yet midday but soon the shadows would deepen in the furthest corners and gradually, over the afternoon, lengthen and stretch out their fingers to grasp back the darkness from the sun's enquiring rays. Christa could not remember when she had last felt this content, her mind delved to sort out if she ever had and there it was, the memory, the first time she had felt what it was like to be safe, needed, and loved. In the back of their van at Litchfield National Park Drew had held her and her body had melted into his, he had whispered their future into her ear. It was there her guard had dropped completely and she had known she no longer had to do it alone. From that day on she'd had someone to rely on. The feeling had been deep, not of the fun and support they had shared with Emily on the road, but a deeper more solid truth of all that had gone before and all that was to come. A tear rolled down her cheek and she flipped again to slowly make her way back to her belongings. Christa felt sad, though it seemed it was with a new acceptance. These memories would always be with her but it was time, as Josh said, time to move forward with them in her heart, but not in her life.

Chapter 24

Drew

Drew returned every day he could. Emily came and went, though the times between had lengthened and he could feel her settling in a way that surprised him. The edge of grief was finding its place, and he could see as she stared across the landscape, the way her body now relaxed and melded with the surroundings. She caught him watching at times and with a cheeky grin would drop her shift knowing he could not resist. He made love to her with a new vigour, a need to give her all he had to compensate for the long hours she waited for his return. Drew's emotions slapped across his heart and mind, confusing both as Emily filled his desires and made him a home. At times he wondered if this had been the dream, as the station life consumed him, and Emily slowly edged her way into a comfortable position in the crevasses of his heart. Maybe she had come to show him what he had, and each day as he woke the torment to let the past go consumed him. The Gap gave him solace, a peace so heavy it was almost a religious experience. Each day he could not wait to go back and cursed the days his chores took him elsewhere. Drew could not explain it but for some hidden reason, he was not yet ready to share the find with the woman in his life. Somehow the spirits were telling him to hold back, heal himself before he made his discovery known.

It was so unexpected he saw her, and he wondered if it was the magic of the gorge or wishful thinking that had brought him here on a day when his duties lay in fence line further afield. On other days he had seen traces of another person or people, broken twigs on the path and the flattened grass along its edge an indication of their visit. It had irritated him as if this place was his, and technically part of it was, but in a holistic way, a belonging more than an owning.

The first time he saw her was like a dream, his mouth had opened but no sound could be released. He had slid into the shadows suddenly cautious and unsure, from here the girl looked so much like her but there were subtle changes. She was swimming, her hair floating, longer than he remembered, then turning back she had released her breasts from her bra flinging both it and her panties onto a rock, turning again to float on her back, her breasts rising, cooled by the water, her nipples erect, her body glistening with temptation and his urge to call out muffled into a gasp as his body responded. She paused as if she had heard him, and the shock held him in place frozen in time. Drew dropped his eyes, his body like a statue, solid unmoving, his insides rolling and churning, his mind whirling faster than it could make sense, it's her, it can't be, it is, she just looks the same. The how's and whys spun like a whirlwind in his head, and it was the noise of a vehicle muffled by the distance that brought him back to awareness though still unable to move as the thoughts slowed and unravelled themselves to make sense. It couldn't be, she had aged, not much but her body had filled out, there was a roundness there, the curving of womanhood filling the hollow gaps she had carried before. Her breasts appeared larger, smoother, and more sensual and his mind touched the places he could not. It had to be her, the turn of her head, the angle of her jaw, the reaction of his body, the way her hips had swayed as she walked away. Christa, his Christa was alive or was this a fanciful dream dealt to him by the gods of the Dream-time to tempt him to some kind of fate? The mirage had walked away while he had been frozen in time and the sound must have been her vehicle, the noise filtering back so he knew it all had been true. It was on the other side, too far to give chase, and the terrain would block him on most fronts. The magic still glowed about him and making his way back, he knew he would have to leave before it stole back what it had held out.

As he reached the narrow path, the sun bit his skin and blinded his eyes, shining the red reflection of the rock straight into his heart like a dagger, wake up it seemed to call, the light's fading, and we have more important things to do. Drew glanced back as the softening light changed the colours in the Gap smoothing and hiding the raggedness seen in the bright light of day. Drew found the ute and then wondered how he got there, he sat sideways in the driver's seat his feet resting on the trim of the footwell, elbows on knees and his head resting in his hands. It wasn't until the last rays disappeared that he raised his head and let the exhaustion of the shock take over. So many times he had envisaged this moment, so many times he had stood in his dreams, looking into her eyes in disbelief before taking her in his arms and covering her mouth with his in a kiss that would take them to the heavens and back. The mechanics of nightfall took over and he threw down the sticks of wood he had gathered and put in the back. Soon the fire was crackling, and a steak sizzled in a pan, two eggs resting nearby waiting their turn shining orange in the glow. The moon rose early, and the stars seemed to shy away allowing it to have centre stage as Drew rolled his swag out in the back of the vehicle and settled in to watch the nightly performance. All thoughts of the future were erased, he only had one now and it was to find her. The road beyond led to an almost abandoned town. He had been there once and remembered the nosy shopkeeper, though he had supposed he was probably the highlight of her week, a conversation to speculate about in the days to come with another traveller passing through. It had been getting late when she left so deduction would have him think she lived not far away. What if she was camping out? No, he had heard the vehicle, too far away to follow and she had seemed relaxed not in a rush to have set up for a night somewhere. He pondered whether to abandon everything to find her and give up what he had. Maybe he could have both, would she still be willing? He wanted to call Emily and tell her the news but there was no service here and the nagging in his stomach knew he didn't want to.

Sleep evaded him as the stars winked, taunting him with their cheekiness as they hid behind wispy clouds only to jump out and sparkle again in a game he had no desire to play. He knew it was her, every fibre of his being told him it was true. Should he have called out? The answer was yes but still she would have run, naked and probably as shocked as he. The relaxed feel of her made him know she would return, as the days grew warmer she would return. He could search, but the hours may take him further away, so he would wait, and if he had to leave he would come back whenever he could, leaving her a sign he was close, and waiting. The circle of the night finally consumed him and on waking, thinking he would feel refreshed and full of life ahead, he only felt drained and weak from the restless turns. Emily had filled his dreams, disjointed and troubled she had taunted him tossing him this way and that, her features changing at every movement, so he no longer knew who she was or who he longed for the most, the dream or his reality.

Chapter 25

Emily

Emily's hair glistened in the fading light, it felt light and fluffy, and she was glad she had taken the time to wash it. There was a settling inside her, a knowledge of what she had learned some of which she would reveal tonight once he was home. It had worked out, the two of them, and she was happy. At times the isolation dragged her down and fleeing south had been her haven though the longer she stayed there the more repressive it felt. People moved on, their lives changed, the party animals of the last decade were now mums and dads and a catch-up for drinks was now a playgroup of babies and toddlers and tea with fruit. Thoughts of him always pulled her back, he was her rock and although she had danced around him, played up to him, and played up away from him, she too was maturing, looking for change and the steadiness of life she thought she craved. To be honest, Emily thought she was tired, tired of the smiling, tired of the effort, and tired of pretending she had not already found what she had always been looking for. Her father was not even a memory and yet the qualities she had bestowed upon him were ones she never thought she would find.

Drew had matured into that man, a man of integrity, honesty, and loyalty. He was her goal. Christa had been his light, his first love, and bit by bit he was letting her fall away and looking forward to their future together. Tonight it would be sealed, the planning of telling him excited her, his reaction she anticipated would be one of joy. Emily paused in her chore, the sweeping was never ending anyway, to stare out into the distance. It was true - this land will steal your heart they'd said - but she knew it too was devious. If you tried to reject it, it would sneak under your nails first then spread like a slow-moving mist, twisting and turning beneath the surface, edging slowly towards your heart breaking you down until you admitted defeat and she could draw you in and never let you go. The earth was both a manipulator and a dominatrix, a prowler in the night come to capture your heart when you least expected it. It had surprised her to a degree, the urge to get away reversed with a stronger pull to stay. The isolation suited her, the constant push from her teens to be strong, popular, and brave had now been replaced with contentment and satisfaction with her days. It was not as lonely as she thought and some days when he stayed close by, she had almost wished he would go, so the pace of the day would be her own. Emily still had her secrets, some too big to tell and the thought of bringing him pain was too much to bear. Their lovemaking of late had been beyond her dreams and it was with the mix of fierceness and tenderness with which he took her and left her breathless and wanting more.

Whether it was maturity, or a decision to move on at last Emily did not know, but each day as he approached she was filled with an excitement for the future, one laid solid by the past they had shared and a future they were now building together. The struggles, the tears, the triumphs, and the heartaches had all combined to bring them here and nothing now, would stand in their way. They were their own family and soon, she rubbed her belly unconsciously, they would be three.

The sound of the vehicle could be heard long before it approached, Emily wondered now, how the sound of one taking her away, had once been a joy. She felt nostalgic, whether it was the pregnancy or Drew's insatiable desire for her of late, Emily felt the need to sift through the past before she packed it away never to be dwelt upon again.

The days in the south had not been the parties and frivolity he would expect, as each friend moved on and her constant absences and isolated position did not fit in with their weekly plans. During the days she had searched, haunting the library for its internet and walking beaches and bars she thought might be a source of gossip from the road north. It had occurred to her that if she found Christa, Drew would move on, realise she was different now, their paths had crossed but their junction in the road had come. Emily's only fear had been if Christa did return and show up unannounced before Emily could prepare a story, a plausible excuse for her actions. By now and the longer time passed, Emily knew Christa would have changed, moulded into a new life, hopefully with someone else and they too could continue a friendship with no animosity on either side. Knowing Christa was alive, was like a knife turning in her side. On that day in the café long ago, when Drew had assumed the worst with her words -I'm sorry, she had watched him turn to stone as the depths of his grief waited to take hold and she had, in that moment, had the chance to correct his misinterpretation, to tell him the truth, but she had not. The moment had passed and then he had left suddenly, struggling to hold in the tears before he could get out of the public's eye. Emily had sat for a moment debating to herself whether her decision would define her future and her fate. To follow was to commit one way or another and for the truth or the lie, to stay hidden for another day. To leave and walk away without him, allow him to continue on his quest no matter how fruitless it now would be, had been her decision to make. One would leave her free to choose a new life, maybe a better one with new beginnings and different windows of opportunity. The other would be a life she stole from another,

Christa's life, and karma could be the issuer of the punishment for whatever sins it deemed were committed.

Emily remembered how little time it had taken to make the choice. Ever since Drew had crawled into her swag she had known her truth and as much as she had loved Christa and sacrificed her feelings, even encouraged him to give chase, Emily had also known she would always be waiting in the wings for them to fail so she could legitimately pick up the pieces of him and for him.

In the months as they had grown and travelled Emily had watched as his muscles strengthened and his body matured into manhood. A few times after Christa had turned in for the night, she had flirted and teased, knowing full well the reaction he tried to hide, though occasionally he had given in and taken it almost to the point of no return. It had become a game she enjoyed as much as the result, though the flirtatiousness had not been shallow, only a way of hiding how deep her feelings were. The three of them had each needed something from the other at the start, and for Drew, his need to feel like a man, the protector role, something he'd had beaten out of him in the past if he had tried to speak up, had fulfilled him and helped him move forward. Emily and Christa had allowed him to protect them, laughingly calling him dad at times when they knew they could hold their ground, or they thought he had overstepped. Christa had been the quietest, the shyest, the more unsure of their moves, and the most grateful for them taking her along. As they watched her, she had blossomed like a flower in the spring allowing her soft centre to ooze out catching both of them in her web. Christa had relied heavily on them both for their unspoken support and Drew had risen to the occasion and it fed him in a way Emily could not control. As loud, and outspoken, as Emily had been, it had niggled her hurt when his attention to Christa turned to one of a romantic nature. Drew could not see how it was the chase that lit him up, how mixed up he was in the thought he had found everything he was looking for. Emily had been willing to wait, wait for the deepest parts of Christa to show their true self. The time would come when the hidden, deep ramifications of being dragged from pillar to post would rise to the surface, and in her short time under government care, Emily had met no other long timer who did not have hidden agendas.

She could see the dust now, no matter the season good or bad, green or brown there was always dust. It spiralled behind before dispersing in a haze and settling in a new place for another day. Today was the day to take hold, declare her love, and show him in every way she was the woman of his dreams. Time to move on, from the emptiness her mother's death had left in her heart. The hardest was the torment of loving one while he thought he loved another. Once Emily had realised her feelings, they told her not to rush, drag him away too soon where he could hold any regrets or the what ifs of the sliding doors of life. Chance had stepped in and given him to her in another way and since she had last seen Christa, she had known the time for fate, her fate and his, had come to step forward together. With a little nudge it would all work out and her final fear of Christa's reappearance, would be pushed aside.

They had always had a spark, she and Drew, and as the dust settled behind him she searched his face for the remnants of the day. He looked grim, a funny word which was not usually in her vocabulary, but grim it was as if pondering on bad news or a disappointment he felt. He slapped his hat against his pants before returning it to his head and the dust from it shimmered around him. The smile came and as his eyes reached hers she could see a decision made, an agreement he had forged internally which settled whatever debate had raged in his head. The smile came too, and she stepped down to embrace him though a part of her felt his response was mechanical. 'You're back' he said as he sat on the step to remove his boots, Emily brushed her disappointment aside and her excitement oozed out as if catching him by surprise.

'What is it, what's got you all bubbly and excited?' Em's face fell slightly, and the doubts jumped in too quickly. Would he be pleased, what if he wasn't? He looked up with concern. 'What is it Em?'

'I've got something to tell you, I've known this for a little while and didn't know how to say it, I wanted to be sure but ..' Drew stood up swiftly and facing her put his hands under her elbows, so her forearms laid along his as if to steady her, his head tilted down now, and his eyes searched the ground as if looking for something he'd lost.

'I know' he said solemnly. Emily bent her knees trying to look up into his face

'You know, about the baby?' The words she had practised fell away and she had a sense of dread. If he had known and if he had been pleased, now would be the time to show it.

'Baby?' He was staring at her now, mouth open, eyelids blinking in confusion. 'Baby.'

Emily started to dance now, she couldn't keep still, her feet were marching on the spot as her hips wriggled and she gripped his arms. 'Yes a baby Drew, our baby, can you imagine, I'm sort of scared, terrified but excited at the same time.' Emily could see the light hit his face and what could only be excitement as it spread through him trying to push away the disbelief. It faltered for a moment as a dark cloud scurried across his face but then it was gone in the blink of an eye and picking her up he spun her around and it was as if every fear for them she had ever known was being blown away. When he finally put her down he cupped her face in his hands and she could see the longing for this, the torment of the life he'd had, and the future life he was seeing now The dark storminess of his eyes was new to her, and Emily knew her news had changed everything, and Drew would give it all to this new little soul. He could now change the future by being a better parent than the ones he had known. As his lips touched hers, Emily melted into his arms and into a bond she now knew would last a lifetime.

Later in the night as a light snore escaped his lips and the breeze fluttered the curtain, Emily lay quietly soaking up her emotions. Some of them were new, others enhanced by what they would now share. Fulfilled by their lovemaking, and he had been so gentle and hesitant until she reassured him their un-born child would not object. Emily could feel the deeper level they had reached and knew she had been right in only telling one of her secrets. Eventually, one day she would tell, the baby would give her the timing, once he held his child in his arms there would be no going back, the longing would be gone and the love he had would be channelled in a new direction. One day Emily hoped to clear her conscience but then again, if the opportunity never arose, her mind debated, would it ever really matter? Emily had lived with the secret long enough so maybe it was time for the truth to stay in the past.

The stars twinkled and winked at her through the window, and she wondered if they could see her evil heart or were they too, naughty little imps condemned to taunt and tease for eter-nity from above. The burden of her guilt was lessening, there was nothing wrong with taking what you wanted, and there had been no one to object, Emily had made sure of that. It had taken only time to see it play out and so far everything had gone in her favour.

It had been on a visit south and a shortcut, though why she had been hurrying Emily could no longer remember, when had discovered the truth. Emily had seen herself flashing by in the fancy shop win-dows, her black heels and caramel-coloured coat tied at the waist, blending in with the other city dwellers though it was the clasp on her bag that shone out and made her notice her image. It had made her falter, almost stumble and then the familiar face which had her stop dead in her tracks. Drew. The cattle in yards, the background, his leg up on the bottom rail and face, grinning, turned back towards the artist. Both arms, sleeved rolled up above the elbow, were stretched up grasping the top rail so you could sense the motion he was about to make. The Akubra shaded his eyes, but it was unmistakably him. Emily was thrust forward by an apologetic passerby. The faces of others looked down on her and the shame again rose showing on her face to the silent stares. Cookie, even from this angle Emily could see it was him, and Johnno, Emily had only met him once as the bore running had kept him away from the homestead and quarters, but it was him, the details of his face so perfect it could almost be a photo. Tiny highlights of background colour glistened in his eyes and his mouth was not open but set in an almost comforting way as if he was telling you a yarn whilst sharing a part of himself. It was the highlight piece positioned perfectly to catch the eye of the passersby, a friendly face in a busy street. Others paused as she stood, to admire the crinkles at his eyes and the friendliness of his features, a reminder of a long-lost family member, a favourite uncle, or a father gone too soon. Impulse motioned her in the door before she was even aware she had done so. Suddenly afraid of seeing what her mind was scrabbling to make her acknowledge, Emily had fumbled with her bag while trying to scout the interior for the face she could not believe she would see.

A tall woman had approached, manicured and elegant, and Emily felt the elevator look she gave, almost as if she had physically run a hand from her toes to the top of her head judging her by the value of her clothes before a word had been spoken. She too, could rise to the occasion.

'Hello, I was just admiring your window. What talent, could you tell me,' she lowered her voice as if they were conspiring a plan 'Who

is the artist, I almost thought it was an,' Emily had paused as if her knowledge of art was extensive, 'no, too modern for him.'

Emily glided over to the paintings for a closer look while the woman judged whether she should break into her thoughts or wait it out. Raising one eyebrow and giving a look that could have made her an actress, Emily had encouraged her in.

'A new artist, and I have been fortunate enough to have been a part of her journey which began with our initiative of having an artist at work here in the gallery.' Emily again gave her an encouraging nod. 'Christa Manning has been one of our in-house artists many times, people just adore watching her and it is a way for the artists to have feedback from their buyers as well. The detail around his eyes draws you in doesn't it, I have some others here,' she paused placing her index finger across her mouth in thought, though not yet ready to reveal them. With a sweep of her arm the woman led her towards the one of Drew. 'It was only yesterday we received this one back from the framers. Look at the movement, you could almost be there couldn't you? I know I can feel the heat and the flies, the dust from the cattle, and this young stockman makes you wonder who his smile is for, a workmate, a lover, see how she has positioned just enough shade from his hat so you cannot read the complete story in his eyes.'

Emily felt like she had stepped back in time, the woman's voice narrating a story she already knew. It took her a moment to realise she had stopped talking and was looking at her quizzically. 'Oh sorry, they are captivating, aren't they? It is amazing how many emotions she has been able to filter in each stroke. A local Perth girl?'

'Yes she was and used to work here as well before revealing her talent. I feel I almost discovered her, an artist couldn't turn up one day and Christa took their place, fate works in mysterious ways. Already word has spread, and frankly, I receive calls almost daily about commissions to present to her. Between you and me, and this is not a sales pitch, if you are interested I would jump in now Christa's ca-

reer is on the way up, and not only would you have a lovely piece for your home, but the value of her work is set to skyrocket so it would be a secure investment as well.'

A face appeared from behind the counter, apologetic for interrupting but obviously in a hurry.

'Sorry Joan excuse me, I've just dropped off a canvas, Christa said can you have a look and let her know if you need another, it's not finished but would give the idea of it being a, um, collective?'

'Excuse me, Miss. Yes thank you, Josh, I understand. Actually we were just talking about Christa and admiring her work.' Joan acknowledged Emily as she stepped away. Emily turned to catch the conversation. 'I need to give her a call soon anyway just waiting on a few contacts to get back to me and fingers crossed I'll have some discerning collectors clambering for her work. Now if she was back here it would be easier, you know.' The young man had shaken his head as if it was something he had heard before and good-naturedly indicated it was not going to happen before raising his hand to Emily and retreating the way he had arrived.

Focusing again on her potential client the woman, Joan, had zeroed back in.

'To answer your question more, he is why she is no longer local though the isolated outback seems to be her happy place and,' waving her hand, 'her inspiration. Now, have you been able to choose a favourite, I believe this is the one which caught your eye?'

'It is this one which made me come in, I worked on a station once and he looks so much like an old friend I feel like I'm looking at a ghost.' The woman looked sympathetic. 'The boy died, in a car accident, and I think it was a shock to see his face.'

'Maybe you know Christa then, she worked on a few stations I believe, hence it being her inspiration.' Emily shook her head.

'No I was the only girl there, but she certainly is very talented I almost feel like I'm back there.'

Joan, Emily later thought, had used her sympathetic tone to push her towards a sale, the ultimate professional moving to the goal she had set out to achieve the minute the bell jangled on the door. 'I have a pricing list over here on the desk if it is to be a guideline for you but believe me, this one is quite reasonable considering her talent, and if you purchase any one of Christa's works you will never regret it.'

Knowing she was getting in way over her head and experiencing emotions she hadn't expected at seeing Drew's face, Emily accepted the catalogue and retreated with excuses about the time and an empty promise to return.

Time had filled in so many days and months since then. There had been times Emily thought she should tell, if Christa was happy and settled there was no danger of her returning to their fold. Josh had looked nice, obviously caring and helping to support Christa in her career. Emily had researched her. Joan's Gallery web page filled in a few questions and the catalogue gave more details which someone else would never pick up the hints from. Tiny details in the art revealed scattered wildflowers which only grew in the north of the state and the red in the dust a tint unique to the same area. Emily had never returned to the gallery and rarely ever again to Perth. The lights of the city had dimmed for her. Finding Christa had once been something she had wished for, but the moment Emily knew, she realised the extent to which it all could change, and running away was something she no longer felt the need to do. Drew was all she wanted. As time moved forward the sense of warmth and security she had from being near him had grown, every quality he had, Emily admired. When he had searched for Christa, and instead found her, she had taken it slow and eased herself gently back into his arms. Emily had felt more than the physical attraction stir, this is what she desired, someone to love her above all else.

Christa had run at the first challenge and Emily knew she would run again, frightened by giving too much of herself to him in case it all came crashing down again. Christa would flee rather than fight. Matt had been her second choice, not entirely the man Drew was, but one who Emily thought she could rely on if by chance their romance lasted. The accident had changed the outcome and although at first, the property had not been her dream, it was with surprise some days that she realised how easily she had given in to the pull of it. Boodja the aboriginal people called it and Boodja was what Emily felt. The earth, sand, and country worming their way in, to be part of her forever if she relinquished all to it. Emily could feel the blanket of the spell it had cast.

It was a miracle their paths had never crossed, and if they had, surprise would have covered any knowledge of her existence. Emily felt leaving the past in the past and moving forward to the future she craved with the man she had chosen, was worth the risk. Now this baby would seal all the loose ends. The look that he held in his eyes on the days she felt he had gone back in time and was drifting away from her, the days he was sifting through the torment for clues, all those moments would be wiped away as this little one captured his heart.

The breeze lifted the curtain higher and a rattle on the tin roof reminded her of the rain they would like to come their way. The drop in birdlife and the kangaroos with no joeys were early warning signs of a season that could break those who were unprepared. One more good season and they may be able to weather any storm, the saying the opposite of what they would need. Storms and rain are either a saviour or a curse depending on the season. The long hot summers parched the surface but when the water table beneath ran low and the underground streams disappeared, no longer able to rise to the surface and draining deeper into the soil beyond the reach of the plant's roots, the fight for survival for some, could become too much to bear. The bores would still slowly draw this precious resource from the earth's depths, but the vegetation would be gone and the cattle clambering for moisture would exhaust themselves in their quest for food while the one thing a drought is short of pumped in abundance from the depths below. Emily crossed her fingers in the dark silently praying for luck to finally run in their favour and knowing in her heart Christa, wherever she was, would be happy, happy with her new man and moving forward to a life better than the troubled one she had come from.

As sleep evaded her she slid out of bed and tiptoed her way to the kitchen. Tea made, Emily eased open the door hoping it wouldn't creak, and sat on the top of the stairs, the warm liquid spiralling steam into the night air. The stars seemed larger, somehow closer to her. No matter how hard she tried she could not evict Christa from her mind. Thinking about the day already gone she played out the telling again in her head. He had looked grim, the word came to her again, his steps hesitant at first but gaining speed as he approached, the Drew she knew, returning to his face. I know, he had said, but he hadn't. Know what, she wondered, she hadn't asked, the thrill and surprise at her news had taken them away from the moment. What secret had he hidden away between the vehicle and the house was filed away as her news blotted out the unimportant. Emily knew it would not be anything too significant, surely, yet the look on his face and the shadow across his eyes was leaving a doubt. Leave it Em, move on, the past has always sorted itself so the future can have its way, leave closed cans unopened, for the worms inside might eat you alive. The moon shifted and several stars waved their goodbyes. Emily could not wait for the baby to stir inside her, it would not be long until it let her know it was there and stretched its tiny growing limbs in impatience. It was peace she now knew she had sought and tonight felt it descend as all her stars aligned and all the fears and the what ifs, faded away. Grow strong my little one, she whispered, you will need it out here, but we will keep you safe your daddy and I. Wherever your Auntie Christa is I'm sure she is happy and would be excited for you to be coming, and if you two should ever meet, I know she would see I did what I had to, to save him from himself and you were the angel sent to help me.

Shivering slightly Emily made her way back inside. As her eyelids settled and the cloak of sleep circled, her last thought was, if Christa surfaced again, it would be like a story you hear on the news, gone tomorrow now unimportant to those not involved. As the world pulled them back into their bubble he would know he had made the right choice, his child, their child would tie them together in a knot which now could never be broken.

Chapter 26

Drew

The second time he saw her he had been hiding in wait. With light steps and basket in hand, there was a freedom about her he did not recognise. This time he only wanted to watch, to refill himself with the sense of physical pleasure she had planted and had been growing steadily inside him. It was a desire he had not discovered in the past, the thrill of watching, imaging, yet not pursuing. He sensed a relaxed feel about her as if the water was washing away any tension she felt and as he eased his way along the rock wall he could see her basket was full and knew she had come better prepared. Crouching down slowly he adjusted his feet into a comfortable position and double-checked the surroundings hoping the shadows would remain his friend. He knew it was wrong, wrong to watch her without her knowledge but it felt like a drug, a dose of which he needed to continue and to get through each day since he had found her. The property lay behind him, its vastness so great he had yet to reach every boundary, pain had pushed him back here, back to the north, the dust, the flies, and the loneliness he had craved. Here before him the Gap was delivering the future he had always dreamed.

Perhaps he should have known, from the buildup of their relationship, the long-drawn-out months as he had watched her from a distance, gathering fruit in the orchards, laughing in the kitchen with Cookie, stealing a kiss to whet his appetite for what was to come. The desire had been enough for him to wait, and he had both savoured and relished it, the buildup he was now realising had been as intoxicating as the consummation. As he watched he could see she was planning, moving rocks, and after finding a concealed crevasse had stowed some items before departing, so he knew she would be back. Drew raised his hand now, but she had turned away and the thought she would be back, kept him silent.

Drew sat in the ute, head down reliving the images of her as if they were a drug his body craved. Guilt was weighing heavily, Emily's news had unexpectedly torn him. He could not deny he had been over the moon, this baby could be the block to cement their future in a way he had never imagined and if he had not seen Christa in the Gap, he knew he would have been happy, happy with Emily and the family they were creating. The Gap somehow changed it, cast a spell he had been unable to resist, luring him back and then offering to him what he had desired the most. So close to his dream, the property, the cattle, the life he knew he should have been born to, and then one sight of her had ignited a flame he could not extinguish. What price was he willing to pay to gain what he had always desired and what was he willing to lose? These questions were what held him at bay.

Drew had nearly told Emily and had decided he would, it was only fair so she would have time to adjust once he told her the news. In the confusion of the day and the questioning of himself as to why he had not called out to Christa, the why's and why nots of keeping it a secret had circled. All of them had been listed in his head. They'd had a good relationship, but he knew Emily understood this place now was his life, he had used her for companionship and affection, another human being to touch and use as a centre pivot. It had been with her full unspoken consent and as much as he had used her, Emily too had used him until they had reached this plateau of un-

derstanding and acceptance of what they both wanted from the future. He had been happy to see her meld, become a part of the land, or let it become part of her. Drew loved her, he truly did, but would he ever love her the way he knew it could be? Now he wondered if she would be enough and if eventually it would end anyway. Either way was a chance that may never end as planned. News of the baby had stopped him in his tracks and made him swallow the words he had carefully been planning out in his head, setting them aside as the universe threw what seemed at first, another hurdle for him to navigate. Would sacrificing a child, his child, be too much of a trade for the happiness he had craved? Whatever demons had haunted his past they now seemed to be conspiring against him to show his true self.

Long ago now when he had slid into Emily's swag as the cattle's low sounds and the snores of the stockmen had broken the otherwise silence of the outback, he had run his hands across her breasts and entered Emily's eager body, moulding with her past and with the future they both had before them. They were the same yet different, two sides of a coin both rolling in the same direction, but both independent with their different strengths to bring with them. Both of them were driven to move forward and away, to grab the chances and then push them through until they no longer could. The parts that pushed him forward were known to her without him saying, she had known his needs, seen them for herself in the darkness, and in the soft words they had spoken afterward, she had told him she had known, both where they were going, and where they had been. His youth had wanted him to start afresh, meld a life with someone, and Christa had been the one he had chosen and the one who filled his visions and dreams. His dreams had become hers and yet he had wondered if she would stay. Had it been the freshness of young sweet love that had enticed him, given him the clean slate to work on, and when Emily had smudged the edges, thrown at him elements he had not known he desired, had that been a clue to show him there were more paths from which he could choose? In the morning it had been shame, shame on the faces of his fellow hands, shame in his heart for using her to fulfill his sexual desires, and shame for being exactly as his father would have expected. It was this last thought which had driven him to make it right and when Emily had encouraged him, he had put all his effort into finding Christa and begging for her forgiveness.

It was the colours that lit up the Gap behind him and told him the sun was getting low, she was casting shadows and painting the highlights from her pallet of oranges and reds across the Mulla-Mulla turning their pink display to the colour of a ripened peach. The side mirror flashed glimpses of her glory, and the kangaroo grass bowed down to her beneath his wheels.

The drive home tormented him, he knew it was her, Christa, risen from the dead in some kind of miracle and returning to him. His heart should be full, this was all he had longed for and yet he was pausing, waiting, letting her slip through his fingers.

Emily plagued his mind, her expanding belly would be a daily reminder of all they had shared. Together they had struggled to get to this place, to this point in time and she had supported him in every decision since and through every hardship. Now in one movement he could throw it all away, abandon her for another life, and lose his child for another love. The stakes were high, and he did not know, if he revealed himself, if any of them would survive the fallout. Drew was caught between two worlds, and it would only take one small movement from him and the door could close on both of them.

A full circle was coming. Drew could feel it and was confused as to how it would all end. To tell Emily was to crush her, take away what they had been slowly building in their grief, but she had loved Christa too, had been her sister as well as her friend. To not tell was to deny himself of the future he had long dreamed and had thought was buried in some unknown place with her. As the veil of darkness lowered in the west Drew knew whatever their destiny, it could not be changed.

Chapter 27

Drew

Drew opened the door and stepped out, pulling his sock guards down to stop the burs and placing his hat firmly on his head. Yesterday still seemed surreal. Drew remembered staring at the ground as he tried to recover from the shock, a baby. Hesitating he knew then he couldn't tell her his discovery, not now and not until he had sorted out what he wanted to do. The surprise had made him mirror her reactions, giving Emily what she needed when all the while his head was full of reuniting with Christa. Emily was as used to his quietness, as he was to her prattle, so the evening had been endured without much response until sleep gave him the shield he needed. Drew had felt her rise and then heard her making tea, he had remained still feigned sleep, not wanting his thoughts to become words spoken. When he heard the outside door Drew had rolled over to look at the night sky and ask for advice. To have one was to lose the other and the choice was now almost too much he'd thought. Who do you love the most the stars had twinkled as the moon solemnly stared. Why do you think the choice is yours he heard, as truth made her entrance.

In his wakefulness in the night he knew to make the decision there was one piece he had not yet considered. Christa. What did she want, had she moved on with both her life and her heart? It was as if a sword plunged through his heart at the thought. To plan without knowing all sides would be foolish, to walk away from Emily and his child and then still be left with nothing would be stupid, he knew Emily well enough, and she would now have the ultimate bargaining tool. Drew chastised himself, he sounded cruel and yet a life of watching a bitter and twisted man turn against his family made him want to make the right decision for himself, with no regrets to play out in awful ways to others. To punish his child for his unhappiness would be like repeating the past and he would not let it happen. Drew wanted his children to be strong, happy, and independent, and to learn by being true to themselves, made the ruler by which they would be measured. Yes, he had hesitated, and because Christa was clouding his mind, when Emily had said she wanted to talk, he had thought in some distorted way, somehow, she had found her also.

A breeze rustled the scrub, make up your mind it said as it flicked the leaves and bowed the heads of the scattered remaining wildflowers, the chores were mounting, and love to the breeze, was only a whisper it knew nothing of. To confront her was the only way to find his truth and in her initial reaction, she would show all he needed to see his future.

The daily wear from his boots had not given the grass enough time to stand up again and the dirt one was now clear of tiny stones that had been thrust aside on earlier visits. Today he only went halfway then skuttled down the ledge to jump across a narrow flow of the water where it dammed up before running over and out to disappear beneath the gums around the bend. He had done this before on days when it was clear she was not around, and he had explored the rock face from the other side. He had sat on the rock in thought and once stripped off, slipping into the water to feel the sense of freedom it gave. The path out to where she had parked was examined and it was where he now headed hoping to spy a spiral of dust so he could get this done now the decision was made. The sun beat down and distracted by an eagle gliding on the rising air currents the noise as the vehicle rattled up along the dry creek bed startled him and he withdrew back down the path and slid into the shadows.

The breath left his body as she appeared, her easy steps showing how relaxed she was feeling now she was here. Placing a small esky and arranging her basket on a towel Christa slipped her light dress over her head and without even a glance removed her bikini top and bottoms. Drew's body responded, his whole body aching just for the look of her. She slid into the water, and he could see the relief and calmness it created. Every movement was relaxed, a slow unwinding of a life on the other side he knew nothing about. He could only watch now, every fibre wanting to speak but naked and alone he did not want to frighten her away. Refreshed, a smile playing across her lips she pulled herself out and reached for the towel. Drew craned forward, his eyes glued to the body he had so long dreamt about. The twig snapped, startling them both and she turned snatching at the dress but in the end, only holding both it and the towel awkwardly in front of her.

'Who's there?' Christa's eyes were wide, caught, a deer in the headlights who had not given a thought to safety. 'Is anyone there?'

Drew knew he had no choice and stepped out, one hand rising to remove his hat.

'Christa.' The shock slammed onto her face. 'Christa, it's me, I've been searching for you.'

The towel dropped on the sides and mechanically she wrestled with it to cover herself, no conscious thought was aiding her, and her mouth had dropped open. Fumbling she managed to pull the shift over her head and again clutched the towel under her chin, the drapes of it falling as an extra layer of cover.

Drew took another step forward as the urge to sweep her up, cup her face, hold her close, and never let go pushed him. As the roar of emotions fought, bursting beneath his skin and demanding to be released he knew he could not let them, not yet, she needed time, time to take it in, time to remember all they had been. Christa looked frightened, trembling in disbelief beneath her scanty clothes. He inched forward again and reached out a hand. The round unblinking eyes had never left his face, her lips, now returning some colour to her shocked white face.

'Drew.' The sound slipped out, though her mouth never moved.

'It's me, Chris, I've missed you, I couldn't believe it when I saw it was you. I thought you were...' She put her hand up as if it were too many words to take in and dropped her head so he could no longer see her eyes nor read the confusion in them. It was a double step this time, this close was still too far but he realised he'd had time to adjust, time to think what this would mean and sort through some of the outcomes.

Christa sank to her haunches and then rose again to wrap the towel completely around her. Brushing her hair back behind her ear, she rolled her neck slightly then again crouched, balancing unsteadily on the balls of her feet and her hair released itself again to cover her features. Drew crouched too.

'I know it's a shock, take a breath, oh my god Christa you're beautiful.' His hand touched the back of her head and slid down her silky hair and she pulled back as if the electricity between them was too much to bear. Drew backed off, standing and moving a few steps away before sitting on one of the smooth rocks and pressing his hands against its coolness. The shock was still with him also, this close, and a glance at every one of her features gnawed at his fingers in the need to touch.

Christa raised her head now and as if calculating the distance gave herself some more space by stepping back and mimicking his position. Her shoulders were dropping, and her eyes looked like they were reducing slowly back to normal size. 'Drew.' Again she repeated his name with no more to add.

Leaning forward slightly Drew clasped his hands in front of him resting his elbows on his knees, his shoulders were relaxing as he watched the shock ebb away and the reality of him being here be absorbed. Closing his eyes for a moment he smiled as a sense of relief washed over him. Found, she was found, and safe, the agony of her loss releasing itself while hope poured in she still felt the same.

'I didn't know what to do, you were gone, and they wouldn't let me find you.'

'Who wouldn't let you? My parents?'

'Everyone, I couldn't find your parents or Sarah. I searched for her along every beach, we never talked much about where you had lived or what school you went to. I had no clues, and my phone was crushed in the crash, I waited for you to find me, but you never came.' The stricken look tore at his heart.

'I came as soon as I could Christa.' He spoke her name as an endearment and thought he could see a spark at the back of her gaze. 'They took me to Perth and then Sydney, I was out of it for a long time, and I lost a lot of memories, some are still a struggle to get back.'

'I dreamed of you today and when I was coming here I had to shake away the feelings you were close by.' Christa's state- ment sent a surge of hope through him and Drew lessened the distance between them kneeling in front of her and tentatively reaching out a hand to connect it somewhere on her body, desire surged through him, and it was an internal fight to hold back.

'Then here you are, how did you know Drew, oh my god so much time, so many things told me you were gone, but in here,' closing her eyes she placed her hand flat across her heart, 'in my heart I always held a thread of hope.'

Lowering his hand to her knee, and with no sense of rejection from Christa, Drew pushed himself up before turning to sit beside her. Again, with caution, he placed his arm across her back gently drawing her closer. As she turned her head their bodies relaxed into each other and their faces so close a breath of air could not have passed between them. As their lips parted, their eyes telling each other all their doubts and fears, Christa raised her hand to touch his cheek. 'You are real' she whispered, and her fingers felt like a warm blanket, a thousand stars and a lifetime of memories. Drew closed his eyes and his whole world shrank to this one moment as his lips touched hers.

Long after he would remember almost every microsecond, not like in a moving picture, only each feeling, as it rolled into the next fearing it would not feel as good as the last, but then each one had only felt something, so much better, words could no longer be found to describe them. In the following hours they had captured it again and again, their bodies remembering and rejoicing with every touch. Slipping into the cool water they swam, slowly, close so only the movement of a finger would see them joined again. They smiled and turned in the water, playful now, wanting to laugh and shout to the world their news. Our news, Drew thought, though if I did, no one would hear us, and he silently wished reality would stand back for another day.

The line of shadow had crept up the eastern wall and Drew knew he must face it now, he was not scheduled to be away for the night and Emily would worry if he didn't return. Emily deserved to be told, and Christa did too. As he watched her pull herself up on the rock, turning sharply so her eyes did not leave him for too long a time, Drew duck-dived under, stretching his arms to pull himself down as the realisation of what was to come, hit. Christa was something he couldn't hide, and the reunion was everything and more than he had ever dreamed of in the time they had been apart. Rising slowly to the surface he released air bubbles hoping each one would give him the answer he needed. Drew knew, now Christa was found he could never lose her again, not when she made him feel like this. Emily was now carrying his child, something he and Christa had daydreamed about, but the closer he got to the surface he realised it was not a future he had ever envisioned with Emily. As the vision of Christa rippled from above, Drew knew which sacrifice he would make, today had shown him he no longer had to choose.

Drew's face broke the surface, and he shook away the excess drops while pulling himself up beside her. In the end, he knew, it would not be his choice and there might even be the chance, he would lose them both.

'I have to go. Emily will be waiting.' They had not even spoken about anything before today and the surprise registered on her face.

'Emily.' Christa clutched his arm frowning as if recalling a conversation from long ago. 'Our Emily?' The silence spoke more than words and she turned to look directly into his eyes. 'Are you ... together?' Drew nodded.

'She's pregnant.' The colour ebbed from her face, and he could see her recoiling remembering their day. Drew took her hand. 'We'll work it out, I thought you were gone, we both did. Once I found her we stayed together. Emily had been told you had died, so we clung to each other for support, and as time went on it has become a habit.'

'A habit! She's pregnant Drew. It sounds like a bit more than a habit to me.' As her voice rose he clutched her hand tighter, he could see all the dreams he had given to her today being snatched away one at a time as each thought moved to the front of the line. Drew glanced up at the shade line again. 'I'll talk to her and tell her I've found you. I want you Christa, I always have, and we can sort this, look after Em, have a baby ourselves.' His voice trailed away as he realised how badly he had chosen his words. After today he could not imagine being without her, today his world had righted, and he never wanted it to tilt again.

'You're having a baby Drew, it is hardly the right time.'

'Come home with me. Emily will be shocked, but in a good way, you're her friend, her best friend, we'll sort this out over the next few days, but it will work out Christa. I love you I always have. I want to show you the station, work it together Christa, just like we dreamed, she'll understand, and we'll take it slow, as long as we are together. I never want to let you out of my sight again.' Drew's sentences ran together, the light was fading and yet he didn't want to leave but knew, for Emily's sake he couldn't stay. No matter his feelings he would not leave her on her own.

Christa gathered her things and then ran up to her car to get a few more items and to make sure it was locked and secure. Together they made their way towards Drew's vehicle, and he guided her carefully along the narrow ledge, navigating the way while balancing her basket and holding her hand. Drawing her closer as the path widened out and the ute came in sight, he was not game to look in her eyes in case she was changing her mind, afraid she would turn back and disappear again like a mirage and shatter all his dreams. Bouncing along the track he had expected a million questions, but the country held her view and he sucked in a breath for what was to come. The homestead came into sight, and they could make out Emily's silhouette as the lights shone through the windows throwing shadows across the yard.

As they waited for the dust to settle, Christa slid her hand away into her lap. The door of the house opened now, and the light spilled out behind her, hiding Emily's face in the darkness. Opening the door Drew slid out and they saw her step forward in surprise as the passenger door opened as well.

'Who's with you Drew?' she called and for a moment both he and Christa hesitated behind the open doors before stepping into the light.

'It will be fine,' he reassured her, and her soft reply carried itself across the seats between them.

'She knew I was alive.'

Chapter 28

Christa

Drew. Christa couldn't believe it, he looked real but how could that be? The touch of his hand had been like a firecracker exploding under her skin, the sparkling colours igniting every nerve. As he had nestled beside her, drawing her close, every memory of their time together gathered inside her, and as their lips had touched, an emotion surfaced so deep and raw she would never find the words to describe it. Rippling across her body it had made every pore tingle with an intensity of desire and made the rest of the world disappear. As their bodies came together it felt so familiar and the hidden unquenchable flame they had both held on to roared to life like a bushfire out of control in the scrub.

The swim had washed clean both her body and mind. For a moment as she watched him dive, the magic of the Gap felt so strong Christa had a fleeting thought it might all be a dream. Watching as Drew pulled himself up out of the water, his muscles rippling and body gleaming from the moisture, her body stirred again, and Christa knew it was not. The light cast a halo around him and Christa promised her soul to the gods who had guided them back to each other. The shadow had made its way up the cliff face and Christa's thoughts had turned to the night ahead and the joy tomorrow, when he would still be here. Four small words had shattered her dream the moment he voiced them, 'Emily will be waiting.' All her thoughts had scattered as the past raced to catch up.

The homestead looked almost familiar, a wide verandah giving it a settled look and the light spilling out the windows a beacon of welcome. Christa had let her mind go blank so the shock could settle. Emily was here, with Drew, and they were having a baby. From the moment he had uttered the words, with so many unspoken behind them, Christa had felt frozen, robotic, her body automatically manoeuvring her actions with no direction from her brain. The giant fog of white silenced her and although she felt his gestures and the movement of the vehicle, she would never remember the journey until this point. Once she had opened her mouth to tell him but had closed it again as the words scrambled to string into a sentence. He looked so happy and confident as if all would be perfect in a world he had created in his head, a mythical, dreamtime where everyone walked away happy and content with the outcome. Drew had always been a dreamer and his dream of living out here with a station of his own had come true. If he was owed one more favour in this life, maybe this would be it. Christa was far too realistic to believe it could be so.

The shadows had been Emily's saviour, her expressions hidden for the number of seconds it took to recognise, register and work out her response. Surprisingly for Christa it was only a tiny part of her that wanted to spring forward, rejoice at them all being reunited at last. There was too much water under the bridge, too many hidden worms of memory surfacing that would no longer bury themselves. The frivolous fun they'd had on their journey, as their confidence grew along with their sense of freedom, was now part of their youth. The pie-in-the-sky dreams had been replaced with struggles, pain, and loneliness with the accident revealing people's true selves, no matter how hard they had tried to hide them.

There was an uttering of surprise and while Christa could feel the eyes boring into her body she was as yet unable to see them. It was obvious Emily had never told. After today, the love they had shared, the touches she had felt, Christa knew Drew would have come to her, and her choice now was to stay silent and let Emily make all the moves. Should she let Drew remain oblivious to the deceit and protect him from the hurt? Or lay it directly on the table and expose the lies before more were added. The words had slipped out before her decision was final, she knew I was alive. Christa glanced to see a response, but Emily was already stepping forward and Christa was unsure if he had heard.

'Drew I was worried.' Emily stepped slowly, not running toward her in delight or faking the smile which would not reach her eyes and exclaiming the shock Christa was both alive, and well. Christa wondered how she was going to play it out when all along she had known the truth. Emily had always looked after number one, every decision they made had eventually gone her way or somehow would lead to it, and to not entirely lay blame, they had allowed her to. On the way here Christa had regretted her decision to come, they had discussed so little letting only their emotions live for the moment and the time in between had taken a backseat so as not to steal the moment. Should she have taken more time to think it through? The baby was a surprise, though once he spoke her name she had known they were a couple, and Emily had achieved the result she had pursued.

So much had rumbled in her head under the euphoria of finding him but she had consciously pushed any doubts aside giving in to enjoying every moment of the dream. Reality did not knock until the homestead was in sight and the last glower of the sun was behind him as he had looked at her across the breadth of the vehicle assuring her it would all be fine. The words had slipped out and so her only course now was to make him believe them.

Christa had never forgotten how much can happen in a short time. It took no more than a millisecond to act on your response, she had learned it young, and it would never leave her. A glance her way and she would know to flee, tone changes in a voice, the reason to react. As awkwardly and unworldly as she had been, her world had taught her skills she hoped few would ever have to know. As Christa stepped away from the door, she did so now with a new confidence, one neither of them had witnessed, and with a wisdom that had come painfully after she had seen the security camera footage from the gallery.

Everything was still raw, surreal and this could all be too soon, but her feelings had never changed. As soon as she saw him she knew her destiny was back on track. Take the bull by the horns her many mentors would have expressed, and Christa was hoping this would be easy, but this was Emily, so knew it would not.

Emily had moved to the top of the steps, a post giving her support as she reached out to it with one hand and turned her body more towards Drew than Christa. Drew rounded the front of the ute putting his hand out toward Christa and she moved forward taking it with confidence in both the grasp and her stride. Drew's face was set, and she could see the dashes of confusion starting to form as whatever imaginary words he had planned for this scenario, did not fit with the tension being projected.

'Em look, it's Christa, we've found her.' Christa's heart pounded as he moved his arm around her shoulder and pulled her closer. As her hip brushed his and they moved forward together, Emily leaned more toward the timber support a look of disbelief on her face.

'Christa, oh my god, it is you, they said you were going, and I couldn't wait, I couldn't watch, I thought I would not be able to stand the pain.' Christa's head shot back in surprise. So this was the game she thought would play out in her favour. In the moment she made her decision, she would protect him if she could, but she would let Emily tighten the noose all by herself.

Christa felt her anger rising, the memory of her face on the screen when Joan had replayed it. Christa remembered the pain of knowing Emily had been so close and had walked away, her empty promises of returning soon another lie to tuck in her belt.

Josh had said someone was looking at her work and he had felt embarrassed at the way she had stared at him, though it was nothing he could pinpoint. Joan had relayed the emotions evoked as the young woman had told her story of loss. I think he looked like her boyfriend, killed in a car accident she'd said, such a terrible thing. She was certainly impressed with your work, and I could see how it touched her. I thought I almost had a sale but then she seemed overwhelmed by his likeness.

Christa had interrupted and asked if she could view the tape explaining the story rang a bell and it might indeed be an old friend even though Joan said she was not. The image had shocked her, even before seeing her face, every movement was recognisable, and Christa remembered gasping aloud. Joan had been stunned as Christa told her story, of three friends lost forever and now one incredibly was found, drawn in by a snapshot of their past.

Christa had waited, waited for days and then weeks and then months for her to come back, Sometimes she had wished she'd never seen the tape, to not know would have been better than the silver thread of hope that had begun to grow, the hope maybe there were two. The tiny doubt had grown, Emily had told Joan he was dead, but Emily had been gone too and now she was back. Why didn't she come again? Didn't she know Christa would at least want some answers? The questions had plagued her, built a barrier she knew Josh would never break through, and raised a huge stop sign for her emotions to move forward.

Chapter 29

Drew

The words had stunned him to the core. Emily knew. How? Why hadn't she told him, brought Christa here so they could all be together? The whisper across the seat was a can of worms he did not expect and one, if it was the truth, which could have changed it all.

Emily came to him now, acting surprised. Carefully she negotiated the few stairs, her hand free to hold against her stomach in a gesture he had seen her use last night for the first time. Drew frowned as it now looked orchestrated, and he wondered what point she was trying to achieve. Why did she not go to Christa first? This was not the scene he thought it would be. Christa too, was holding back though Emily did look shocked and the hand on her belly purposely reminded him of where his responsibilities should lay. This child was innocent, and it was in those few moments Drew realised while he had been searching his memories for truths, they had only fabricated a fairytale.

Chapter 30

Emily

Emily moved toward Drew first, she was shocked, Christa was here, and with Drew. He had put out his hand to her and it was easy to see what had passed between them. They were both glowing and even under the cover of darkness their bond was a light they could not extinguish. Why now she thought, though the baby news was probably perfect timing, why now when life had finally mellowed, and a balance had been reached. Drew had moved on, they had a future planned and none of it had included Christa. What fate had made her appear today of all days?

As the required words left her mouth, the exclamations of disbelief and the where, and how's questioned, Emily was striking each off her list to see if her deceit would be discovered.

She had never gone back to the gallery and couldn't see how her appearance would give any need for conversation. The guilt had weighed her down for a while, keeping the secret from Drew. The one thing he desired most in the world, above the property, had been Christa. To find her he would forsake all else if needed. Emily loved him, had secretly always loved him and as his and Christa's love had blossomed the tendrils of jealousy had formed and slowly wrapped themselves around her heart. When she had left the gallery that day a part of her intended to return, but as the hours ticked away and the second coffee became a third as the shock of her discovery sank in, the ramifications for her, had also sunk in. To tell Drew would have been to lose him, lose the security she now had and the affection they shared. Josh had looked nice, but she had seen them together too often to know if Drew walked in, Christa would move heaven and earth to be with him. Soulmate was an expression Emily had seen in action. Drew was security, a safe place, and a constant. He was one of the few people who accepted her for all the chatter, the scheming, and her overload of confidence. Beneath it all Drew also recognised the hurt, the sadness and the need to belong, and he forgave her the rest, because of it. As Emily had motioned for a refill, the decision was made and she was able to tuck it away, her love of Christa was the sacrifice, but Emily was determined to protect herself and her future. After all, she almost said aloud, I'm the only one who can look after me and I will do it, no matter what it takes.

Chapter 31

Christa

Awkward could not be a more perfect word. Emily's embrace not long enough to be sincere. Drew had stood back looking confused, if he had heard what Christa had said, she would have understood, but no words were uttered to show he had. The Christa from long ago kicked in, she had been added to by experience and some maturity, but the turmoil from her youth had taught her to play the role and let others become their own fall guy. The whole day now seemed surreal and as they made their way inside, Emily was fluttering and fussing, making noise and speaking words which were irritating because of their insincerity. The interior was quite stark with a few high-end ornamental pieces which Christa could see had been Emily's input. Thin blankets lay across the lounge and a fine layer of dust gave a grey look to most of the room. A small kitchen was visible through an opening and as they had come down the short hallway Christa had seen an older style bath in a room and another room with a bed which was most likely theirs. Two more rooms whose doors were closed but they did make her notice the low wooden door handles which looked shiny from wear. An aroma of roasting meat filled the room, and she could see saucepans set on the stove ready to be turned on for tonight's meal. Christa tuned back in.

'So there will be plenty, I hope you still like lamb and the vegetables should be enough. You're staying?' As of old she didn't wait for an answer and continued with the decision she had made not ever allowing for the consultation. 'Come and I'll show you where to put your things, now this is our room and I can make this one up after tea, it's comfortable, I slept here for a while, before we became a couple. I was thinking of making this a room for the baby, but the other one is closer to ours.' There it was, Emily staking her claim in one sentence and showing Christa all the boundaries veiled with a smile, though the underlying threat was clear.

'Drew told me about the baby, congratulations. I will admit I was surprised at first, though we did talk about grandchildren one day, remember?' Christa saw the memory flash across Emily's face followed by another emotion. Could it be regret? The charade continued while Drew stayed silent, frustratingly so. Emily fussed around the kitchen her chatter filling the space Christa thought other questions should fill. There had been no mention of how she got here, how Drew had found her nor when or where. The situation was almost bizarre as if each of them was waiting for another to make the wrong move. Christa knew Emily would know the score, as much as she circled Drew, running her hand along his back or arm each time she passed, they all noticed the slight flinch as his nerves rejected her touch and the silence spoke of his inner turmoil now they were all together.

With dishes done and the compliments made, an awkward silence hovered as Drew made a cup of tea still seemingly undecided as to what he should say. The day they'd had, full of the love they had shared and the catching of all the emotions they had missed, was coming to an end and the touches and the kisses full of their wonder were now fading onto a meaningless plateau of uncertainty. The day was losing its grasp on her and

Christa, impatient now for Emily to play her card and admit the reality of what was to come, was slipping into the night. Tomorrow, if nothing was said would only be harder and Christa was no longer willing to let the moments she had long dreamt about slip away. Emily feigned a yawn and Christa knew the time had come to bring it to a head. Emily's refusal to confront the situation and Drew's unwillingness to make his decision known was not only frustrating her but also added feelings of distrust she had not allowed in for a very long time.

'So Em, you haven't asked when Drew found me today, aren't you curious?'

'I'm, ... I was so shocked at seeing you, and of course we both thought you were dead Christa. It is taking a while to sink in.' Christa almost felt queasy, the image of Emily at the gallery flashed in her head. 'Of course I want to know, every detail, but it has certainly been a huge day so maybe we can leave it until tomorrow. Drew will have things to do, and we can have a nice quiet chat, just us girls.'

Christa felt the heat rising inside, was she meant to fight for the man who would always be hers, why wasn't he speaking up, had the day been false, a mistake he now was regretting? Was he not the man she had dreamt about for so long? Drew's lack of action was certainly filling her head with doubts. Christa turned to glare at Drew, trying to prompt him into confessing so at least the sleeping arrangements would not become a farce as well. The years of longing, self-doubt, and growth as she had spread her wings and how these two had taught her to fly spun in a ball Christa wanted to throw at the world. For so long she had bowed her head, taken what the rest of the world had thought her due, and now the one thing she had ever truly wanted in her life was here in front of her. Art had brought to her confidence and Joan had encouraged it, drawing her into a world so different from any she had ever known. In the art world she was valued, admired and praised. The love of creating had held her there and yet her dream, this one dream, had always left her with one foot outside of the door she could now have. Drew had been the rock she held on to, the axis to pivot herself to as she flew always knowing he would be there, that was, until he wasn't and then she had used the dream of him to hold herself back. Christa observed the facial expressions as they flitted across their faces. Emily tried to hold his gaze and repeatedly he pulled away. Christa's stomach was churning, today had been a dream, the pinnacle of all she had imagined their reunion would be, maybe it was time to push the dream aside and look again at all she did have and learn to live with what she could not. Christa pushed her chair back from the table.

'I don't think it's wise that I stay.'

'No, don't Christa, please, we'll work it out.' Drew pushed himself up as well but then stood awkwardly still torn as to which way he should sway.

'Well Drew you are hardly trying, and Em is acting like she has something to hide, why don't you just blurt it out Em, confess. Whatever this is,' Christa waved her arm as if surrendering defeat, 'you didn't want to include me, so I'll go and when you two both work out your future let me know but as it stands I don't think any of this is what I want to be a part of.'

Drew looked stricken. As he stuttered and struggled for words, Christa thought Emily's best defence was silence although all she wanted was for her to tell the truth for once and admit she had known where Christa was. It might be for the best Christa thought, she could wind him up in her lies and the more he floundered Christa could feel her faith in him draining away.

'Take me back to my car Drew, I've spent years dreaming of seeing both of you, a dream I thought could not be realised and even after seeing Emily in Perth I still convinced myself it was a mistake, a weird illusion captured by my desperate need to find you both.'

'Perth, you saw Christa in Perth?' Drew's bewilderment was rolling into anger as her words sank in. 'You knew Christa was alive Em and didn't tell me, how could you, where, when did you find her?' His hands made agitated movements, his fingers clenching trying to hold their grasp so as not to form into a fist as his anger grew. Turning he unleashed on Christa as well. 'You knew too, why didn't you come to me, I thought you loved me and what was today, you looked surprised, overwhelmed at seeing me, I don't understand is this some deluded joke you have both been playing?

'I didn't know Drew, I saw Emily on a security footage.' Christa glared at Emily, never in her life had she been this quiet, it was hard to work out what her game plan was. 'My boyfriend told me someone had been looking at my work and then my boss made some comments I didn't understand so I asked to see the footage.

'Boyfriend!' - 'I couldn't believe it when I saw it was you Emily.' Their questions and explanations overlapped as each of them absorbed the situation. Christa continued. 'I waited Em, I waited for days then weeks. Every time I walked down the street I looked for you, I knew you wouldn't abandon me, not again.' The tears came now, the hurt, the longing, the ache of every day since she had thought they were gone seeping out through the cracks until her walls broke and the sadness and disappointment flowed out crashing in never ending waves that didn't recede. Every element of her dreams was here and all of it should be so good and yet it felt so very wrong. Christa sank back down onto a chair covering her face as the sobs took control and shook her body in time with the moans, which she could not hear above the roar in her head, escaping her mouth. Drew's arm was around her, his familiar voice in her ear, it's ok, I'm here, we will sort this, I love you. As endless as the waves, the endearments came until her dam was dry, empty and only the shell of Christa remained, hollow and fragmented. Emily's protests started, quietly at first and Christa wondered if she was hoping it would be heard and not listened to, not until later when it would then seem like some knowledge from further back in the past.

'I wasn't sure it was you, it's not like the paintings were of you. One reminded me of Drew that was all and after I left I decided I would only be bringing back old hurts, and it could all have been a mistake.'

'A mistake Em,' Christa was calm again, resigned to letting go of the future she had always dreamed of. 'We were a family, you knew those paintings were mine and Joan told you my name, you only had to look in the corner of the works to see my signature there. You knew Em, and as usual you decided to look after yourself first, take what wasn't yours,' her voice was rising in crescendo. 'It's the story of your life, you had a chance Em, with us you had a chance to escape the life you lied about.' Emily looked shocked and began to protest but Christa was on a roll and could see only the truth would save them, all of them. 'What, you think I didn't work it out. A dead mother brings a lot of sympathy, enough money you could not have made legally so I figured you blackmailed the other boys, what did you have on them Em? All I know is you had an attitude to mask it all. I looked for you too Em and what I found backed up all the doubtful feelings I ever had when you talked about your past. You're as much a victim of the system as I am, your mother is certainly a piece of work, just admit it and let the chips fall where they will, we never cared where you came from, we only cared that you chose us as your family.'

Emily stood, finally unable to deny the truths being revealed. Drew was shocked, his naivety to it all falling away as he realised how he had taken it all at face value. The doubts and niggling feelings in the beginning had gone by the wayside as their friendships had grown and his attraction to both of them had become his battle.

'You can't have him back, he belongs to me now, to me and this baby. Why did you have to show up now?' Emily's anger was also escalating. 'Yes I knew it was you, your boyfriend looked nice, and I thought you were fine. I walked away intending to come back but then I knew you would take him back, ditch it all to take him away, he always loved you more and do you know what Christa? I was happy with being second best because the rest of the world out there was too scary to contemplate without either of you in it. If I had come back you would be living here and then where would I go, where?' Emily broke down, Drew edged away not toward Emily as Christa thought he should. Poor broken Emily was finally admitting her truth, dropping her mask. Christa had seen behind it on cold dark nights after Emily regretted too many beers and a roll in the hay with some random guy who had liked her smile. When Emily had dipped into the darkness of regret for seeking comfort in the arms of a stranger and allowing her ghosts to take over, Christa had been there, holding her, comforting her, and storing away all the snippets of information for another day until the slurring softened into snores and sleep had eased Emily's pain. Eventually Christa had pieced it all together and as always in the mornings, Emily's smile had risen like the sun, chasing away and hiding her dark clouds in the shadows for another day, Christa had kept her secrets and allowed herself to be pushed forward with the optimism Emily used to breathe each day.

This was the moment, the moment to bring their past, present and future together. The losses, her losses, had made her who she was, Christa realised. The people she had met, her art and the opportunities which had come her way had moulded her into the person she had become. All of it may not have happened if she had found them earlier. Again the sliding doors of life opened, the new path was to the life she had made or this one she had never let go the dream of. These were the options on offer. As Christa watched her friend shed the hidden anguish of her life, Christa felt torn, torn for the child and surprisingly, in spite of her anger, torn for Emily and Drew. Christa looked at him now, her sweet man who had appeared before her so few hours ago. There was no choice she admitted, he had always been her choice and always would be. The baby they would care for, and Emily, they would care for her too. As she and Drew had moved forward from their past, learned the lessons and applied them to their future, Emily had hidden hers deep so they still clawed on the outskirts of her mind and ate away at who she really could be, no matter how valiantly she fought them. One small piece at a time they had gathered until eventually when she would become so broken, they could again take control and the supply of optimism she had been assigned, and had shared, would be depleted and no longer enough to move her forward.

Drew finally spoke, this kind man who had cared for them, defended them and protected them could now see he had not acknowledged the reality as he had drifted with them always on the alert for their safety, he had been their ultimate protector. It was only now he was realising he had not been able to protect them from themselves. The clock ticked loudly and as midnight came and went a new day would soon dawn and a solution had to be made, no more fluffing around to keep everyone happy, it was time now to decide their fates and move forward.

'I love her Em, I always have. I know this baby will change our lives, but we can do this together, Christa and I will always be here for you I promise.' Emily looked at him with the saddest eyes as if her battle had been lost and the past was not worth gathering to move on. 'I found Christa in the most magical place and tonight as I sat here I did wonder if it was the spell of the Gap where we were today or were my feelings still the same. We slept together today, I won't lie to you, and as much as I love you Em, and want this child, I will not sacrifice Christa for either of you. I'm so, so, sorry. To see her sitting here fills my world and I know I would give it all to be with her. This place, this friendship and as much as I don't want to, this baby, if that is what it takes, I will relinquish them all.' It was now he moved towards her and Christa's heart was singing as he put his arm around her, he then moved and knelt in front of Emily taking her hand gently in his.

'I'm so sorry Em,' he said softly. 'I think we got caught up in a dream which was never going to last. We both know it. Baby or no, we would never have worked, at least not for a lifetime. One thing my parents did show me was staying with someone you don't love with all you have, only leads to bitterness and regret. I never want to feel either of those things about you, forgive me if you can, but this is what I want the most.'

Christa held her breath waiting for Emily's reply. Drew had told the truth, it was the one thing they had both taken from their childhoods. To hide behind a lie became poison in the end and as they had grown, matured and lived, truth had been the base of all they had learned and experienced. Christa remembered the men she had met, Cookie, Johnno and Tom. Truth had been their lesson, one they had learned for themselves the benefit of, and one they now lived by and passed on by being the good men they were. As Emily shed the last of the tears for tonight and searched the room for her reply, Christa felt a deep sorrow for accusing her friend, instead of being there for her. The days had been many where Emily's laugh had dragged them through the unknown, unafraid of the outside world she had taught them to plunge forward, and to edge aside the barriers in their way. This would hurt her, slightly on the surface but deep,

deep, down the rejection would add another flammable layer to the turmoil bubbling inside. Christa hoped the cauldron would burst, bubble over to let the hurt run free like a river of lava until the atmosphere turned it to stone, and Emily would at last be able to walk free and away from the past to unlock the tender heart she had always tried to hide. As they waited Christa also knew, this might be the rejection that would tip her over the edge.

There it was, the smile, and the almost visible crushing of the pain behind it, collapsing down as an accordion would, hiding there to wait for the next time to spring open, wider and louder than before when the clips holding it tight, could no longer take the pressure. Emily's deep breath told Christa they would not believe her but knew this was always her first line of defence. Distract, laugh, make it look like your armour had not been penetrated, then distance yourself until the pattern repeated. Watching it all Christa despaired as Emily began to play her game, because this time she had no idea the rules had changed, as had the players.

/ Chapter 32

Christa

Christmas Day was awkward and each of them seemed to be
in a corner trying to work out the next move. Christa had
stayed only because of the lateness of the hour. Each had slept
in separate beds and the sun was high before any of them
showed their face, though it was obvious little sleep had been
had. Emily had hugged her wishing her the greetings of the season and it was only the occasion that held Christa back from
shaking her, hoping to evoke an emotion behind the mask she
had firmly in place. Drew tried to edge her away but the
thoughts in the night, the evaluating of what she had, what she
had thought she wanted, and the reality of this situation was
something she wanted to decide for herself with no pull in any
direction which might blur her final decision.

Christa needed time alone in the brightness of day where
no creeping shadows could claw their way in. Taking her tea
to the verandah she leaned back against the post, closing her
eyes and absorbing the sun's warmth before it turned harsh as
the day moved forward. The decision was fairly straightforward,
Christa would depart, go back to the Gap and let the peace
she had craved meld with her body and clear her mind back
to level ground. It would leave them to sort out their own decisions in the surroundings they were both familiar with. The
rush of dreams when she had first seen him, the day they had

spent together when everything else in the world had disappeared was now mixed in a cloud caught between two worlds. They had eaten in awkward silence, and it was then Christa had announced her plans. Every day of her life she'd had to look after herself, since she was a small child each thought had considered both her physical and mental safety. When Drew and Emily had eased some of the burdens, she had locked it away and given, in the end, far more control to them than she had realised. The freedom it had released, the tension it had unwound in her body day by day, she now felt had made her weak, and after she had left them it had been a struggle to regain some of the strengths she'd had in the past.

Drew was reluctant for her to go, and Emily was insistent she come along with them to see this magical place which she felt, was about to steal her life away. Christa watched their every move, each gesture between them was familiar and unnoticed by them, but a glaring reminder to her of the life they had made together. Between them, they had exchanged gifts, and Christa again saw Emily's determination to highlight the relationship they had forged of which Christa had no knowledge. Emily's gift to Drew contained items relating to his impending fatherhood and it puzzled Christa as to how she had been able to receive them so quickly. As far as she could ascertain the pregnancy, and the news of it was a recent event, a matter of days since Drew had been told. Christa tried to draw on her feelings of old, the ones when they had all been together, young, free and unafraid of what the future may hold, as each minute ticked by, it was getting harder to hold this mask in place and not let her real thoughts play across her face.

At last they seemed ready to go and sitting three abreast, Emily in the middle, hints of memories of the fun they'd shared eased the tension Christa was feeling. As they bumped and rattled along the station tracks Christa wondered if they could work this out, was there a remote possibility it could be something like before? No, in truth, that would be a dream, each of them had changed, grown and hopefully matured, and it was time to let go of what might have been and move forward with the reality they would all have to face. Emily prattled as usual filling in the gaping holes of silence from Drew and Christa. It was mainly directed at Drew, reminders of this or that, highlights they had shared out here together, there were even references to intimate moments and Christa saw her snake her hand across to rest on his knee as she did.

Christa had a mixture of everything inside. If she and Drew had not shared the day they'd had in the Gap, it may have been easier. Were these raw emotions from the past still valid or was that day meant to be their moment to move on from? The closer they got to the Gap the more Christa believed this was the case. Drew was hovering in the middle, sitting on the fence as they say and for all he'd said last night, was still not making it firm about which side he would stand on. Yes, her mind argued as the spinifex thinned and the camel trees lined the track, last night he had said he wanted to be with her and had told Emily so, but his actions this morning said otherwise. Christa knew she could live without him, without both of them because she had, and had survived. Maybe now was the time to let it go, let them go, knowing they were fine and moving on with the life she had created but as yet not embraced. The ghost gum's leaves seemed to rattle in the light breeze and as the ute pulled up at the very spot Christa had first seen it only yesterday, the faces of her mentors, the men she had come to hold dear in her heart came to blur her vision. Their voices filled her head, swirling and curling with advice. 'I think you just found you' Johnno had said after he encouraged her to paint. 'What he does now will show you ... don't let them leave a scar.' Macca, remorseful about his actions in the past but so willing to be truthful and embrace the future, and Cookie with pies full of love for his mates and a sense of family extended to her she would never forget. 'You ever need me, this is where I'll be' he'd said, and Christa knew he would be.

'Come on sleepy we're here.' Emily nudged Christa out of her abstraction. For a moment Christa forgot all the in-between and flashed her a smile as she would have in the past, one of conspiracy and excitement at the adventure ahead. It was only a moment and then she realised it was time to decide. To walk in the Gap and relive the moments from yesterday and to stay, or to bid farewell to a fictitious life she had dreamed of, both before and after the accident and since then, never thought could be realised.

The path was narrow and Drew guided Emily protectively. The spell cast itself on her also and once inside the magic of it filtered down across her upturned face. It was the colours and the stillness in the air Christa thought, a peace which was almost visible and yet as you moved, it was like stepping on a beach for the first time with not a footstep in sight. The Gap let you own it but also took you captive. Christa led the way once the path widened, brushing through the ferns and shivering slightly at the coolness in the shadows. The rock platform looked just as inviting and it took a moment to realise Emily had not spoken since she had entered. Drew had carried her basket and taking it from him, Christa made her way up the eastern path to her car. It was exactly how she had left it, but she busied herself checking inside and out trying to stall time and digest every second of the last twenty-four hours. It all seemed like a long time ago when in reality it had only been yesterday. The sun was biting at her skin and after the coolness of the Gap, felt nasty, prodding her to retreat one way or the other. The keys in her hand though were never tempted to be inserted in the ignition, and Christa locked the car up again and turned to start down the path, as a plan formed in her head.

Drew turned when he heard the pebbles on the path scuttle under her feet, his brows were drawn in a worried look and Christa realised they had both been in the water to cool off as droplets of it still clung to their hair. Emily looked relaxed and was in the process of laying out a towel to sit on. Christa had a vision, a daydream from above, she was looking down, the dark narrowness of the Gap a contrast to the land beyond, she was swooping now like a bird, and she could see them all down there hiding in the coolness and the greenery. From here they looked happy, and she wondered if indeed it was all a dream and soon her eyes would flutter open to the life she had before. It was gone in an instant and he was there, reaching out to bring her in close and squeezing her hand transmitting unspoken words in a code which was all their own. Emily lay back relaxed, her belly flat above her bikini making Christa again wonder about the truths being told.

Chapter 33

Emily

It was beautiful here and Emily was sorry they had not taken the time to explore this end of the station sooner. The southern visits were now another era and once she had set her sights on making this place her home she had found a settling inside of all that had gone before. Some people would never understand there were parts of this great land that had never been stepped upon and without Google Earth, many still would have remained hidden like the Gap, behind an unimpressive exterior. Water was the key and although locals on the other side had known about it, the distance from the homestead had made it unworthy of investigation. Once the water left the Gap it mainly travelled underground except in a season when the way here would be impassable anyway from this side.

Christa would be leaving, or at least that is what Emily presumed she would do. A few days here under the spell of this place would be enough for Drew to grieve and move on, he knew she was the right choice. Christa was now accomplished, her career and choices already made, the boyfriend had been skimmed over but Emily had seen him, seen his support of her and she suspected the tie there would be harder to break than Christa was making out. Emily had proven herself to Drew in this life he had chosen, her support of him over the last few years in good times and bad, should be enough and his need for her physically had been shown many times over. Christa would have no more than her to give. It was now time for her to make a final plea, show him how much she had come to mean to him, what they had was stronger and more mature than their childish antics of the past. Emily feigned sleep but watching through veiled lashes she saw him reach out to take her hand, it was immature the way he looked at her, a dream from the past he must be made to realise had come true in a different way. The longer Christa stayed the harder it would be for Emily to drive the final wedge. It wasn't fair, finally she felt safe, finally she knew her future was secure and then Christa reappeared to spoil it all. Emily stirred, stretching her arms wide more to catch their attention than to relieve her muscles. Waiting was her plan, to see Christa's next move and like a game of chess have hers ready to play either way.

The gorge was breathtaking, the walls so steep and jagged were the perfect backdrop for the varying shades of green in the foliage. The pool's mirror-like surface reflected the myriads of deep reds, rich orange and yellow brown oche layers making it look as if the cliffs plunged deep into the earth below, and yet a tiny touch of a finger could quickly shatter the surface, as well as the illusion. Emily felt calm here, a sense of home deeper than any she had ever felt at the homestead. There was a freedom, a peace the Gap gave but a tiny piece of her wondered what eventually, would be the price. Nothing in this life, she had learned, came for free. Rubbing her eyes Emily struggled to pull on the mask, she knew they saw right through it, but it was all she had and these two were the only ones she had ever allowed a peek beneath. In another life, it would have been easy to cut one or the other away. At last she could see what it was like to care with an emotion so deep, no one could fathom its depths, so they gave it the common name of family. A family she was reluctant to cut away as she had her own, these two had been her world. For Emily survival was the key, being second best was something she had never excelled at.

They were quiet now but there was no awkwardness in the silence and in her heart she knew she had lost. It was as if they moved as one, graceful but purposeful, determined but with an ease Emily wished she could find. It did not make her want to bow out, it only made her more determined to have what it was they took for granted and would not guard as well as she would if she had it. You don't have it her mind argued, this is not something you can take and yet here we are fighting for something he is unable to give. Emily argued back, for this I am willing to be second best.

Behind her they had stepped away their voices were now slightly raised, not in anger, but more a frustrated need to feel they were being listened to. I need you he said, she is having your baby she argued back, I think I should go, please stay, we will work it out. Back and forth it went but as Emily watched them their body language backed his argument all the way. All the time they had travelled Emily had watched it grow, so many times, many unknown to Christa, she had intervened, tried to tempt him, and occasionally succeeded. It was a jealousy of sorts and a fear, a terrible fear they would find their life and move her on, just as all the foster parents had when the cuter child or helpless baby had moved in to take their attention away. Yet here they all were, and she was the one who had finally found the life she wanted, and they were the ones who were so unsure.

Emily walked to the water and her reflection looked back. Her own eyes searched hers for the answer, she looked wise, so full of all the answers and bereft of any fears, if only this was true. Trailing her fingers the ripples reached out shattering her image and the truth she knew had lain there. There were times the truth must be placed aside she determined, so the future could unfold in the path it was meant to, after all, the truth did not always know all the facts. Christa's return was not meant to happen, and this baby had changed the course for them all. Emily was determined to protect Drew and the life they had created. Most of all Emily was determined to protect herself.

'Who's hungry' she called, and they both stopped their discussion and turned towards her. Drew slid his hand down Christa's arm and Emily could almost feel the shiver of delight as it tingled across Christa's shoulders, and she couldn't ignore the glance which passed between them. He was blinded was all and soon would see the light again, once Christa was gone Emily would ensure she never returned, it was for the best. Sometimes when fate stepped in it needed to be guided in the right direction, that was all she was going to do, guide them all to the right outcome. Turning back to busy herself with the lunch the reasoning side of her slid away and the other side did not blink an eye before it turned the invisible key to lock it safely away.

The sandwiches they had brought were tasty and Emily devoured several before realising the others did not seem as hungry. Drew had persuaded Christa to remain camping as she had originally intended for a few days and as much as she protested, in reality there was nowhere else for her to go. The boyfriend it seemed, was long forgotten and in spite of them wanting to restrain themselves, their touching and giggling made her stomach churn.

Chapter 34

Christa

'We should stay as well.' Emily's words caught them by surprise. 'You could go home and grab some more things and then we can all camp here together. It would be like a holiday, our last time to all be together, like when we were young. It will be fun.' For a moment it did sound fun, but as much as the smile on Emily's face was as broad as ever, there was a tightness attached which held a hint of her tension underneath.

'Do you think that's wise Em, your condition and all, I could run you back and then come and get you tomorrow.' There, he had laid his decision directly in front of her. Christa smiled at him, the whole situation was so awkward, but each indication of their future together flooded her body with excitement. This is almost the perfect place Christa thought, it has settled in all of us, and it is almost supporting us all as if the ghosts from the past and the future have reached an agreement to grant our wish. Christa tuned back in deciding to give Emily her one last wish, after all she was the one who was losing the most. For all she had given them the least Christa could do was start to forgive. Emily seemed to be beginning to accept the undeniable and Christa returned her smile burying some of the doubts and angry thoughts from yesterday away in a bid to move forward amicably. This baby would tie them all together forever and it would be the best thing for this little one if they could all agree.

'Em's right Drew, let's have one night together, we can light a fire and talk about old times, it is Christmas.' Both of them looked at him in a way he knew he could not overrule. 'Bring some marshmallows if you have some.' He laughed, she knew they were a favourite.

'Just bring me a swag and you and Christa can sleep in her car.' Emily was admitting defeat, bowing out with less resistance than they had expected. Despite the lifting of her spirits she knew Emily would be boxing it up to be dealt with on another day. Christa felt herself soften, Emily was hurting and although she was covering it bravely in her usual way with sarcastic comments and an air of indifference, Christa knew she would always be there to catch her in the fall, they had shared too much to let anything since the accident get in their way.

Christa was glad Emily had decided to take the high road, it could be motherhood was exactly what she had needed, someone to love her unconditionally and be loved by in return, with no regrets or remorse attached. A family of her own with them to support her in any way they could. At last Emily may have found exactly what she had always been searching for.

'I don't like leaving you alone.' Drew looked at her with pleading eyes and Christa raised her shoulders slightly to give a visual to him of how she was relaxing in the situation.

'What about me?' Emily's indignant look took them all back to their teens with her rolling eyes, dramatic gestures along with the endless plans for the future. Drew and Christa could not help but laugh and a tiny piece settled inside her finding its place to let her know it would all work out eventually.

'Ok then I have to check on the dogs and feed them so if I go now I'll be back before dark. What else do you need?'

The girls rattled off both needs and wants making them all laugh as Drew copied Emily's antics with rolling eyes. Drew took Christa's hand and led her under the canopy of the ferns. Giving her a kiss which was hard to drag away from, he looked deep into her eyes, concern written across his brow.

'We'll be fine, go but hurry back I don't want to be away from you for too long ever again.' With another swift kiss he only paused to call back to Emily.

'No leading her astray Emily and no exploring, climbing or anything a pregnant woman shouldn't do before I come back Ok?'

'You're no fun Drew... and never have been,' was the reply and they both grinned as it reminded them of the million memories they had shared. Christa watched as he disappeared down the path, it made her feel empty and she closed her eyes willing the feel of him to return. At least this time she knew he would, and it was with that thought she turned back to start to rebuild her friendship with Emily and hopefully cement a pact for the future.

Emily had moved further up the Gap. They had all walked through the southern end and in all her visits here Christa had never explored any further than the pool.

'I don't think that's a dead-end Em, come back and we'll go for a swim, I haven't been in yet.' Christa thought back to when she had come here with a crowd and could not recall anyone venturing up that way. 'Drew said no exploring so let's just sit and talk or I have a billy and can make us some tea. We can talk babies and sort some things out before he gets back.'

Emily gave a muffled reply and as Christa squinted to see her in the shadows she realised it was distance which had lessened the sound and not Emily mumbling. Blowing out a breath in frustration Christa followed knowing Emily was deliberately defying a direct request because it was in her nature to do so and always had been. The water looked as if it had simply appeared, barely visible under the huge smooth boulder that had been hidden by a curve in the craggy walls. The smooth shallow stream ran flat across the rock plateau beneath it running into the deep pool with no sign of a fall, no splash or bubbling just an emersion of the two in a meld that defied gravity and tricked the eye with its beauty. Christa scrambled over the first few smaller boulders calling to Emily and her frustrations increased when she received no reply. Part of her wished Drew had not left, they could have managed until tomorrow with the small supplies she had in the car. A few rocks rattled to her right and finding a foothold in one boulder Christa hoisted herself up as far as she could hoping to get a view of what was ahead. Glad she still had her dress on over her swimmers as it did give some protection to her skin as she stretched and wriggled in her efforts. Finally she was up and taking a moment to catch her breath and to laugh at what she must look like slung over a stone, a big one but essentially a smooth round river stone. Christa carefully pulled herself up onto one knee and then the other before using both hands to get into a position to be able to stand upright. The largest one still blocked her view but what she could see was what looked like an endless tiny mountain range that had been smoothed and sculpted by the water over millions of years. A garden of boulders all a different shade of grey lined up like soldiers in the creek bed for as far as she could see.

'Emily.' A faint cry to the right again turned her in that direction. 'Are you ok Em, where are you?' A few stones, as if she had thrown them, made bell-like sounds as they hit the different sized rocks and scattered between them. Again Christa cursed and carefully managed to head their way making sure at each step her foothold was secure. At last she managed to circle the largest one and looking back realised the pool and opening of the Gap could no longer be seen. The sky here was more visible, and the heat of the late afternoon sun had not lost its bite. The rocks felt cool beneath her feet, and she stopped again to survey her surroundings.

'Come on Em, It's not funny anymore.' Christa stretched her body as tall as she felt safe to do, her eyes searching for Emily and her heart starting to pump faster as panic edged its way in. 'Emily. Answer me!'

It was the intake of breath that warned her. Turning, the look on Emily's face flashed all the feelings Christa had seen last night as she had watched Emily step from the verandah and before she had been able to hide them in the darkness. Emily's arms were stretched out as she lunged, and Christa only had milliseconds to calculate her fall. Fate was here and karma was a step back. Christa put her arms up in an automatic self-defence move then thrust out a hand managing to grab one of Emily's arms. They had each other's hands now pushing with their full weight while trying to maintain their balance on top of the rounded surface of the boulders. Christa was screaming but could not hear the sound. Stop. No. Em, we can work it out, but Emily looked possessed, her face the demonic portrait of a lifetime of buried hate and neglect. The struggle was real, and Christa felt her back foot slip, she glanced back to see the drop below and the narrow gap between the boulders. Christa summoned all she could, but in those moments knew it may not be enough. They both seemed to give their final push. He's mine she said, think of the baby was the reply. The world blurred and the look of surprise was as much to absorb the shock as it was to realise there was no saving herself from the fall. Fate had made her final call.

Chapter 35

They found her body on a Sunday, and it was with surprise they each commented on how all the two hundred and six bones seemed to be in place, no wild dog or other scavenger appeared to have disturbed the corpse at any stage of its deterioration. The investigation resulted in the female body being listed as a Jane Doe. The local storekeeper recalled a woman who had been living in one of the abandoned looking houses, but it had been years before and they thought she had moved on when her boyfriend's stint at the mine had been completed. Unfortunately she did not know of anyone else who would know of more information to pass on, and she could no longer remember each passerby. The increase in back packers and grey nomad travellers searching for remoteness had her busier in the last twelve months than in the whole decade before. Also, she had thought to herself, and not wanted to voice to the authorities, chances were out here, if someone chose to get lost they certainly had plenty of places to hide. The store owner's husband had nothing more to give and with the total population of the town now reduced to two permanents and a drifter, he was never going to be an avenue of questioning they would pursue, although the constable did privately question his non-committal answers and seemingly overanxious willingness to assist in the search for any more belongings or clues. The boyfriend of the woman had been contacted through the mine records and said the relationship had ended amicably and, as far as he knew she had intended to live up north on a station somewhere, though the Gap had been a place she liked to frequent. A google search had found the art he had spoken about was still for sale and it was obvious she was alive and well somewhere, so their concentration turned back to the task at hand. At least the enquiry had tied up a loose end and no further investigation into him or her was deemed warranted.

The weather had worn away any tracks over time and the backpackers who found her were cleared to go within hours. They were probably still wishing they had not been so curious to discover the beginning of the water source that filled the billabong in the Gap they had stumbled upon in their travels. A wetter year and the path may have taken them in an entirely different direction. A wetter few years and her skeletal remains may have separated to wash away, sending some of her into the deep pool and catching others beneath the bed of rocks. Fate. Fate and karma are two words that could stand side by side, maybe luck could stand there too, but in this case, it would never be regarded as luck they had found her, more fate, which had placed the backpackers here and maybe in some way to teach them a lesson they would need later in life. Who knew? No one ever would. Whatever it was, this had been her fate. Karma for one so young did not sit well with the investigating officers, it never did. Bad luck and fate had come together at the same time to see her fall in a place so remote help would never have come her way even if she had been able to call. Out here there was no one to hear. The girl with her skull smashed and her arms broken would at least now be treated with the respect earned by the dead. The tired investigators had been glad to leave the heat behind and head back to cases not so straightforward and which brought greater satisfaction in solving. Time and weather were the only ones to know the truth, and both had combined to camouflage any clues. How she got here was unknown, where she came from was also unknown and sadly, no one else had showed up to say they cared. The file would make its way to the bottom of a pile in a computer somewhere, only to surface again if a known relative came to light to be informed or another body was found in the vicinity. The few decaying belongings had been removed to eventually be destroyed when no claim for them was made.

Chapter 36

Drew

Drew thought about it at times, on dark days when the world shrank, and he could no longer see the light ahead. He wondered if he should have told, told how she must have fallen even though he had warned them not to climb, the way she had laughed when he had spoken, her smile pushing away any thoughts of fear. He had known her secrets, the moment he first saw her he knew them, and the details were something he feared. They had loved each other, been a family of sorts, more of a family than most had ever known, and he had grieved the loss as a family member would. In part it was for the best, he had made his choice long before, though her acceptance of it had been a struggle to reconcile. He had loved her and nothing more, it was something she could not accept and had used all her wiles to tempt him once she found him again. The journey, this journey, had been long and as many times as this land tried to break him, it had been these two women who nearly did.

Back at the homestead, the children would be bathed and ready for bed, she would wait for him on the verandah, her neck stretched back as the sun said its last goodbyes. As he turned for home, the light fading and the flies finally finding their beds, Drew felt better. Now she was found, her body would be cared for and hopefully, her troubled soul soothed and calmed by the angels in heaven. She would be happy for them, smiling, no longer having to hide her fears and they, the angels, would know her, this soul who had been lost both in body and mind, and of her front to the world that had covered the torment which raged beneath. Up there, this world would be gone, and hurt would fade away, but he still hoped one day, when their paths crossed in some ethereal place, she would pause and ponder his presence and know he had once cared.

'Goodbye, my darling friend' he murmured.

As the dust shook off the door frames and trailed, curling behind only to settle again for another day, Drew released his pain. Deep breaths cleared his head and slotted things into place, justifying each one of his actions accordingly before filing them away, he felt lighter, his muscles not as tight as they had been these last few years. To look forward now was what they would do, his part in all this had been shameful at times and although he blamed Emily, the she-devil in her had always had a way of catching him out and casting her spell at just the right moment. Deep down he knew he too had been at fault, for falling into her grasp and forgetting what was important. It couldn't have gone on, he had too much to lose but fate had stepped in and made the decision for him. He would never forget her smile, the roundness of her hips, her courage and tenacity, and the vulnerabilities hidden behind a brave exterior. For him, she had been a force to deal with and the force that had propelled him forward and pushed him into this life when he had thought she was gone. Grateful was a word, but there were so many more.

The last of the rays were sliding over the horizon in his mirror and as the homestead came in sight he knew the world, their world, was finally finding its balance. The children had levelled it, balanced the lows with unexpected highs with their innocence and joy for life. Now it felt the pendulum which had at one time swung so wide, was still, locked in place for the time ahead. Drew pondered the thought and then filed it away as his mind turned to the future. All they had to do now was wait, wait until the rains came so they could wash away the past, and bring new life to the future.

Chapter 37

It was four a.m. when they woke, the little ones crying, frightened by the noise as the thunder broke with a furious sound and lightning flashed her blades of light across the sky. The heavy drops echoed through the ceilings as they held them tight, and tears flowed in the darkness as their prayers were answered from above. It took away her breath, the sound meant more than grass in the paddocks and water in the tank, the sound was a future, the future they had planned, dreamed of, and now, might have a chance of making. Today of all days it had come, a sign of forgiveness to her heart from the heavens, the punishment was over, her love for this man had been her only sin and she'd had to pay heavily for the price. They could hear the water as it trickled down the pipes, filling the tanks with the lifeblood they so desperately needed, and as he squeezed her hand she felt him turn toward her.

'It's a day we'll never forget, the day the rains came.' She could almost see the relief exit his body like a ghost, then in a whisper, intentionally meant only for the heavens. 'She'll be safe now.'

As the thunder rolled into the distance leaving the steady beat of the rain behind, she closed her eyes and wondered if he knew the truth, the truth which must stay hidden forever only known to herself and Emily. Emily, her dear haunted friend caught wanting the life she could not have, yet capable of doing whatever it took to get it.

Christa knew this place could never have provided Emily with the peace she craved. Beneath the laughter, her agony had lain wrapped around a soul that was scarred from a shattered childhood she refused to accept, and a family stricken with temptations that played with their minds and destroyed their thoughts. Emily, beautiful, tortured, and troubled. The mask she held up to the world had become too heavy to bear and as Christa had watched her unravel, she had known there was now only one exit. To be relieved of this life would have been Emily's eventual decision. Had Drew been there she knew Emily would have faltered, and she would have too. It was her deep love for Emily that had shown Christa she must guide her on her way to a better life. In that final decisive second she had released the hand flung out in desperation by Emily and as her balance faltered her eyes had shown the moment Emily realised the table had turned, and she was about to lose it all.

As gravity played its part Christa had leaned back to watch her fall, her head smashing into the solid granite sides, her arms flung up grasping for a hold, but instead flailing against their hard surface. Christa had felt no emotion and no desire to clamber down to give aid if it was needed. Emily's eyes had captured hers as she fell, her mouth remaining open after her final words were released. The world seemed to stop turning for a millisecond as she hung there with them and before her body smashed into the ground. I love you she'd said, and Christa knew that she had.

As the rain continued to hammer its tune of redemption, Christa spoke quietly into the darkness no louder than Emily's last breath.

'I did love you Emily, but he was always mine and never yours to take.

Chapter 38

Emily

Slow motion is what killed her in the end, the world choosing to stop turning for a split second had unbalanced her. As she had tried to grasp Christa's hand again, the decision to forgive the things she could not change and let fate have the final say, had come together. The battles had been fought, some had been harder than others and in this one she could have been triumphant if her opponent had not been Christa. For all the love Christa had pushed her way, Emily had still held it at bay, pushing back in her game of self-preservation. Christa's pure heart had almost saved her, and in return Emily had taken all she had. It was time to give back and return to her dearest friend all she had stolen, but never owned.

The pain was short lived. As her eyes closed for the final time, the doors to the afterlife appeared though refused to open until she had forgiven herself for all the things she had never done.

The small flow of water beneath her disappeared and her skin wrinkled and dried across her bones as the endless sun fingered its way into the shadows each day. Most days she was content, happy for its light and a reminder of her living life, on others, it parched her limbs and threatened to destroy tiny pieces when all she wanted was to feel whole. The seasons came and went but still the rain withheld itself, and she was glad. To be washed away, divided and spread to hidden crevasses and deep caverns beneath the earth's crust was her deepest fear. One last time she wanted to be noticed, to shine in, or be the focus of someone's world for just a moment. Her memories were fading but love stayed with her and allowed her to remember their names.

The clambering on the rocks had stirred her and the unknown faces had looked shocked to see her skeleton there. Hope had flared that they would come back, and when they did, her day to shine was announced. Emily appreciated their care, to reach her had been a task and when they finally brought her out, the shallow murky pond explained why visitors had been so few. The angels came now, opening the door and inviting her to join them. One last wish they said, and she did not hesitate in her reply.

It was more freedom than she had ever felt, her arms spread as she soared over the invisible mountains in the sky. The homestead was close, and he was striding across the yard. Happy sounds rang out from inside but as she came close she could see the worry etched across his face. The land was dry and as parched as the bones she had left in careful hands. A rifle lay across the seat of the vehicle and as he looked up before entering it, she knew the task he had today. As his eyes searched the sky for rain, she hoped he could see her there, and she would feel him one more time. The door closed and although tempted to follow him, she knew her time was short, and the angels would soon beckon.

Forgiveness had been given, they had stayed the one night to be near her and then with solemnness in their hearts had left her, their decision made and a life ahead. They knew she was safe and there were many stories which could be told if she was ever found. Drew was told she had fallen, Emily knew she had been pushed. The biggest thing in their favour was, they knew no one would ever come to look.

Two tiny boys ran out and a girl, slender like her mother. 'Emily' she called and for a moment as Christa appeared, Emily thought she had been seen. The child had turned and as they spoke words she couldn't hear, a joy like no other filled the vessel she now was, and the heart she had been allowed to keep. The baby she could not keep with her had returned, and they had honoured her journey by naming her after her mother. Emily's own journey was over now, and as the angels ushered her through the pearly gates their smiles said her wish had come true. Inside the child they had named for her, was a piece of each of them, and her family was finally complete. Emily only looked back once and as the child turned, her smile lit up the heavens and Emily could smell the sweet pungent scent of rain in the distance.